HE WAS WALKING ALONE

HE WAS WALKING ALONE

ZACHARY GOLDMAN MYSTERIES #4

P.D. WORKMAN

ISBN: 9781989080498 (IS Hardcover)

ISBN: 9781989080481 (IS Paperback)

ISBN: 9781989415535 (IS Large Print)

ISBN: 9781989080467 (Kindle)

ISBN: 9781989080474 (ePub)

pdworkman

ALSO BY P.D. WORKMAN

Zachary Goldman Mysteries
She Wore Mourning
His Hands Were Quiet
She Was Dying Anyway
He Was Walking Alone
They Thought He was Safe
He Was Not There
Her Work Was Everything
She Told a Lie (Coming soon)
He Never Forgot (Coming soon)
She Was At Risk (Coming soon)

Kenzie Kirsch Medical Thrillers
Unlawful Harvest

Auntie Clem's Bakery
Gluten-Free Murder
Dairy-Free Death
Allergen-Free Assignation
Witch-Free Halloween (Halloween Short)
Dog-Free Dinner (Christmas Short)
Stirring Up Murder
Brewing Death
Coup de Glace
Sour Cherry Turnover

Apple-achian Treasure

Vegan Baked Alaska

Muffins Masks Murder

Tai Chi and Chai Tea

Santa Shortbread

Reg Rawlins, Psychic Detective

What the Cat Knew

A Psychic with Catitude

A Catastrophic Theft

Night of Nine Tails

Telepathy of Gardens

Delusions of the Past

Fairy Blade Unmade

Web of Nightmares

A Whisker's Breadth (Coming soon)

High-Tech Crime Solvers Series

Virtually Harmless

Stand Alone Suspense Novels

Looking Over Your Shoulder

Lion Within

Pursued by the Past

In the Tick of Time

Loose the Dogs

AND MORE AT PDWORKMAN.COM

To those who walk alone, no matter what they have done to get there

Zachary was standing staring out his window at the businesses across the street from his apartment building, where an old man with a ladder was stringing up Christmas lights when his phone rang. He was startled out of his trance and nearly did a face-plant into the window before he regained his balance.

He put his hand on the glass to steady himself and pulled his phone out of his pocket with the other. A glance at the screen showed him that it was Mario Bowman, and he didn't hesitate to answer it. Since moving out of Bowman's apartment, the two of them had usually gotten together every couple of weeks for a drink. A year ago, they had been acquaintances, just friendly after the various times they had met while Zachary had worked cases the police were involved in, but after the fire that had destroyed everything Zachary had owned for the second time in his life, that had changed. Bowman had graciously allowed Zachary to stay with him until he got back on his feet, which had turned into months rather than the 'few days' they had initially talked about. Bowman had never complained about Zachary being underfoot, and even after Zachary had moved into his own place again, they had continued to get together, cementing the friendship.

Years before, Zachary had accepted the fact that he would

never have any real friends. Moving constantly from one foster family or institution to another, battling with learning disabilities and childhood trauma, he had not found it easy to break into the circles of already-established friendships and had remained on the outside. Not having developed those skills as a child, he had remained a loner as an adult. He'd never expected to have a 'best friend' like Bowman.

"Mario!"

"Hey, Zach. I didn't get you up, did I?"

Zachary pulled the phone away from his ear to look at the time to better compose his answer. After ten o'clock in the morning, a time even night owls were normally up by. "It's halfway through the day. You know I don't sleep that late."

"I know you don't usually sleep," Bowman admitted. "You're like a vampire. Except, I guess they sleep during the day, and you don't do that either. You could have been asleep though, if you had some kind of surveillance job last night."

"Well, I didn't. I've been up for hours. I thought you had night shift this week; aren't you heading to bed?"

"Yeah, I'd better knock off before long. But I have a possible case for you."

"Oh! What kind of case?"

Zachary worked everything from skip tracing and insurance fraud to money laundering and, in a few cases, death investigations. While he was trying to avoid the cheating spouse cases, he always seemed to have a couple of them on his plate.

"Why don't we get together later to discuss it? I'll introduce you to the potential client and you can see what you think."

"Uh, sure." It sounded like a much bigger case than just a background check. "When and where?"

"Old Joe's before I go back on shift? Say, seven?"

Zachary didn't know how Bowman could eat a steak dinner for what was essentially his breakfast. Zachary had a hard time with heavy meals at the best of times. His meds tended to suppress his appetite, and the most recent mood stabilizer added to his cocktail left him nauseated most of the day. But he knew that dinner at the steakhouse wasn't about the food. Bowman would enjoy being treated, as Zachary would pick up the tab for a client dinner. Hopefully, his client would feel at ease at the town's iconic steakhouse. And Zachary was going for the case, not the food.

"Yeah, that sounds good." He didn't need to check his calendar. He knew he wouldn't have anything that couldn't be moved. "I'll see you there."

"Perfect. See you tonight, then."

Zachary thought about it after he hung up. It was late for Bowman to still be up when he would have to be up again at six. He would not get a full eight hours in, and when he was working shift he was very careful to get the sleep he needed so that he wouldn't get worn out and sick. Despite asking Zachary if he'd been asleep, he knew that Zachary was normally up before dawn and he could have safely called hours before. That suggested that he'd worked past the end of his shift, which meant a big case. If that was what they were having dinner to discuss, Zachary might be looking at quite a profitable file. Something he could really dig his teeth into to help him to forget about the holiday season.

The man across the street was working diligently at getting his Christmas lights on. They would make a festive display for Zachary in the coming weeks. He drew the curtains to shut out the sight.

The client who accompanied Bowman was a woman. That was the first surprise. And not just a woman, but an attractive one. At first glance, he would have put her as college age, but on closer inspection, the dim lighting at Old Joe's had softened the lines of her face. She was probably in her forties, like he was. Taller than Zachary. A dark blonde, rather than the almost-black hair that Zachary kept cropped close to his head. She wore no makeup as far as he could tell, and grief was plain on her face. It was no corporate case. Whatever Bowman had brought him, it was personal.

"Zach, this is Ashley Morton. Ms. Morton, Zachary Goldman."

Zachary shook hands. "Nice to meet you, Ms. Morton."

"It's Ashley," she informed him. "Thanks for agreeing to meet with me on such short notice. You must have a busy schedule."

Zachary glanced over at Bowman to gauge his reply. "I've always got cases on the go, but I can make room when something important comes up."

She nodded, looking relieved. "Good. Mr. Bowman said you'd be able to fit me in, but…"

Bowman motioned to an empty booth. "That's our table, shall we sit down? Did you want a drink, Zach?"

"No." Bowman knew he wouldn't have alcohol for a case meeting. Even when they got together to watch a game, Zachary was mindful of his alcohol consumption.

They made their way away from the bar to the quiet corner. Bowman and Ashley slid in with their drinks. Zachary sat across from Ashley.

Bowman took a sip of his beer and talked to Ashley about Zachary's qualifications. He touched on the cases Zachary had worked in the last year or so that had made it to the media. The drowning of Declan Bond, the only son of local TV celebrity *The Happy Artist*, the institutional abuses at Summit Learning Center, and the death of Robin Salter. While Robin's death had not been particularly newsworthy, the subsequent kidnapping of Zachary's ex-wife, socialite Bridget Downy, had been.

Ashley nodded solemnly throughout Bowman's recounting of the cases, her wide eyes going from Bowman to Zachary and back again. She didn't seem inclined to jump in immediately with her story. They ordered their dinners and discussed the menu for a few minutes. Zachary looked at Bowman, waiting for the signal that it was time to talk about Ashley's case. Bowman took a long draught of beer and wiped his mouth with the back of his hand.

"You want to tell Zachary about Richard's case?"

Ashley chewed on her lip.

"Do you want me to give him the broad strokes?" Bowman prompted.

She nodded. "That would be good," she said in a weak, watery voice.

Zachary hoped she wasn't going to cry. He was never sure what to do about tears. A lot of the women who engaged him to catch their cheating husbands cried. He had come to realize that the best thing to do in those cases was just to nod and push through for the details. Trying to comfort them didn't help. It seemed that those tears came from anger rather than sadness, and trying to be sympathetic just caused increased anger and outrage, putting him in the crosshairs in place of their husbands.

But he didn't think Ashley's case was for infidelity. She seemed too brittle, stretched too thin. Grief, not anger.

"Ashley's partner, Richard, was the victim of a fatal hit and run," Bowman said, confirming his suspicion. "It's a little more difficult to investigate than your usual MVC, since there were no witnesses, no cameras, and the body wasn't even discovered immediately. That has all made it very difficult for Miss Morton—Ashley—to deal with."

Zachary nodded. The waitress had brought him a glass of water. He took a sip, waiting for the rest of the story. Bowman sounded confident of the facts, so Zachary suspected he wasn't looking for Zachary to do an accident scene reconstruction. The police had probably already done their own, or had plans to, depending on how long they'd had to work the case.

"They're calling it an accident," Ashley said. "They said the driver isn't at fault." She shook her head, sputtering for words. "There's no way it was accidental."

Zachary considered. "What were the conditions? Was there alcohol involved?"

"All they have is the driver's word for it what time it was.

There aren't any witnesses. No proof. The police couldn't do a breathalyzer three days later."

"No," Zachary agreed. He pulled a notepad out of his pocket. "Do you mind if I make some notes?"

She nodded her permission.

"Your boyfriend's name was Richard...?"

"Harding. Just how it sounds."

"And the date of the accident?"

"Well, we don't know, do we? All we have is his word for it. And it *wasn't* an accident."

"Sorry. Incident. When did this allegedly happen?"

She was mollified and gave him more details. It had been a week since she had seen her boyfriend last and the police suggested that it had been that night he had been killed on the side of a rural highway.

"But you don't believe that's when it happened?"

"Well... I guess I do. I mean, Richard just dropped off the face of the earth, and that's not the kind of thing that he did. He was very reliable."

"So it probably was that night."

She nodded. Zachary wrote down the location and the date. He could look up weather conditions, sunset and sunrise, and any surveillance camera locations later on. The police might have missed something. They were usually pretty thorough, but every now and then, Zachary managed to tease out new information from a suspect or the available evidence.

"And you didn't know that anything had happened to him, just that he had disappeared."

"I knew something was wrong. I reported him missing in the morning when I woke up, but they said I would have to go to the police station and make a proper missing persons report once he had been missing for twenty-four hours. I know they can start an investigation sooner than that." She flashed a glare at Bowman.

Bowman shrugged. "In the case of a missing child, or someone we have evidence was kidnapped or in danger. But just a routine missing person… no. They tend to show up on their own and we don't want to waste precious police resources on someone who just went out on a drunk."

"He didn't go out drinking! He was hit on the road!"

"Yes." He had a sip of his beer, which was almost empty. "We know that now, but we didn't know it then. To start with, it was just a routine missing person with no evidence of violence. No ransom. No sign that there had been a fight. No witnesses that he'd been taken by force. He just disappeared off of his property."

"His car was still there. Did you think he just walked away? Off of a property twenty miles from the nearest town?" Her voice rose accusingly.

"It's just policy, Ms. Morton," Bowman reassured her. "You were not wrong to suspect that something had happened to him. Your instincts were right on."

She nodded, seeming appeased by his words. She fiddled with her drink for a minute, making tracks in the condensation on the side with her finger.

"So, they started an investigation after he had been missing for twenty-four hours," Ashley said. "They got people out searching the property, even though I had already looked everywhere for him. And they got scent dogs out to see if they could track him."

Zachary nodded. "And that's when they found him?"

"He was in the ditch beside the road, but you couldn't see him because it was overgrown with weeds and grass and bush. They just covered him up." Her voice was cracking like an adolescent's.

Zachary gave her a sympathetic smile. He didn't reach out to take her hand, too awkward when he had only just met her. "I'm sorry. Do you need a minute?"

At that point, the waitress came with their meals, a welcome distraction. The plates were delivered and they each took a few bites of their dinners before attempting to continue the conversation.

"Why don't you tell him the police findings?" Ashley suggested.

Bowman nodded. He took a big bite of steak and chewed it vigorously for a few minutes before offering any comment.

"Date of death was the night he disappeared. Exact time unknown. Gross examination suggests he was hit from behind and to the left, which is consistent with him being found in the right-hand ditch if he was walking away from the farm, toward the highway. As Ms. Morton said, the body was hidden by the overgrowth. Both she and the police had driven by the location several times without seeing him from the road."

"Any tire tracks?"

"It's a rural road, but it is paved and gets a fair bit of traffic because it joins two highways. If you know it goes through, you can use it as a shortcut. But there was no fresh rubber along the stretch of the highway before the collision to indicate an attempt to stop. There was a minor skid mark and tire tracks where a truck had pulled over after the point of collision. Since it's just a rural road, there's really no shoulder to pull onto and it isn't a safe place to stop in the dark."

"So someone might have stopped after hitting him."

Bowman agreed. He glanced at Ashley and continued. "The driver says he got out of the truck, looked at the damage on the truck, and looked for any sign of an animal he had hit along the side of the road."

"But he didn't see the body because it was hidden in the ditch." Zachary pushed the food around on his plate. "Is this the driver who hit him, or someone who just happened to be along? I thought you said it was a hit and run."

"As it turns out, it was more of a 'hit and stop and have a look around and then leave'," Bowman said with gallows humor. "As he didn't know he had hit a person, he didn't call it in. He got back in his truck and drove away."

"He really didn't know what he had hit?"

"Apparently."

"He knew very well!" Ashley insisted. "It was no accident!"

"You asked me to talk about the police findings. That is the police finding."

Ashley closed her mouth, pressing her lips into a thin, straight line. Bowman gave her a moment in case she wanted to say something else, then went on.

"The driver self-reported. Not for a couple of days, but later when he got suspicious that maybe it wasn't just an animal he had hit out there."

That seemed a little suspicious to Zachary, but he nodded and made a note of it. "You don't think that he was just waiting until he would be clean of any drugs or alcohol before reporting it?"

"We followed up with his insurance company. He had filed an insurance report the morning after the accident—er, MVC— saying that he had hit an animal and giving the pertinent details."

"That could have just been a complete cover-up," Ashley broke in.

"Sure," Zachary agreed. "I would have to look into it further to see how well his story held together. But he could be telling the truth. If you hit a person in a small car, you're going to get a lot of damage and know for sure what you hit. But a bigger truck… it wouldn't do as much damage to the vehicle."

"It was a semi taking a shortcut," Bowman informed them. Zachary nodded. A lot of inertia behind something like that. He would have to hit something pretty big to make a big impact on a truck of that size.

"And you've interviewed this driver and decided that you believe his story. It was just an accident."

"I didn't interview him personally. But interviews were conducted. The final autopsy results are not in yet. They'll want to run a tox screen and see if there is anything else suspicious, but chances are, it's going to be ruled an accident pretty quickly. There are, as yet, no indications of foul play."

"Richard didn't drink," Ashley said.

Zachary smiled politely at her. "What?"

"They aren't going to find anything on a tox screen. Richard didn't drink. He didn't take drugs. He didn't take anything. He was very careful."

"Did he have some kind of history of alcohol abuse?"

"No, of course not!" Her reply was vehement. She shook her head and put her fork down loudly on her plate. "He did not have anything to do with alcohol. Not ever."

"Religious? Personal decision? No family history...?" In Zachary's experience, people weren't teetotalers for no reason. It was the society norm to have a drink now and then, particularly on social occasions, and people didn't fall outside the norm without a conscious decision.

"He just didn't think it was a good idea," Ashley said primly. She took a sip of her own drink and picked up her fork again. "There's nothing wrong with that."

"No," Zachary agreed, glancing down at his own glass of water. "Nothing wrong with that."

"So would you take the case?" Ashley asked him tentatively. "Would you look into it, dig down deeper than the police did, and prove that it was really an intentional homicide, not an accident?"

"I can't guarantee the results," Zachary said. "I can't tell you what my findings are going to be or whether you're going to agree with them. Is there really a case to be made for intentional homicide? What are you reasons for thinking it wasn't just an accident?"

Ashley took a bite of her salad and chewed it slowly. "The driver got out of the truck and went to have a look," she said. "That tells me that he knew exactly what he had done. He got out to make sure Richard was really dead."

"Or he got out to look for the animal he had hit, but not seeing one, decided to go on his way."

"I know Richard. He would never be careless like that, walking with his back to traffic. He would have walked on the other side of the road so he was facing oncoming traffic. He would have gotten off of the road if there was a truck coming. He was very careful to avoid traffic accidents. He would never have let something like that happen."

Zachary scratched down a couple of notes and closed his eyes, thinking about it. "Were you there that night? Did the two of you live together?"

"I have my own place, but I stayed over with him a lot. It just depended on what our schedules were like. That night… I went home."

"Because you wanted to? He wanted you to? Whose idea was it?"

"I don't know… I don't think either one of us said specifically. It was just one of those things… mutual. I had things to do, he had things to do. So I went home."

"And you realized he was missing when? The next morning."

"Yes." Without prompting, she went on to give him the details. "I called him every morning. We always chatted for a few minutes over coffee. Just touched base, talked about how our days were going to be. Couples stuff. It didn't matter whether we were together or apart, we always had that talk."

"So you called and he didn't answer."

"Right."

"How often had that happened before?"

"It wasn't unusual… he would be getting breakfast ready or shaving and he would call me back once he was free."

"But he didn't."

"I waited a while, then called again. Over and over. He still didn't answer. I texted him. I didn't know what else to do. I went to work for the morning, but I couldn't keep my mind on my work, I was so worried about why he wasn't answering. So I took the afternoon off and went to see him. I thought… maybe he was sick in bed. I really couldn't think of anything else. It never occurred to me that he might have left the house."

"He didn't normally go for a morning jog or walk?"

"No. We both thought that was a little silly. Not that there's anything wrong with it if that's how you choose to get your exercise! But we both had fitness equipment and club memberships. No need to brave the weather and the traffic if you could just take a spin on the stationary bike while watching the morning news. It just seemed a lot more… civilized."

Zachary looked at Bowman. "How was he dressed?"

"Comfortable, casual. Not dressed for the office, but not dressed for bed or for a jog either. Jeans, t-shirt, warm jacket. Sneakers, not loafers."

"Where did he work? Did he have a stressful job?"

Ashley gave an uncomfortable shrug. "He was… a janitor. Well, somebody has to be! It was a good, steady job. It paid his expenses and he was putting a little away. I bring in good money from my job, so if we got married…" Ashley swallowed hard and didn't finish the thought. She was still in the process of figuring out how to manage without him. She still thought of him as being there, present with her, and the thought that they didn't actually have a future together anymore was startling and tragic.

"Nothing wrong with a good, honest job," Bowman asserted. "We checked him out and there were no indicators that he was into anything illegal on the side. One hundred percent legit."

Zachary was glad that the police investigation bore out what Ashley had to say about her deceased partner. But that didn't mean he wouldn't find something more when he had a chance to really look for any issues. He smiled and nodded at Bowman.

"Good. It helps with an investigation when I'm told everything."

He looked at Ashley. She didn't jump in with more details. He had a feeling she was holding back, but he didn't know what kind of information it was she was holding back. She claimed that Richard was clean, no drugs or alcohol, holding a custodial position. No problems with the law.

"What was Richard's background?"

"What do you mean?"

"Custodial jobs are usually entry-level. People don't stay there unless they don't have a choice. Did he have any education? Did he grow up with his family or in the system? It doesn't sound from his name like he was an immigrant whose qualifications were not accepted here."

"No. He just... I don't know. That's what he could get, so he stayed there. He and his family grew up in Minnesota."

"Are they still around?"

"No."

"Hobbies?"

Ashley's brows drew down. "I don't understand what that has to do with anything."

"I wonder how he spent his time. If he wasn't doing something he enjoyed for work, then I assume he was getting satisfaction from something else he was doing at home."

She gave a helpless shrug. "No... no hobbies. I guess he just... we did things together. Went out to eat or watched TV. Nothing... special."

Zachary tried to think of what else to say. He still didn't know what made her so sure that it hadn't been an unfortunate accident. Was she in denial? He didn't like to take a case just based on the fact that she was in shock over Richard's death. She'd come around to it and then wouldn't want to pay him.

"I'll need a retainer," he said. "If you really want to go ahead with this. But I don't hear anything that leads me to believe it was an accident. I'll need money up front, and you need to be prepared for the fact that I might not find anything that supports your feeling that it was accidental. The police are pretty thorough..."

"But you've solved cases before that they thought were accidental when they were really murder."

"Yes. I have."

"That's why I need you. I need someone who is willing to suspend disbelief and not just follow what the police say. If you come back with it being an accident... I guess I'm going to have to live with that. But I'm not going to find out anything if I don't pursue it. I really need to know. I need to know what happened to

Richard. He wouldn't have just gone out walking in the middle of the night and gotten in an accident like that."

"Okay." As Zachary's dinner got cold, he outlined the financial terms and conditions for Ashley, and she nodded and ate her meal and didn't blanch at the rates he gave her and the upfront retainer. Eventually, Zachary had given her all of the warnings he could think of. "Well, if that sounds okay to you, I'll write it up. You sleep on it tonight and make sure it's really what you want. If you wake up in the morning and have changed your mind, no harm done. Just let me know. If not… I'll start in on what the police have gathered, and see what else needs to be done." Zachary looked at Bowman. "Can I get access to the case files?"

"You know how it is. It's an active investigation, so no. But talk to the right people and push the right buttons, and that could change. Your friend Joshua Campbell is on the case, so it probably won't be too hard. He was happy with the work done on the Salter case."

Zachary nodded, relieved. There were plenty of cops at the police station who didn't like him or didn't want anything to do with a private investigator, but Campbell was not one of them. He'd always been civil toward Zachary. Sometimes, like in the Salter case, he had even given Zachary a tip or given him leave to investigate in a direction he knew his own officers wouldn't be able to pursue.

"That's great. He won't give me any trouble."

"Good," Ashley approved. "You always hear stories about how cops and private eyes can't get along together, or cops and the FBI. I'm glad to know that's just pulp fiction."

Zachary exchanged looks with Bowman. "Oh, it's not always fiction. But it shouldn't be a problem on this file."

2

The first thing for Zachary to check, once he had his retainer from Ashley and was sure that he was okay to go ahead and begin his investigation, was what Richard had been wearing the night he had been killed. There was a big difference between a jogger out with a headlamp and reflective vest and a man walking down the shoulder wearing black pants topped by a black hoodie. In the middle of the night, with no streetlights, a vehicle would be almost on top of him before their headlights picked him out, and then it would be too late. It was easy for a quickly-moving vehicle to outrun its headlights, especially a big, heavy, fully-loaded rig with a deadline to meet.

After talking to Joshua Campbell, Zachary sat down in a meeting room with the first file from the case box, and read through the description of the body and the initial evidence gathered at the scene.

Richard Harding. White, six foot one, one hundred sixty pounds. Body found in the ditch of a secondary highway that ran along his property line. Probable cause of death, pending the autopsy results, blunt force trauma from an MVC. The pictures of the body at the scene did not show a lot of bleeding or bruising. Death had probably been instantaneous.

He was in stocking feet. One shoe had been recovered at the scene and the other was missing. Fashionable red sneakers. Zachary didn't want to guess what they had cost him. Dark blue jeans, white t-shirt, dark green winter coat. The coat would have covered up the white t-shirt and didn't appear to have any reflective embellishments.

The evidence suggested that he had been hit with a powerful force, which had blown him right out of his shoes. Zachary knew from his past investigations and accident scene reconstructions that it indicated a fast-moving vehicle. Had Richard not even heard it coming? Zachary didn't see anything in the file indicating that he'd been wearing earphones that might have blocked the noise of the approaching vehicle. His phone was in his pocket. If he'd been wearing earbuds, they had been torn from his body by the force just the same as the shoes had been.

What reason would he have had to be walking or standing on the road at that time of night? Had he been meeting someone? Walking to a neighbor's? Had he pursued a trespasser or burglar from his property out to the highway? Was he investigating a sound or an animal? Or had he just been out for a walk, unable to sleep and hoping that the exercise and fresh air would help him to reset and get some sleep?

It hadn't sounded from his discussion with Ashley at Old Joe's that walking outside had been a normal activity for Richard. He did his workouts inside where there weren't big rigs to mow him down.

Then what *had* made him decide to go out the night he had died? Zachary made a note in his notepad to check later and see if there had been any trouble Ashley wasn't aware of. Threats or a break-in. Any previous police reports or alarms with his security company. Just because Ashley said there wasn't anything going on, that didn't mean it was true. Richard might have hidden it from Ashley or Ashley might be hiding it from Zachary. He never could understand why a person would want to hire a private detective on a case and then keep secrets from him. But everyone seemed to hold something back.

———

In the evening, he was transcribing his notes from his notepad to the computer. He supposed he should make notes on his phone or get a tablet or a notebook that he took to the police station or other research sources with him, but he preferred the notepad. It was idiot-proof, the batteries didn't run down, and he hadn't yet lost his notes taken in a physical notepad, other than the ones he lost in the fire, along with everything else. If he'd taken those notes on a cloud-connected app, he wouldn't have lost them, and would still have been able to get them back. But he hadn't had anything backed up to the cloud. Not his computer, not his photography, nothing. He was happy to find that his phone had automatically saved his contacts, and he'd had his email, but that was about it. Everything else had been lost in the fire, and Zachary had once again been left vulnerable and homeless, just like after the first fire, when his mother had decided that she couldn't take it anymore and had kicked him out of her life.

Zachary's phone buzzed. It was a few moments before he could tear his eyes from the computer screen to look at the display on the phone. His heart leapt when he saw Bridget's name. He swiped quickly before picking it up, to catch it before she hung up.

"Bridget?"

"Oh, you're there. I was beginning to wonder, Zachary."

"Sorry. I was just in the middle of writing reports. Needed to finish my thought."

"Are you home, then?"

"Yes."

"Mind if I stop over for a few minutes? I have something to give you."

Something to give him? While she still sometimes tried to take care of him, monitoring whether he was taking his meds and eating properly, he couldn't think of what it was that she might want to give him. But he didn't really care. He still welcomed any opportunity to see her again. No matter how many times Kenzie told him that he needed to just cut off contact with his ex, he couldn't do it. Bridget was a big part of his life, and even as an ex, she still had a place in his life.

"Sure, Bridget. I'm around all night."

"Great. I'll pop by a little later, then. Maybe an hour or so."

"I'll see you then."

The call had completely broken his concentration and he wasn't able to focus on the case notes again. He tried for another twenty minutes to get back into them and eventually gave up.

He went to the fridge and looked for something he could serve Bridget when she stopped by. But he didn't entertain much and he didn't think she'd be interested in a frozen dinner. He should start keeping a few bottles of her favorite drinks on hand so he'd always be prepared in case she decided to stop by.

He could just hear what Kenzie would have had to say about that plan.

It wasn't much past the predicted hour when Bridget got there. Zachary could hear her footsteps in the outside corridor and looked out his peep hole to make sure it was her, then opened the door as she drew closer. Bridget raised her eyebrows.

"Well, you didn't need to wait right at the door for me," she said dryly.

"I just happened to be there. I was looking to see if I had any drinks." He motioned to the fridge, giving a little shrug. "Not really anything interesting… maybe some tea?"

"No, I'm not going to be here for that long."

That was one of the reasons Zachary had been hoping to have something for her. Having a drink would encourage her to stay longer than she would otherwise.

"Oh. Well, come on in." He led her to the couch and the two of them sat down side by side. Zachary was careful not to crowd her too much. He didn't want to make her uncomfortable.

Bridget settled into the couch, taking a minute to look around the room for something to compliment or comment upon.

"It's starting to look lived-in," Bridget said. "Not like you just moved in."

"You mean it's a mess?" Zachary tried to keep his possessions orderly, knowing that they would quickly get out of control if he wasn't disciplined about putting things away where they belonged. But his home didn't have the decorator-magazine look of Bridget's home with Gordon. He couldn't function in something that was so antiseptically neat. He would find it just as distracting as an apartment with clothes and food wrappers on the floor.

But he didn't always succeed at keeping everything tidy, especially if he were working on a major case.

"No, I don't mean it's a mess. I mean it looks… like it's yours. Like you've settled in a little bit."

Zachary nodded. "Yeah. It's starting to feel like home."

"That's good. I didn't like it when you were at Mario's. I mean, it was nice to know that there was someone around to keep an eye on things and notice if you were going off the rails, but I think it's important for you to have a place of your own. It really is important for you to…" She shook her head, wrinkling up her nose as she fished for a way to explain her thoughts. "It's important for you to have a home base. An anchor."

Zachary nodded his agreement. He had lived so many years with uncertainty and unstable living arrangements, it was one thing that he craved and really couldn't live for long without. With his own place, he felt better mentally and was better at taking care of himself. Relying on someone like Bowman had allowed him to let things slip, and that wasn't good. He didn't have a lot of room to slip before hitting bottom.

He looked at Bridget, waiting for her to announce the reason she had showed up. She had said that she had something to give him. Bridget stiffened her backbone and reached for her purse.

"This was sort of strange. I didn't know what to make of it."

She inserted two fingers into the mouth of her purse and came out with an envelope. Not a number ten envelope, but the personal size, like grandmothers used when they wrote long rambling notes on flowery stationery. Bridget hadn't opened it, and Zachary's eyes immediately narrowed, wondering if she was worried about a letter bomb or harassing note. She handed it across to Zachary. He held it by the edges, not wanting to get his fingerprints on any evidence.

The envelope was made out in Zachary's name, not Bridget's. At an address that was a couple years old, from when they had been living together in wedded bliss. Or not so much bliss.

"I still have the mail forwarded," Bridget explained. "I know I shouldn't keep paying for forwarding from an address that neither of us has used in years, but then every time I think of letting it expire, I end up getting something that wouldn't have reached me otherwise. Or... you."

Zachary looked over the envelope to see what other information he could gather from it. His name and address were printed. Not exactly neatly, but clear enough to read without a problem. A hand that he would have identified as male rather than female, when women were the ones who usually sent personal notes by postal mail. Handwritten mail—did anyone really do that?

There was a return address, printed in tiny letters, but not so small that Zachary needed a magnifying glass to make it out.

T. Goldman.

Zachary's heart started to pound. He looked at Bridget in disbelief. "T. Goldman?"

"I know, I saw that. I didn't think... well, you haven't had any contact with anyone, have you?"

"No." Zachary hadn't had any communications with anyone in his family since that fateful day when the social worker had insisted that Zachary's mother come to the hospital to see him before making the decision to dissolve the family and relinquish them all to foster care. Mrs. Pratt had hoped that by bringing

Zachary and his mother together again one more time, she would see the error of her ways and would agree to look at other solutions. There were other social programs, other ways the family could be given support and help. But Zachary's mother had been adamant. She had called him incorrigible. She had looked him in the eye and told him, "You don't deserve to be part of a family. None of you do, but you most of all. Every time I turn around, you're getting into some kind of trouble. Don't give me those sad puppy dog eyes. You know I don't want you."

Her words cut him to the heart. He had tried so hard. Even after that, he had tried to be well-behaved in the hopes that she would change her mind and take him back. He wanted to prove to everyone how well he was doing. Show them that he could be a good son and a good brother. They could reunite him with his siblings. Maybe once their mother had had a bit of a rest, she would feel strong enough to take them again. She'd see that he could be a help to her instead of causing her more stress. But that wasn't the way it had turned out. She had never changed her mind and, in spite of Mrs. Pratt saying that he would be able to see his siblings again, he had never laid eyes on any of them since the fire that had burned down his childhood home.

"Zachary." Bridget touched his arm to try to bring him back to the present. "Zachary. Why don't you open it? See what they have to say." She hesitated, searching his face. "Do you know who T is? Is that a brother or a sister? Or a more distant relative?"

"Tyrrell. Younger brother. His nickname was T. At least, that's what I called him sometimes."

"Remind me of the names of the others. I know you've told me before, but I don't remember. There were two girls…?"

"Two older girls," Zachary corrected. "The oldest kids were Jocelyn—Joss—and Heather. They were like… they were supposed to take care of the rest of us. Like… second mothers."

"And then you?"

"Yeah. Me, I was ten. And then T was… I think he was in first grade. Six years old. Then Vincent. And Mindy. She was just little.

Not a baby anymore, exactly. A toddler. Maybe two. Not quite two, I don't think."

It was hard to remember back that far. So many things had happened in between. His memories of those early years with his family felt like a dream. Not a happy one, but distant and blurry.

"Wow, that's a lot of kids. You haven't had contact with any of them?"

"No. I don't know where they are."

"Well, apparently you do now," she indicated the address on the envelope. "Besides, you're a private detective, you could find them anytime you liked, couldn't you?"

"I don't know. They might have changed their names. Been adopted. Moved out of the country."

"But you've never looked for them?"

"No."

She sat there looking at him. She didn't pry, but it was obvious she wanted more from him. They'd been married for two years, and he hadn't told her any more than the absolute minimum about his biological family. It would be easy to say he had forgotten about them, but he hadn't. He'd been ten. He'd held as tightly to those memories as to his own name and identity. They were all he had left of his family.

"I'm afraid," he admitted. "If I contacted one of them, and they said they didn't want anything to do with me, I don't know if I could handle that. And if they blamed me for breaking our family apart and ruining their lives… well, I did. It was all my fault. Everything that happened to them from that Christmas Eve when I started the fire until now. It's all my fault."

"You never intended to start the fire. And I don't think you can say that you were the reason your mother and father decided to split the family up. That's on them, not you. There have been other families that have gone through worse tragedies and toughed it out together. None of you were killed in that fire. None of them were even injured, were they? Just you."

"Yeah." He'd spent weeks at the hospital recovering from the burns and the damage done to his respiratory system. But everyone else had gotten out of the house without any injuries, he had been told. "But she told me. She said it was my fault, and that it was because of me that she couldn't do it anymore."

"If it was because of you, then why didn't she raise the other kids and just have Social Services take you away? That doesn't make any sense."

Zachary shook his head. He looked down at the envelope in his hands.

"Open it," Bridget prompted.

"I can't."

"Then give it back to me and I'll open it."

He didn't. It was his. It wasn't Bridget's to open. It wasn't even hers to read or to insist that he open it in front of her. Just because it had gone to her house, that didn't give her any claim over it.

"So… you're just going to sit here looking at it. You're not going to open it."

"Uh-huh."

"Because you're afraid of what he'll say."

Zachary nodded. He flipped the envelope over in his hand, turned it back around again, and studied the postmark and stamp as if they were important evidence in a case.

"You think that he's waited thirty years to tell you how much he hates you for something that wasn't your fault."

"It *was* my fault."

"He was a little boy. He's trying to reach out to his big brother. It isn't about blame. He wants to get in touch with you."

Zachary pressed his lips tightly together and shook his head. He looked at the clock on his DVD player across the room. "I didn't realize how long I've kept you," he said. It wasn't a total lie because he was surprised at how much time had passed. He must have withdrawn into himself for a long time. He shook his head, as if that would clear his sense of disorientation. "Gordon will be wondering what happened to you."

Bridget recognized a dismissal when she heard it. She stood up slowly, looking down at Zachary on the couch.

"I'm here because I want to help, Zachary."

"Thank you for bringing the letter. I appreciate it."

Kenzie had said to cut his ties with Bridget. This was exactly what she had meant. Bridget thought that she had the right to be involved in Zachary's life and to make decisions for him. She thought that he owed her something because she had put up with him for two years and had brought him the letter. But she was the one who had chosen to break up. That hadn't been Zachary's decision.

Bridget huffed out an exasperated breath and headed for the door. "Are you just going to sit there looking at it all night?"

Maybe. Probably.

"Thanks for bringing it," he repeated.

Bridget's heels clicked all the way to the door, and she pulled it shut behind her with force that wasn't quite a slam, but not exactly a sedate departure either.

Zachary put one hand over his face, elbow braced on his knee, and tried to figure out what to do.

3

Rusty Donaldson was the trucker who had hit Richard. Zachary didn't know if Rusty was his birth name or a nickname due to his orange beard and hair. He was a pleasant man, around Zachary's own age, but much bigger, his chest twice as thick as Zachary's, towering over him by a least a foot. A hearty man's man.

"Uh, hi." Zachary forced a smile and offered his hand. Big men made him nervous. Sure, he'd known a few gentle giants, but more often he'd been bullied by the bigger boys as he grew up. There was lot of competition in foster homes and institutions, lots of opportunities for physical and emotional torture by the boys who were bigger and stronger.

Rusty took Zachary's hand and shook it warmly, without squeezing the life out of it. Though he had a naturally cheerful face, it turned grave as he looked at Zachary.

"I'll answer whatever questions you might have," he said. "I'm just sick over this thing. I'd never intentionally hurt someone, much less kill them. I feel awful for his family, and I'll do whatever I can to... make some sense of this for them."

Zachary nodded. Rusty had picked out the meeting place, the lounge of a truck stop. It was clean, quiet during the day, and upholstered in a dark red. They sat down and Rusty leaned in, eager to get started with the questions. Zachary felt a little disconcerted, used to witnesses who were a little more reticent.

"Why don't you tell me in your own words what happened that night, and then we can go over some additional details as questions come to me. You don't mind if I take notes while you're talking?"

"No, man. Go ahead."

"Thanks." Zachary opened his notepad and nodded for Rusty to begin.

He started off with a lot of technical information about the run he'd been doing, which meant little to Zachary, but he wrote down the details he thought were pertinent. Rusty's deadline and destination, the route he'd followed until he got to the secondary road where Richard had been killed.

"You'd been on that road before?" Zachary asked. "You're familiar with it?"

"Oh, sure. Been on it a dozen times before. A good shortcut, if you know the road goes all the way through. A lot of experienced truckers take it."

"And you'd never run into any trouble before."

"Nah. It's quiet. No accidents, no mechanical problems. The road itself is in good condition; paved, no potholes or ruts to deal with."

"But no shoulder, either, if you did run into any problems."

"No, you're right. Have you been on it?"

"I'm going to drive out to take a look at it after I have your story. No point in going out without knowing something about what happened."

"So you can check out my story," Rusty said with a bit of a grin.

Zachary returned his smile. "Of course."

"Good man. So... there's not really that much to tell. I was flying along, no obstacle or problems, nice straight stretch of road. Then I hear a bang and feel the truck take some kind of impact.

So I hit the brakes and pulled over the best I could, in the dark with no shoulder. Got out the old Mag flashlight and scouted around the truck to see what had happened. Figured maybe I hit a deer. Not like it hasn't happened before."

"And what did you see?"

"A new dent and a bit of blood on the front right. No significant damage, lights were all intact. Maybe an animal smaller than a deer. A coyote or something."

"Did you have a look around to see if you could see it?"

"Sure. Walked back along the road maybe half a mile, sweeping my light across the road and off the side into the ditch. But I couldn't see anything suspicious. Couldn't find the place where I'd hit it, couldn't find any sign of a hurt animal. Sometimes they just run off into the woods and there's nothing you can do. I looked again on my way back to the truck, still couldn't see anything. So I got back in and kept going."

"And you had to have your load delivered the next morning," Zachary said, looking at his notes. "So you must have driven all night."

"We've all pulled an all-nighter now and then. I'm sure you have too."

Zachary hadn't slept a wink the night before. He nodded. "Yes, a few."

"Company's got rules about night driving and the number of hours you can drive at a time, all aimed to keep sleepy drivers off the road. Most guys are pretty good about following them."

Zachary noticed that Rusty didn't exactly say that he had followed them.

"I dropped my load and headed for home. I was just a couple of hours further on, then I could flake out in my own bed."

"Right. The police said you reported the possible collision to your insurer that morning?"

"Sure. You have to get these things taken care of as quickly as you can. No one is going to give you any breaks if you put it off. I called, told them I figured I hit a coyote, all the details, and went to bed."

"But it was a few days before you called the police."

Rusty nodded grimly. "I got my sleep in, took a couple of days' break, just like the company policy states. I was lined up for another run, so I went out to check out my truck, make sure I hadn't missed any damage in the dark that night."

Zachary cleared his throat and waited. Rusty was scowling, his bushy eyebrows drawn down fiercely over his eyes.

"There was a dent and blood spatter on the front, like I said. I took a picture with my phone and grabbed the high-pressure washer to clean it off. While I was washing it off, I was looking for any other damage or clue to what I had hit. There was a torn bit of cloth in the fender. It could have gotten there some other time. I didn't know for sure. But it seemed… out of place. Like it wasn't just someone who had brushed by it in the parking lot and got their jacket caught."

"So that's when you called the police."

"Yeah. Didn't get much response when I first called it in. It was just kind of a routine report, they didn't seem to think there was anything to be worried about. But then I got a call back from the police detective who was in charge of this Harding case. Told me I'd better come in and give a statement. Answer some questions." Rusty sighed. "So that's what I did. You might think that all truckers are naturally law-breakers, always in trouble with the police, but we're not. There are some rowdies out there, and everybody's had a traffic citation at some point, but most of us, we do our best to stay out of trouble and just live our own lives."

"Sure. So you were pretty anxious about having to go in and tell them about what had happened. You wondered why they had called you back after the reception to the initial call was so cool."

Rusty nodded earnestly. "Yes. Exactly. That's it exactly. I go in, thinking they want me to just write down in triplicate what I had told them on the phone, and it turned out that they had found a body in the ditch. I'd actually hit a person, and I had no idea." He blew out his breath noisily. "You have no idea how that feels."

"The police followed up on the call you made with your insurer. They examined your truck, even though you had already washed it off."

"I guess there was still some blood that I hadn't gotten off. In cracks. They charged me with hit and run, but released me, and the DA is reviewing it now... I guess deciding whether I did everything right, or whether there was something else I should have done. I swear I looked in the ditch, but it was dark, and I must have missed him. If there was something I could have done..." He had a haunted look. "I can't imagine him, lying in the ditch there, dying, thinking that nobody cared and that I had just gone on..."

It was a macabre thought, and Zachary didn't envy Rusty his nightmares. He had done everything right as far as Zachary could tell. He hadn't known that he had hit anyone.

But Zachary had been hired to look into Richard's death from the other angle. To look into the possibility that Rusty Donaldson had intentionally killed Richard on the road that night.

"Did you know Richard Harding?"

"Know him?" Rusty shook his head. "No way. I'd never heard of the guy before the police told me he was dead. I guess I'd driven down his road before, past his farm, but I had no idea. I don't know anyone who lives along that route. Not that I know of."

"His girlfriend doesn't think it was an accident."

"Not an accident? What, she thinks..." Rusty's florid color drained. "She thinks that I ran down her boyfriend on purpose?"

"Yes."

"Why would she think that?" He seemed truly astonished. Apparently, the police hadn't told him about Ashley's theory.

"I haven't quite figured that out yet. There may be something she isn't telling me. Maybe he got threats or had something on his mind. Maybe it's just the shock and grief. I don't know. But that's why she's hired me."

"She hired you to prove that I killed Harding on purpose?"

"Yes."

Rusty's expression changed so rapidly Zachary was reminded of a board game spinner cycling through options. Where was it going to land? Anger, astonishment, regret, fear, more anger, directed at Zachary this time, confusion, guilt, more wide-eyed fear. Finally, he just stared at Zachary, blanking all expression out, staring at him with lifeless eyes, as if Rusty himself had left his corporeal form and gone far away.

"I never met Harding before in my life. I don't know what he was doing out on the road that night, but if I'd seen him, I would have avoided him. I would never have hit him on purpose. The thought that I hit and killed a man... it just makes me sick. Whenever I think of the thud that night, my stomach is all in knots."

"As far as you know, you never talked with him, never emailed or texted him, never ran into each other at some social event."

"No. Nothing. I've never heard of the guy before in my life."

"You never dated his sister or his girlfriend."

"Uh..." Rusty shook his head. "I have no idea who his girl-friend is. How would I know that?"

"Do you know an Ashley Morton?"

"Is that her name?"

"Do you?"

"No. No, I don't know anyone named Ashley Morton. I don't date a lot, and when I do, it's usually ladies who... hang out around the truck stops. If your girlfriend is one of those gals, then maybe we've hooked up before. But I don't remember an Ashley."

"I'll try to find any connections between you. And I'm a good investigator, you should know that. If you've had any contact with Richard Harding or Ashley Morton before or after the accident, you should just tell me now."

"No. I swear, I've never heard of either one of them before."

"Would you mind giving me all of your contact details? Any

phone numbers or email addresses that you use? Your home address, anywhere you use computers regularly?"

"Why would I do that? You could set me up!"

"I'm not trying to set you up. If you haven't had any contact with him, then you have nothing to worry about."

Rusty motioned for Zachary's notepad and pen. Zachary flipped to a fresh page and slid it across to him. Rusty wrote down several lines of information.

"Anything else?" he demanded. "Social security number? Blood type?"

"If you want to include those, and your birth date, that would make things easier for me," Zachary agreed, keeping his voice and expression flat.

Rusty looked up at Zachary in surprise, then broke into a grin again, the mask of indifference falling away. "It's not in my best interests to make your job easy." He looked down at the information he had written down. "So why am I giving you all of this?" He pushed it back across to Zachary as if he were afraid that he might tear the page out and crumple it up. "If I had contact with Harding, do you really think I would give you that address or phone number?"

"No. I don't. I don't think I'll find any of these numbers or addresses on anything with Richard Harding's name on it. But eliminating them is one more step. One more thing I can do for my client."

Rusty shook his head. "Helluva job you've got there, Goldman. Helluva job."

Zachary knew that if he wanted to avoid another sleepless night, he was going to have to open the letter from Tyrrell. Bridget hadn't called him or contacted him to see if he'd opened it yet, but he was sure she was thinking about it, wondering how long it would take him to pull himself together and simply rip the envelope open.

He wore gloves and slit it carefully with a knife, treating it as if it were important forensic evidence. And it could be, couldn't it? There might be DNA in the saliva that was used to seal the envelope, if it wasn't a self-sealing envelope and if the sender hadn't used a sponge-top bottle to seal it. There could be fingerprints on it. There could be other evidence that he wasn't aware of. A hair stuck in the seal. Skin cells. Other transfer evidence.

He slit the end rather than the top, and then pressed the top and bottom of the envelope to make it pop open in a tube shape to examine the contents.

It appeared to be a single sheet of paper. No unknown powders or other contaminants. No letter bomb. Just one piece of paper.

He used a pair of tweezers to snag the letter and pull it out onto the table. Just a plain white piece of paper, torn off a tablet, slightly jagged at the top. Not a densely-written letter, just a few loose lines of print, the same printing that had appeared on the outside of the envelope.

Dear Zachary,

I am looking for my brother.

Do you remember me?

If you are the right Zachary Goldman, please get in contact with me.

T

He had followed with several lines of contact information. An email address, a cell phone number to call or text. A repeat of the return address written on the outside of the envelope.

Zachary read the words over again hungrily, like a starving man who, expecting a feast, had been given only a single cracker. Tyrrell—assuming it was Tyrrell who had written the letter— wanted to get in touch with him. But he had left it up to Zachary.

There were no declarations of love or hate, leaving him to wonder how Tyrrell felt about him. Sorry they had been separated? Angry for what Zachary had done? Maybe he didn't care about reconciling and just needed a kidney. Would Zachary give him a kidney if he asked?

Zachary carefully put the envelope and letter into a plastic bag before taking off his gloves.

4

Zachary ran a full background check on Rusty Donaldson. Criminal record, courthouse search, credit check, past residences, family members, all of the public records he could think of. He owned his truck and rented his house. He didn't have any criminal charges. No DUIs. A few speeding tickets, but none of them at crazy speeds and none of them at night. He'd had stable employment. No marriages, divorces, or paternity suits. All in all, a guy who had been living quietly within the law for many years.

The next task was to check out Harding's phone and laptop, which Ashley had supplied Zachary with. The police had looked at his phone and not found anything of interest, but Zachary knew they didn't usually look at electronics too closely unless there was a compelling reason, and in the case of a man accidentally hit from behind on a dark road at night, there wasn't a reason to give them more than a cursory look. Zachary had called Gerry Birch, his usual tech guy, who had cloned the computer's hard drive to preserve any data. Gerry had also broken the news to Zachary that the drive was encrypted, which meant that a simple boot hack like he'd used in other cases would not be helpful.

The first thing he thought odd was that Harding's phone didn't have any social media on it. No profiles, no instant messaging apps, nothing. The apps built in by default had been removed. The email address that was attached to the phone was a new address that had just been set up within the last year and had only a few non-spam messages in it.

Even the text messages had been wiped. Zachary had looked at dozens of phones that still had every text message since the beginning of time stored on them. People hardly ever deleted text messages, and if they did, it was just a few here and there. The ones that were incriminating. Harding's text messages had been completely wiped. There were only a few messages exchanged with Ashley, in the day or two before he had died. Then the increasingly worried and frantic texts that Ashley had sent when she couldn't reach him the morning after the accident. Zachary followed the progression from casual and routine to really worried, demanding Richard call her.

The phone itself was a recent purchase, within a few months of Harding's death. For anything earlier than that, Zachary would have to see what he could get from the phone company. Getting call logs, text logs, and old voicemail messages from phone companies could be complicated. It sometimes took weeks or even months to get everything. Even a police warrant didn't always get an immediate response from one of the big providers.

Ashley had known the unlock code for the phone, which had saved Zachary the effort of trying to hack it. The computer was another story. Zachary tried a few different passwords, hoping that the computer didn't have any kind of software on it that would automatically destroy data once the limit of password retries was reached. Variations of Ashley's name, Harding's birthday, anniversaries of when they had met and started dating. The phone unlock code had been a simple pattern, but trying to replicate it on the computer didn't work.

Zachary searched through the phone for any note or password keeping app. He glanced at the computer screen and noticed an unlock icon. He turned the phone screen off, sending it into standby mode, and the lock icon disappeared. He could have kicked himself. The phone was a key to unlock the computer. A proximity auto-unlock. Zachary unlocked the phone again and clicked the unlock icon when it appeared on the computer screen. The laptop whirred and the screen came to life. He was in.

At first look, the computer was much the same as the phone. It was of recent vintage and didn't have a lot stored on it. The email address was the same as the one attached to the phone and all messages and messaging apps had been removed.

When he opened the browser, it booted automatically into a private window instead of the usual browser experience. The kind that didn't leave electronic footprints showing what sites had been visited. In Zachary's experience, it was rare that the average computer user even knew about private browsing modes, much less had their default browse mode set to private. He dug into the computer's connection details and found that it was also set up to connect through an IP anonymizer, making it more difficult to track where the computer was logging in from. It was some serious online security, which was surprising considering how easy it had been to get onto the phone and computer in the first place.

Private mode on the browser was set to automatically wipe the history of the sites visited. Zachary switched over to regular browsing, and found that the history had been deleted there.

He switched over to the built-in operating system app that could save and autocomplete passwords, and found that it had not been cleared out. Zachary went methodically through the list. All of the main social media sites. Some news sites. Harding's email address. But there was another email address too, one that neither the computer nor the phone were logged into. Zachary typed the webmail URL into the browser and accepted the autofill suggestion. The inbox had obviously not been checked in some time and was overflowing with unread messages. Zachary stared at the bold black subject lines.

How could you live with yourself?
*You are a piece of s****
You should be ashamed of yourself

You should die

Zachary swore to himself under his breath. He had begun to suspect that there was something strange going on with Harding. The lack of social apps and texts on his phone, the private browser, and a brand-new email address were not exactly red flags, but had made him curious. If Harding was being electronically stalked and harassed, that would explain why he had started taking counter-measures to cover up his online activity.

Zachary started to read through the accusatory emails. They were, unfortunately, vague and rambling and did not outline exactly what the writer believed Harding had done. The accuser had known and had assumed that Harding also knew exactly what he was talking about.

The emails came from a number of different addresses with odd combinations of letters and numbers, obviously from a system that generated one-off addresses. The kind you could use when you wanted to download a free guide without getting spammed by the company afterward. Chances were the email addresses themselves would be untraceable.

Zachary logged into each of Harding's abandoned social media accounts in turn. It didn't take long to find the vitriolic messages in the direct mailboxes of each of them too. It was no wonder Harding had stopped using them. There was no escaping the messages. Harding's banned, muted, and blocked user lists were long, but his stalker had obviously just kept creating new identities and harassing Harding relentlessly.

After spending hours going through Richard's social media and poison pen messages, Zachary was almost afraid to look at his own phone when it buzzed to indicate that he'd received a text message. He knew it was silly, because he wasn't the one who had been getting the harassing messages. The only unusual contact that he'd received recently was the letter from Tyrrell. But after seeing how the stalker had hounded Richard, Zachary couldn't help feeling a little vulnerable himself.

As a private detective, he knew how easy it was to find out all kinds of supposedly private details about the average person, but he had never been particularly careful about protecting his own information. Maybe in the back of his mind, he had hoped that by leaving a trail, one day some member of his family would come along and track him down. If he made himself too difficult to find, then there was no chance he would ever be reunited with his loved ones.

Zachary picked up his phone, and instead of seeing a message from Richard's stalker or from Tyrrell, he was almost surprised to see a message from Kenzie.

Hear you're on the Harding case. Give me a call when you're free.

Zachary stretched and yawned noisily. He unfolded himself from his chair at the desk and made a trip to the bathroom and then to the fridge before calling Kenzie back. If they ended up having a longer discussion, he didn't want to be interrupted by inconvenient physical demands. He'd been hunched over the computer for hours, which was not good for his body or his mind. He walked briskly around the apartment for a minute to get the blood flowing and to clear his head.

He sat on the couch and gave Kenzie a call. He closed his eyes and visualized her masses of dark curly hair and her bright red lipsticked lips as the phone rang. He felt a rush of warmth when he answered and heard her "Hi, Zachary."

"Hi. How are you?"

"What's this I hear? You get a new case out of my office and you don't give me a call? What's going on with you?" Her voice was teasing, not really angry with him. Usually, she was irritated when he asked about a case that she believed was clearly accidental but he thought might just be something else.

"You hear it from Bowman?" he asked.

"Where else? You apparently didn't think it was important enough to call me."

"I don't need you yet," Zachary returned, teasing her gently back.

"Ha. Exactly! I know how it is. The only reason you're interested in me is to get someone to interpret pathology reports for you."

"Kenzie, you know that's not true... I'm getting pretty good at reading them by myself."

She chuckled. "Well, your friend is in autopsy right now, so I thought maybe you'd like to get together for supper to go through initial findings. Full report won't be ready yet, of course, but I can hit the high points."

"Yeah, that would be great." Zachary looked at Richard's phone and computer, and thought he might want to show Kenzie what he had found there. Which meant that a restaurant wouldn't be the best place to meet. The two of them huddled over a laptop at a restaurant would be awkward, even if he waited until after they had eaten. "How would you like to come over here and we'll order in?"

"Oh," she was obviously surprised at the invitation. They really didn't stay in. Most of the time, she was trying to make sure he got out of the house for something other than surveillance. "Sure, that sounds fine."

5

Kenzie showed up on schedule and she and Zachary went through a few takeout menus before settling on pizza and placing their order. They talked in general terms about work and the weather and current events while they waited for the pizza.

"Are you getting ready for Christmas?" Kenzie asked.

Zachary tried to figure out how to respond to her. She didn't mean anything by it, she was just making more small talk, the events of the previous year and what she knew of his past far from her mind.

Kenzie lifted one eyebrow, waiting for his answer. Then he saw realization enter her features, and her mouth formed a small 'O' of surprise. "I wasn't even thinking, Zachary! I forgot that Christmas is a hard time for you. I'm sorry."

"It's okay." Zachary tried to brush it off and move on to other topics. "It's just my thing, you shouldn't have to tiptoe around me."

"Well, since I already put my foot in it, how are you doing with it? Does your therapist have any tips for getting through holidays and anniversaries of bad things happening?"

"I… never thought to ask."

"You know that you're seriously depressed every Christmas,

and you haven't addressed it with him? Don't you think that might be a good idea?"

Zachary shrugged. "I've had so many psychiatrists and therapists in the past... none of them have ever been able to do anything about my state of mind around Christmas. I'm just used to... trying to get through it on my own."

"I don't think that's a good idea. You need to get help and not be left alone with your own thoughts at a time when you know you're likely to be suicidal."

Zachary scratched his jaw, his face and ears burning. "Uh..."

"I'm sorry if being blunt embarrasses you. But it's not a topic to be delicate about. Do you know how many people end up in the morgue because they didn't talk openly about being depressed and having suicidal thoughts?"

"I guess more than would if they talked about it. I'm just... not used to it. People just usually don't want to hear. It makes them uncomfortable." He was aware that he was echoing Bridget's words. How many times had she chided him that talking about depression or mental illness in front of their friends made them uncomfortable, and he should never do anything that he knew would make them uncomfortable. He had grown up knowing this rule in the back of his head and knowing that talking about depression and suicide was taboo, but he'd never had anyone tell him that explicitly before Bridget. It just *wasn't* discussed in polite company.

"Taking care of yourself means letting other people help and explaining when there is a problem," Kenzie said. "If you push everyone away, then you're going to find yourself alone and that's going to be a problem."

"Yeah. I know you're right, but over the years... people have their own family traditions at Christmas. I don't like to impose on anyone."

Kenzie pulled her phone out. "Look, let's start planning now. Christmas Day, you and I are going to get together for dinner. My place." They never went to Kenzie's apartment, so this news startled Zachary. He figured since she had never invited him to her apartment, that she was protecting her own safety. She didn't want someone else in her space. She didn't want someone else to have access to her living quarters. It was a matter of keeping safe. She knew she could always leave Zachary's apartment, but she couldn't leave her own. Kenzie didn't seem to notice Zachary's consternation, tapping the details into her phone. "Don't expect a big turkey dinner. I'll do a two-person version. Turkey breast, gravy, mashed potatoes. But I'm not doing a whole bird, there's no point in that." She looked up from her phone, raising both brows.

"Okay," Zachary agreed. "Sure. Thanks, that's really nice of you."

"Aren't you going to put it into your phone or planner?"

Zachary's guts knotted tightly. He could barely breathe. "I'll do it later."

"You might forget later. Just put it in now."

Zachary looked for a way out of it. He knew that he'd never be able to put anything on his calendar past Christmas Eve. That was always the way. He couldn't plan anything past that cliff.

He swallowed hard and pulled a sticky note out of the dispenser on his desk. Putting it on the desk, he hovered his pen over the note for a few seconds, with no idea what to even write. Finally, he forced himself to scratch out the words, "Kenzie X-mas?" He unstuck the note from the desk and stuck it to the edge of his monitor. Kenzie looked satisfied with this process.

"Good. You know what can really help around Christmastime when you're feeling really overwhelmed with everything?"

She really didn't have any idea how paralyzing it was for him. He didn't just feel stressed at Christmas. He didn't have problems with Christmas lists and trying to buy presents for loved ones. He didn't worry over baking cookies for Santa or some community potluck. For him, it wasn't overwhelming because there was too much to do. It was overwhelming because he couldn't stop thinking about his family and how he had ruined their lives and his and how the pain would stop if he just chose to put an end to it.

He shook his head in response to Kenzie's question. "No. What helps?"

"Doing something for someone else. Taking the focus off yourself and thinking about how you can help someone else to have a good Christmas."

Zachary grunted noncommittally.

"I know. You think it sounds cliche. But it isn't. Reaching out to someone else, taking the focus off of your own problems, it really does help."

"Yeah, maybe."

"You know what would be a really good idea?" Kenzie's voice rose excitedly as the thought came to her. Zachary shook his head. "What about doing something for Rhys?"

Rhys was a young black boy whom Zachary had met on a previous case. Rhys's mother had ended up in prison, which meant he really was going to have a bad Christmas, his first one without her. Or maybe going to the prison to visit with her on Christmas. Not quite as bad as Zachary's experience of burning the house down and losing everything he had on Christmas Eve, but it was a contender. Rhys had selective mutism, which had developed after his grandfather was murdered when he was still just a child. If anyone could compete with Zachary for rotten childhoods, it was Rhys.

Zachary swallowed, his throat dry. "Yeah. He's going to have a pretty sad Christmas this year."

"So let's do something for him. Think about it, okay? We'll brainstorm, and maybe talk to Vera and see what she suggests."

"Yeah." Despite his misgivings, Zachary found that his heart did lift a little at the thought of doing something for Rhys so that his Christmas could be a little better. He forced a smile for Kenzie so that she would see he agreed it was a good idea. "Thanks."

There was a knock on the door and Zachary peered through the peep hole at the pizza deliveryman before opening it. The spicy and sweet smell of freshly-baked pepperoni pizza wafted into the apartment. Zachary settled up the bill and tipped the delivery-man, then put the box out on the table and opened it up.

"That smells great! I could eat a horse!" Kenzie declared.

Zachary had disposable plates and he had nipped across the street to pick up some beer before Kenzie's arrival. He put out the extra items. Kenzie twisted off the cap on a bottle of beer.

"You having anything tonight?"

He considered the possibility, then shook his head. He hadn't slept the night before, and if his thoughts turned to Tyrell's letter he might want to take something to help calm his thoughts and help him to sleep. He wasn't supposed to mix alcohol with his medications, so if he didn't want to eliminate the possibility of taking pills later, he'd have to pass on beer at supper.

"I'll just have water."

"You know, I admire you being careful not to mix your meds and alcohol," Kenzie commented as she took a couple of big slices of pizza from the box and slid them onto her plate. "Too many people just ignore those problems and end up with liver damage or a really bad reaction. Or a toxic combination. I'd rather not see you on Dr. Wiltshire's table."

Zachary shrugged and looked for the smallest piece of the pizza. "It's not a big deal."

"Actually, it is. I'm proud of you for not allowing yourself 'just one' or saying you'll have burned it all off by the time you need to take anything. A lot of people ignore those warnings."

"Well... thanks."

They sat down in the living room to eat. Kenzie lounged comfortably against the armrest and closed her eyes to savor the pizza. "This is great. I'll have to remember them next time I'm ordering in."

As disgusting as it might seem to outsiders, Zachary and Kenzie often talked over autopsy results while they ate, so once they were settled, Zachary started to think about Richard Harding and his sudden death on the side of the road that night.

"So you have some initial autopsy findings on Harding?"

Kenzie took another big bite and nodded while she chewed it. "Yeah. Nothing shocking. Blunt force trauma that shattered everything down his left side. Consistent with what would happen if he was walking down the right side of the road with his back to traffic. Death was probably instantaneous. Not a lot of bleeding despite the trauma."

"That will make Rusty Donaldson feel better."

"Who is Rusty?"

"The trucker who hit him. Having nightmares about Harding slowly dying in the ditch because he didn't see him in the dark, even when he went back and looked."

"Oh. That sounds pretty awful. I didn't know they'd caught the guy. But yeah, Harding didn't likely suffer."

"And there wasn't anything out of place or unexplained?"

"Tox screen was clean. He wasn't drunk or high, so I have no clue why he was out walking on the road in the dark."

"Wearing dark clothing and walking with his back to the traffic."

"A lot of people don't seem to know they're supposed to walk on the left. They're so used to driving on the right, that's what they automatically do. But dark clothing... that's pretty stupid. From what I understand, there's a fair bit of traffic on that road."

"Yeah. It's not exactly a quiet farm road, from what I gather. I'm going to go out and take a look at the scene in a day or two."

"Well..." Kenzie shrugged. "Who knows what his reasons were. Maybe he was out looking for his dog. Or checking on a strange noise. Or a UFO."

Zachary chuckled. He nibbled at his slice of pizza. Kenzie had already worked her way through one big slice and was starting the second.

"The girlfriend thinks it wasn't an accident. She thinks that the driver hit Harding on purpose."

"Is that why you're on the case? Looking to prove intentional homicide?"

"Yeah. I mean... not trying to prove it, but investigating whether it's a possibility. I don't have any intention of railroading the guy."

"I hope not. Not the Zachary I know. Why does she think it was on purpose?"

"She didn't give me a cogent reason. But I might have found it without her help."

"What?" Kenzie inquired, mouth full.

Zachary motioned to Richard's computer. He crossed the room to sit at the desk, putting his plate to the side so it wouldn't be near any sensitive equipment. He hated the feeling of crumbs crunching under the computer keys.

"I've got his computer. A lot of stuff has been deleted from his phone and computer. All of his social media apps. He had been using a new email address recently, but I did get into his former email address." Zachary beckoned Kenzie over. She stood behind his shoulder, keeping her pizza well back from the computer. Zachary switched back to the email screen he'd been looking at previously and waited for Kenzie's reaction. She leaned forward to read the subject lines and her mouth dropped open.

"Holy crap!"

Zachary nodded his agreement. "He tried to block the guy, but nothing worked, he just kept rotating email addresses. So Harding created a new email account and stopped opening the previous one. And he started using IP anonymizers and private browser windows to keep from leading the stalker to the new email address."

"That's pretty hard core."

"The stalker was sending stuff to all of his social media accounts and probably his phone number, and was harassing him through whatever means possible. I mean... look at these."

Kenzie was looking at the subject lines. She shook her head. "Things were really bad. Poor guy. You think this is why the girl-friend said it was intentional homicide? Because she knew he was being stalked?"

"He must have told her about it, right? I can't imagine him just going on with his life and not even mentioning it to his partner."

"You're right. He'd need to tell someone. He couldn't just deal with it without anyone else even knowing."

Zachary nodded. He held a lot of things in. He put up with the pain and didn't tell those closest to him. He thought he could deal with it himself. But keeping the extent of the harassment Richard was dealing with a secret seemed impossible.

"So does the girlfriend think that this Rusty, this truck driver, is the one who was harassing Harding?"

"I don't know. She didn't say anything about it. But that's going to have to be my next step. Trying to trace the cyberstalking back to Rusty. Matching up his schedule with the IP locations of the emails. He's a long haul trucker, so these emails should originate from all over the area he covers."

"Yeah. Good thinking. Unless he's been masking his IP addresses, which I certainly would if I was stalking someone. If he knows how to track Richard's email address and other details, then he wouldn't leave himself open the same way. He'd cover them up so no one could get back to him."

"Even if he did, there should still be a pattern to the timing as well. No emails when he was actually driving from one place to another. More during his down times. And some kind of connection between the two of them, because he needs to have a reason for this. They must have belonged to the same club, gone to the same church, something. And they don't exactly live in the same neighborhood. They must have some kind of shared history. This sounds personal, don't you think?"

"Have you read through them to see what they're talking about? What it was that triggered this guy?"

Zachary randomly clicked on one of the subject lines, opening the email. The subject line was "you should be too ashamed to even live," and when the email opened, it was filled with dark and violent moving gifs. Kenzie winced and pulled back.

"Oh. Yuck."

"There is text in some of them." Zachary closed the email and clicked on another. There were a couple of lines of rambling text. Zachary, staring hard at the words to make them stay still and make sense, ended up just shaking his head. "I can't make heads or tails of it. You'd think that with my experience, raving lunatics would make at least some sense."

"Don't put yourself down. If you're going to catch this guy, you're going to have to outsmart him. You've done that before and you can do it again. He'll have made a mistake somewhere, we just have to find it."

Zachary closed the email again and just stared at the flickering screen. "Do you think it's the trucker? Or do you think it's coincidence that he was being stalked and then got killed?"

"I don't know… Obviously, the girlfriend would disagree with me, but this doesn't have the hallmarks of a stalker or a crime of passion or insanity. It feels like an accident. Like the truck driver was just lighting a cigarette or changing the radio tuner, and looked away from the road in the instant that he might have caught a glimpse of Harding. Night driving, going a bit too fast, Harding is all dressed in dark colors. Rusty wouldn't have been able to see Harding until he was on top of him, and then it's too late."

Zachary nodded. So far, he didn't see anything that suggested otherwise. The fact that Richard had a cyberstalker did not mean that the stalker had killed him.

6

Ashley griped and groaned about having to meet Zachary at suppertime out at Harding's house, and Zachary wondered if maybe she thought he was fishing for a date or even just a free meal. That wasn't what he had been doing, and he tried to explain to Ashley without saying anything that might disturb her.

"I'd like to see the road while it's still light enough to see where they found Richard's body and scout around a little. But I also want to see it at night. How dark it is, how busy it is, how far ahead a truck would have been able to see. I don't want to have to put you out twice, so I thought if I could catch the daylight and the nighttime both in one visit, that would work the best."

"Oh." Ashley thought about this. He didn't know if she were looking for an argument, a way to talk him out of his logic, but if she were, she didn't seem to find it. "I guess... I can see your point."

"You don't need to feed me. I realize it's suppertime and it's inconvenient. I don't want to put you out, so you just go about your business and have your meal like you normally would. I'll want to look around the house about that time. You don't need to entertain me."

"I wasn't thinking that."

"If you were concerned about it, you don't need to be. I'll be around for a few hours, but other than a few questions, I won't need you most of the time."

"Well... okay, I guess. I'll have to get out there to tidy things up for the real estate agent anyway. May as well do it all at once."

"I'm sorry to put you out..."

"No, like I say, I have to get out there anyway..."

So he got his way and showed up at Richard Harding's home after a slow drive down the road Harding had been killed on, looking for anything out of the ordinary. There was no sign of the accident that had occurred there, no marker showing where he had been struck or where his body had been found. Zachary didn't see any significant marks on the pavement, though there were occasional light skid marks, some of them perhaps made as cars avoided wildlife, and one by Rusty Donaldson after something bounced off his front fender, when he pulled his rig over to have a look.

Ashley stood in the open doorway of the house watching him as he pulled into the gravel pad to park. She didn't greet him, but simply asked, "What do you want to see first?"

"I'd like to have a look at where his body was found. I have the GPS coordinates from the police report, so I don't need you to go with me."

"Why didn't you just look at it on your way in?"

Zachary hesitated, trying to work it out in his own mind. It just hadn't seemed like the right thing to do.

"I didn't want to be poking around without checking in with you first." He gave an awkward shrug. "I guess you probably don't care, but it didn't seem proper."

Ashley didn't disagree with his assessment or say it was stupid. She just looked at him for a minute. In the afternoon sun, her complexion was washed out and she seemed older and more worn than she had at Old Joe's.

"You don't need to come with me," Zachary told her again.

"But if you want to be there to supervise or... be where it happened... we can go out together."

"Okay," she conceded. "Should we take my car or yours?"

Zachary grimaced. "I know it's not environmentally conscious, but we should probably take both. I have cameras and other investigative equipment in my car that I might need and you might want to come back before I'm done. If you have your own car, you can decide how long you want to stay."

Ashley headed over to her own car, a shiny blue VW Bug, and got in. It was a far cry from Kenzie's beloved red convertible or Richard's nondescript black four-door Cavalier. He pondered what it might say about her personality. Fun loving? Artistic? Outgoing? It was hard to reconcile in her current grieving state. He slid back into his white compact, which looked exactly like hundreds of other white compacts in the county, commonly used in rental and courier fleets and by people who were concerned with maintaining a good resale value. A private detective's car, intended to be invisible and unmemorable.

He let Ashley lead the way rather than relying on the GPS coordinates, though one thing he would do when he got there was to verify the location against the police records. He couldn't think of any reason Ashley would have to lead him to the wrong location, but people's memories could be faulty. The record the police had made was unlikely to be.

The irrigation ditch was close to the road, so there wasn't much space to pull over. He did the best he could and hoped that the passing traffic would take care and not hit his car.

Ashley motioned to the ditch, her motion languid, her shoulders slumped and head bowed.

"This is where they found him, down there in the grass and undergrowth. You couldn't see him, even standing here and looking down during the day. Certainly not from a car driving by. He wouldn't have been found if we hadn't been looking for him. It isn't exactly a place that hikers come through."

He could see glimpses of black water and mud through the

dense grasses and brush. There was brown grass beside the road that was trampled into the dirt, but it had snowed on and off in the past week and he couldn't see a lot of footprints. Zachary could picture it as it would have been while the investigation was ongoing. Pylons with yellow tape stretched between them. Evidence markers wherever they had found anything that might have to do with the investigation. Examining and taking pictures of the body while it was in situ. Then it would be carefully loaded into a body bag and carried away. He hoped that Ashley had not seen any of these activities close up.

"Thanks. This is going to take me a while. You can stay or go, it's up to you."

It appeared she was going to stay. Zachary did his best to ignore her and go about his investigation like he would without any supervision.

He used a handheld GPS to record a few reference points, drew a diagram, measured the distances between the reference points and various landscape features. He had been involved in accident reconstruction scenes before. He was no expert, but he knew the basics and would collect enough information that he could consult with an expert later if he had to. The police had already done their best estimates, but it was difficult, given that they were out there several days after the collision had occurred and they had little evidence to rely on.

He walked back on the road, keeping a careful eye and ear on the occasional vehicles that approached to ensure that he didn't end up in the same position as Harding had. He walked the side of the road as Harding must have done, feeling the evenness of the pavement, the pitch of the slope, the way the road crowned and then sloped off at the edge. He kept a sharp eye on the ditch, his attention jumping from the road to the traffic to the ditch in rapid succession over and over again. They hadn't found both of Harding's shoes, so the other had to be out there somewhere.

After walking the road both approaching and departing from the site where the body had been found, Zachary geared up and descended into the ditch. There was a crust of ice over the sludgy water and mud. He slogged down its length; it was much harder than walking the road, and he was glad he had thought to bring hip waders. If someone were out there at night, they would definitely have to walk the road rather than the ditch. It would have been far too dangerous and difficult to get through in the dark. Even in daylight, it took at least four times as long to traverse the ditch as it did the road.

He watched for any sign of snagged clothing, anything that Harding might have been holding or wearing and any sign that someone else had been there. Had Rusty descended into the ditch to check on whether Harding was alive or dead? Had there been someone else with him? Had Harding been running away from someone or chasing after someone? What had made him go out there so late at night?

Even after Zachary figured he had gone past the point of collision, he kept going. He started to see trash in the ditch, which meant he had gone past the perimeter the police had established. The police would have collected every piece of debris they had found within the perimeter in case it were relevant to the case. The sun was getting lower in the sky. It would be dusk before too long. Zachary pressed on, slowed by the muck and vegetation and having to stop to examine the bits of garbage. Food wrappers, straws, unidentifiable clothing ground with mud. A "For Sale" sign. Curled black hunks of tire. Shredded plastic of every description. His foot caught on something in the ditch. Probably another piece of tire or a shelf of ice. Zachary bent down to pick it up, glad he was wearing industrial rubber gloves.

What he came up with was a very muddy red high-top shoe. The mate to the one the police had found.

Zachary clambered up the side of the ditch to the road. From his pocket he pulled a large glow stick and snapped it along its length to activate the chemical reaction that would start it glowing. He placed it on the side of the road, then placed a second one for good measure. Zachary briskly walked the road back to his car.

Ashley had, at some point, left him alone there, taking her car back to the house. Zachary was glad she wasn't there to see the sneaker. He put it directly into a plastic bag and left it in the car. He grabbed a small orange pylon and walked it back to the glow sticks and placed it as well.

Another walk back to his car to add the new location to the hand-drawn map. He measured the distance between the shoe and the body, taking a careful GPS read and using a laser sight to get as accurate a distance as possible. He pulled out his phone and searched through his contacts for Joshua Campbell.

Apparently, he was in Campbell's contact list as well, since Campbell recognized his caller ID and greeted him by name.

"Zachary Goldman!"

"Hey. I'm out at the Harding scene."

"You've seen our file, so I'm not sure I'm going to be able to help you with anything further."

"No, I've got something for you."

"Oh." Campbell gave a rumbling laugh. "What did you find?"

"I've got the other shoe."

"Hell! How did you find that? We searched and searched. Even had the dogs out, but they were useless at finding any kind of trail after a couple of days had passed."

"It was outside of your search radius. And underwater."

"Hmm." Campbell cleared his throat and thought about that for a few minutes. "That's going to have an impact on the reconstruction wonks' calculations, isn't it?"

"Yes. The rig was heavier or going faster than they figured."

Campbell swore. "You're on the scene now?"

"Yes. I planned to go through the house next, then come back out here after dark. Maybe seeing the scene like Harding would have seen it that night will trigger something else."

"It will be the same, except dark."

Zachary laughed. "Well, yes. And the traffic patterns will be different. Animals coming out. I don't know what else, because I haven't seen it yet."

"If you're going to be out there after dark, do me a favor and light yourself up. Like a Christmas tree. Lights and reflectors from head to toe."

His mention of a Christmas tree made Zachary remember the other tree. The tree that had blazed with fire. Whenever anyone said 'lit up like a Christmas tree,' that was what he remembered. It had been bright; like a burning torch. He gripped the phone hard and tried to focus on the feeling of it in his hand. He took a deep breath of the chilly air. "I'll be sure to be visible," he agreed weakly.

"Just leave the shoe where it is. I'll have a couple of guys come out to take photos and forensics. They can bring out the big lights. If you just give me the geocoordinates—"

"I already moved it," Zachary confessed, after a split-second consideration of whether to toss it back into the ditch. "Uh, sorry. It was underwater, stuck in the mud. I pulled it out to see what it was, and when I saw… I figured I'd contaminate it more by putting it back. Maybe wash off something that was stuck to it."

"So now it's got your fingerprints and transfer on it," Campbell growled.

"I was wearing gloves. I put it directly into a plastic bag without letting it touch anything else. I've done my best to mark the location for you."

Campbell grumbled, but couldn't come up with an argument for that. "Alright. My guys will come by. Beam me your coordinates. They'll have to find it in the dark."

"I've got glow sticks out. As long as they slow down when they're getting close, they should be able to see it. I'll be back here once it's dark."

"Is it safe to leave the scene unsecured?"

Zachary took a slow look around. He didn't see any other houses close by; it was pretty isolated. There were occasional vehicles, but no one had paid any particular attention to him. Without his car there attracting attention to the scene, there was nothing there to indicate it was a crime scene. No reason for anyone else to be poking around.

"Yeah, I think it's fine. The only person of interest around is the girlfriend, and she'll be in the house with me. If she suddenly decides to go out to run an errand, I'll keep an eye on her, make sure she's not tampering with anything."

"Don't tell her that you found anything. She's not watching you now?"

Zachary looked back toward the house, but he couldn't see it clearly. "Not unless she's got a pretty good telescope."

"Okay. Thanks, Zach. I'll be in touch."

Back at Harding's house, Zachary had to knock on the door to be let in. He had divested of his boots and gloves and was fairly presentable. Ashley looked him over warily, as if she'd never met him before or he was someone she thought might be dangerous. Did she have something to hide? He knew she wasn't telling him everything. Like the reason she thought Harding's death was not an accident.

"If it's okay with you, I'll take a look around the house… see if there's anything that jumps out at me."

She didn't react for a few seconds, then stepped back from the door, nodding and opening it the rest of the way. "Did you find anything out there?"

She was his client, but Zachary wasn't ready to divulge everything he knew yet. If he told her about the shoe and she decided to go out for a look, Campbell would not be happy about it. "That remains to be seen," he said obliquely.

Ashley bit her lip. She looked around the living room of the small house. "I don't know exactly what you want to see."

"I'll just wander, if that's okay with you."

"Well… I suppose."

She didn't go back to whatever it was she had been doing, but stood there looking at him. Zachary did his best to again pretend that she wasn't there and just focus on his investigation. It was his chance to get to know who Richard Harding was and what kind of a person he was. Zachary didn't have a good picture of him, only an amorphous impression of a man who had walked off down the road and been hit by a truck. He was a colorless sort of person. A custodian, non-drinker, steady girlfriend, owned or rented his own place, kept to a regular routine. No hobbies or interests, nothing that seemed to set him apart from the rest of the human race. Other than his stalker.

Zachary had seen pictures of Harding, but only after his death, and that was never a very good representation of what someone looked like in real life, especially after a few days decomposing in a ditch. So the first thing Zachary did was look for pictures.

The paintings on the walls were cheap reproductions, mass produced and purchased in some home decorator store. There were no pictures of Harding's parents, or of himself with Ashley. No pictures of his brothers, his college friends, or bowling buddies. Either he lived a very solitary life, or he kept the evidence of his relationships somewhere else. Maybe he felt that they were not for public consumption. Not everyone felt the need to show everything off in the living room.

Zachary circulated around the room, glancing at magazines and books on the shelves, opening drawers in the side tables to poke through an assortment of pens, pencils, rubber bands, and junk. A few phone numbers scribbled on a piece of paper. Pizza delivery, a couple of first names, nothing that looked very interesting. The phone numbers were not ones he had gotten harassing text messages from.

Zachary went on. Ashley was in the kitchen, so he walked past it, leaving her to herself, and checked out the bedrooms. There were two of them. The one Harding used as his bedroom was immediately identifiable. His clothes were in the closet and drawers; the bed was made, but wrinkled; there was a picture of him with Ashley. Zachary picked it up and looked at it. Ashley appeared to be happy and relaxed. Harding did not. He was smiling unnaturally, looking anxious about having his picture taken, as if he might dart over and take the camera out of the hand of the photographer. Zachary didn't like posed pictures. Even before he had become a private investigator, he had preferred candid shots. The pictures that showed people in unexpected moments, looking natural.

"He hated having his picture taken."

Zachary jumped and looked up at the doorway, where Ashley was looking in on him. "Some people do," he acknowledged.

"I had to beg him to get that one. I told him I had to have a picture of him. It was a dealbreaker. So he finally agreed. But I think you can tell, looking at the picture, that he really didn't like it."

Zachary gave her a small smile of acknowledgment. "Yes, I can see that."

"So, this was his room," she made a small gesture to present it to him. "This is where he slept. Where we slept when I stayed over. But there's not really anything… no secrets, nothing that was really… special to him." She looked around the room critically. "I never realized how little he had."

"What was his childhood like? He grew up with his family?"

"Yeah, sure." Her manner was dismissive.

Zachary put the picture down and continued to look. There were no pictures of Harding's family. "Are his parents still living? Did he keep in contact with them?"

"No, they passed a few years ago."

Richard had been forty-five. It was possible that both of his parents had already passed away, but unlikely. Zachary opened and closed drawers, pushing clothes around to look behind and under them. Ashley was right, he had few possessions. She had almost as many clothes in the closet and drawers as he did. And more dresser space for her cosmetics and jewelry.

His clothes in the closet were uniformly nondescript. T-shirts, blue jeans, a couple of blazers. Nothing really dressy for church or funerals. One pair of loafers on the floor of the closet, placed neatly together.

Zachary approached the door and Ashley moved out of the way to let him back out of the bedroom. "I'll just hang out here until you're done."

"Wherever you want, I don't want to put you out."

She picked up a book from the dresser and sat on the bed. Zachary went to the second bedroom, which was a multi-purpose room. A small computer desk and chair, a couch that undoubtedly folded out into a spare bed for guests. An exercise bike and some free weights. Zachary could see by the wires that the desk was where Harding's computer normally resided. Zachary took a slow look around the bleak room. Richard Harding really was an enigma. Had he even existed before he had died? There was nothing of his personality in the house. He could have been someone that Ashley had made up, except for the fact that the police had found a body.

Zachary spent a couple of minutes in the bathroom, looking through Harding's toiletries, which weren't much more revealing than the rest of his house. He did not use generic bath products, but the more expensive brand names. He used a manual razor with a disposable head. The medicine cabinet contained all of the usual products—toothbrush and toothpaste, pain pills, cough syrup, antibacterial spray. But also a few over-the-counter sleep aids, and several prescription bottles.

Zachary was well-versed in the pharmacopeia of mental illness. A glance at the labels showed him that Richard Harding was being treated for anxiety and depression. Not just one of each, but several different types, which meant they had been struggling to find the right cocktail for him. Zachary reviewed the dates of the prescriptions and could see Harding's treatment plan take shape in front of him.

He closed the medicine cabinet and checked under the sink for anything Richard had preferred to keep out of sight. Nothing more interesting there than cleaning products. The last room to check was the kitchen. He didn't expect to find anything enlightening. With the way Harding had kept the rest of his house, Zachary didn't think he'd find a secret stash of booze or evidence of some other vice there. He looked anyway, methodically going through the drawers and cupboards. Ashley returned to the kitchen as he finished up.

"Did you find anything?"

"You didn't mention he was suffering from depression."

She bit her lip, thinking about that. "I don't know if he really was. I thought he was being a hypochondriac. He didn't *act* depressed."

"People who are depressed don't necessarily go around acting sad all the time."

"Then why do they call it depression?" she challenged.

"They may feel depressed without looking depressed. They might be silly and clown around. Look at Robin Williams. It's a way of covering up what they're really feeling, or trying to connect with the world in spite of it."

"Well… Richard didn't seem depressed to me, and we were together. We shared everything."

"He may not have had it before. It might have been the result of the harassment."

Ashley's brows went down. "What?"

"He was probably having such difficulties because of the harassment."

"What harassment? Did something happen at work?"

Zachary searched her features for any sign that she was trying to mislead him. Could she really have not known about the unrelenting harassment her boyfriend had been going through? Could Harding have kept that a secret? If Ashley had known, that would explain why she thought Harding had been intentionally murdered. If she didn't know, where did that leave him?

He couldn't see any deception in her face. She really didn't know what had been going on in Harding's life. It must have consumed him, but he'd kept it from her. He'd continued to go to work and to do things with her, acting like there was nothing wrong. He told her he was depressed—just a chemical thing—and that he'd be straightened out as soon as the medication kicked in. And she hadn't known how some lowlife was driving him to distraction.

Zachary indicated the chairs at the table. Ashley sat down, and Zachary pulled out a chair and sat across from her, making sure he wasn't too close, wasn't crowding her.

"Richard was being cyberstalked. It was… very brutal. Very threatening. He was doing everything he could to keep out of this stalker's reach. He closed all of his social media accounts, changed his phone and his email."

A light went on in Ashley's face. Suddenly, it all came together for her. "I didn't know! He said he was spending too much time online and that's why he was shutting down his accounts. He dropped his phone in the water and had to get a new one. He said he was getting too much spam email and needed to start fresh… I never connected them all. He spread it out, it wasn't all in one day, and I never… I didn't realize what he was doing. He never said a word about being stalked."

"Men tend to feel like they should be the strong ones in a relationship. That they should be the protector, keep bad things from happening. He was probably embarrassed and didn't want you to think that he was weak for trying to avoid this guy instead of 'being a man' and 'taking care of it.'"

"I never would have expected him to act like that. We never had gendered roles or felt like we had to follow those societal pressures. I told him I liked a man to be sensitive and to have real emotions." She shook her head. "He never should have felt like he had to play the big, strong man for me. That's not the way we were."

Zachary nodded slowly. He pulled out his notepad and jotted down a few thoughts and things to check before they could flit away from his churning brain.

"So he never told you anything about this."

"No. I'm sorry. He should have. I would have supported him. He knew I'd support him through anything."

Did he? It seemed to Zachary that their devotion to one another hadn't really been tested. It didn't seem like a passionate relationship, but like a partnership of convenience. Something warm and comfortable, where they could cuddle up and watch a movie together, but didn't have to be totally devoted to each other all of the time. They each kept their own residences, their own jobs, their own vehicles. They were still themselves more than a couple. How could Harding have known how Ashley would react to the news that he was being hunted and harassed?

"Is there anything you need to tell me?"

Ashley looked at him for a long time, her eyes swimming in tears, looking helpless and uncertain. But she didn't offer him anything. It wasn't the depression. It wasn't the stalking. She was still holding something back from him.

"If you don't tell me everything, how do you expect me to find out what really happened?"

Ashley shook her head. "I've told you all I can. I know it wasn't accidental, and this proves it. He was being stalked by someone. That person caught up with him in real life and killed him!"

"You think the trucker was his stalker? Why turn himself in to the police?"

"I… I don't know. Maybe he wasn't the one who really hit Richard. Maybe he hit a deer and someone else hit Richard. Or maybe when he hit Richard, he was already dead. I don't know. But whoever was stalking Richard, *that's* who killed him."

"I'll pursue it as far as I can," Zachary promised. "But you need to tell me the rest if you want me to sort it out."

7

Zachary looked at the letter from Tyrrell, still in its protective sleeve on his desk. Was it really from Tyrrell? His Tyrrell?

He remembered his little brother. So anxious to please, so trusting of everything his parents or teachers told him. The perfect little man, always trying to be well-behaved and follow the rules. More like a firstborn than one so far down the line in the birth order.

Tyrrell cried when their parents fought and often crawled into bed with Zachary to cuddle, too afraid to go to sleep on his own. Zachary would hold him gently and hum to him, trying to drown out any noise from their fighting parents and lull the little boy to sleep. And then he lay awake himself, staring into the darkness, listening to Tyrrell and Vincent breathing, waiting for sleep to come and take him, but it always took hours to come. He couldn't sleep when their parents were still up. He had to wait until they had stopped fighting and had gone to bed, and everything was quiet and peaceful with no danger of the argument blowing up again. Then he could start to relax, but the process still took a long time.

The nights when the police were called were the worst, and they were a relief. It was humiliating for the whole neighborhood to see what was going on in the Goldman home. He hated for the kids at school to know that his parents didn't get along. If it was just arguing, he could have laughed it off. But not when the neighbors saw his mother or father being put into handcuffs to be carted off to jail for assault. The next day, when it had all blown over, the arrested parent would be back, and things would go on as usual, but that didn't stop the teasing and bullying at school.

And on the other hand, it was a relief to have the police come and break it up. Zachary would be able to get to sleep sooner, knowing that the fight was over. While they had sometimes threatened to put both parents in jail, they never had, always picking out the one who they thought had been most at fault and leaving the other at home so they didn't have to call Social Services to find emergency homes for six children.

Tyrrell. Zachary touched the plastic bag. *Do you remember me?* How could Zachary ever forget? He couldn't forget any of his siblings, not ever. He longed to call Tyrrell or to write him back. But he couldn't bring himself to. Not when Tyrrell might blame him. It had been Zachary's fault that they had all been taken away. Tyrrell had been old enough to understand that.

He closed his eyes and tried to remember everything Mrs. Pratt had said about the other children back in the beginning. They hadn't been able to keep the other five children together. It was just too many for one home to take. Joss and Heather had been put in one home, and the littles in another. Had they stayed there? Had they been good homes where they were treated fairly and the parents were interested in adopting them permanently? Or had they been emergency placements that had never been meant to be anything but temporary?

Mrs. Pratt had said it was best to let them settle into their foster placements to start with. Not to disrupt them with visits by Zachary. That meant that they had been meant to stay in those homes permanently. Or at least long-term. Every time Zachary had asked about being allowed to visit them, the answer had been no, and eventually, he had stopped asking, though he had never stopped thinking about them.

———

Joshua Campbell was a busy man, but he agreed to meet and spend a few minutes with Zachary on the Harding case. Zachary had, after all, managed to dig up additional evidence, so maybe he merited a face-to-face conversation when Campbell would normally expect a PI to just be happy to get access to the paper file.

He graciously offered Zachary coffee, which he accepted, even knowing it was likely to be hours old and bitter as grapefruit. He took a sip without wincing and put it down on the offered coaster as he sat down on the other side of Campbell's desk.

"How is the case coming along then?" Campbell asked genially. He stretched and leaned back in his chair as if he were ready for a nap. He'd probably started his day pretty early.

"It's intriguing," Zachary said slowly. "There may be some-thing to the girlfriend's claims, but she's not been completely open about her reasons, so I'm still a bit in the dark."

"Why would someone hire you and not tell you all of the reasons why?"

Zachary gave a shrug. "It's actually not as unusual as you think. People usually hold something back. Maybe it's something inconsequential, maybe it's a secret, or maybe they just want to see if you can find it, so they know you're really putting some effort into the investigation."

Campbell nodded. "I know they hold back from the police, but it never occurred to me that they'd hire you and then not produce."

Zachary leaned forward. "I'm wondering whether Richard Harding ever filed a complaint with the police."

Campbell raised his brows. "A complaint? For what?"

"Criminal harassment. Cyberstalking."

"No… something like that would have shown up when we opened the missing persons report and when we started the investigation into his death. You think he was being harassed?"

"I know he was. Email, social media, texts, calls. I don't know whether he got snail mail or any face-to-face harassment, but he was the victim of some of the worst cyber-harassment I've ever seen."

"You need to turn those records over so we can have a look at them. How did you get access? I'm sure my guys must have taken a look at his electronic footprint."

"He'd closed his social media and replaced his phone and his email address. Recently, he'd been anonymizing all of his online activity. Trying to keep this guy from tracking him down again."

"Okay. Yeah. Pass on what you've got so we can investigate it further. We'll see whether there is any connection between Rusty Donaldson and this cyberstalker."

"None that I can find. I've been through everything with a fine-toothed comb, and it doesn't follow the patterns you'd expect to see from a long-haul trucker. The times he is sending his messages follow more of the pattern you'd expect to see with someone with a nine-to-five job or school schedule. Little or nothing from nine until noon or one until four. A lot more in the early morning, noon hour, and evening. A long-haul trucker… wouldn't follow a distribution like that."

"Unless he was smart enough to use some kind of scheduler."

Zachary shrugged. "I suppose. In my experience, people take a lot of care to cover up the things that can be traced back to them electronically—burner phones, anonymous accounts, stuff like that—but they don't think to cover up behavioral patterns."

"I'll see what we can find. We might be able to trace some of the messages back to the source. I assume you've already done the preliminaries."

"The obvious stuff. With the amount of harassment that went on, it's impossible for me to check everything, but with a few more people following the trail, maybe you'll be able to."

"Might call on the feds for help. They have a lot more manpower and some pretty slick technology."

Zachary nodded. "You'll let me know what you find?"

"Usual answer." Campbell took a sip of his coffee. "It depends. If we have enough for an arrest, we're just going to move in and do it, and you won't be involved. If the feds find something, we might be prohibited from sharing it with you. If it's a rat's nest that I can't do anything with… you're welcome to it."

Zachary grinned. He liked Campbell's open, honest manner. He knew the strengths of the police department, and he knew Zachary's strengths, and he had no problem with feeding information to Zachary if he thought that Zachary had a better chance of coming up with an answer than his own staff.

"Fair enough."

Campbell took another drink, his eyes distant as he thought things over. "Do you think this stalker had anything to do with his death?"

"Right now… I can't see a connection. I don't believe Rusty Donaldson has any connection with the stalker. It just doesn't feel right. Does that mean that the stalker didn't have something to do with why Harding was out there on the road that night? I can think of a few different scenarios that could connect them… but nothing that feels right yet. So far, it still seems like an accident."

"Well, you've proven to have a pretty good instinct for these things, so I'm glad to hear it."

"You haven't heard anything back from your accident reconstruction guys yet…?"

"Early days. They want confirmation of the weight of the truck, so we're in the process of getting a warrant for the weigh station records and looking into the possibility that Donaldson might have added something to his load without telling anyone. Truckers sometimes supplement their incomes by carrying extras they don't tell their employers about."

Zachary wasn't a math guy, but most of the things he could

think of a trucker transporting for extra money didn't weigh enough that he thought they would make a difference.

"How much extra weight would it have taken? Would a passenger have made up the difference?"

"A passenger." Campbell looked at him sharply. "Do you have anything to suggest that he had a passenger?"

"No. I'm just spitballing. Could we put the stalker in the truck? I'm not sure that makes any sense even if the answer is yes…"

Campbell shook his head. "What's he going to do? Tell Rusty Donaldson to run down the guy walking by the side of the road?"

"Probably not. Unless it's a woman and she tells him that the guy is trying to kill her or did something to her in the past. More likely… distracts him at the key moment, grabs the wheel without warning…"

"I'm sure he would have been eager to tell us something like that if it was his passenger's fault. He wouldn't have a reason to protect the passenger."

"Unless they knew each other." Zachary sighed and blinked his eyes a few times, trying to refocus. "No evidence, just trying to think of what would fit."

"Chances are, he was just going faster than he wants us to believe."

Zachary nodded.

Campbell sat up and leaned forward over his desk, his body language indicating that the interview was over and he had other work to do. "Good luck. Get us the information you've got, and we'll see where the evidence leads us. How is Bridget doing, by the way?"

Zachary swallowed and attempted a smile. "She's recovered from the kidnapping, seems back to her usual self." Which was to say, she still had no interest in getting back together with Zachary and hadn't had much reason to call him since the Salter case was closed. While Zachary might occasionally run into her around town, he couldn't make direct contact with her or she might just call up Joshua Campbell or one of her other friends in the police department and take out a restraining order against Zachary.

"Good. It was too bad things didn't work out between the two of you. Cancer is a bitch. I think the two of you might have had a chance if that hadn't thrown a wrench into the works."

Little did Campbell know that things were already bad between them before the cancer diagnosis. It had been the straw that broke the camel's back. It was nice to think that they might have worked things out without the cancer, but seeing the relationship Bridget had with Gordon Drake, Zachary had to face the fact that he could never have been the kind of spouse that Gordon was. Women like Ashley might say that they liked sensitive men who weren't afraid to cry or wear their hearts on their sleeves, but in his experience, they just liked the idea of that kind of man. Bridget's declarations of love had quickly faded as she came to realize just how broken Zachary really was. That he had real problems that weren't just going to be healed by their relationship or her no-nonsense advice.

"Zachary."

Zachary tried to force himself back to the present. He had picked up the cup of coffee as he prepared to leave. He put it up to his lips, letting the bitterness of it shock his senses and help to ground him. He didn't want to get swallowed up in the past. Not even his past with Bridget, where the memories started out sweet but quickly descended into something even more bitter than the stale coffee.

"Sorry," he told Campbell, pushing himself to his feet. "I'll be getting on my way."

"No, I'm sorry. I didn't mean to reopen old wounds. I thought you were over it..."

Zachary tried to say that he didn't think he'd ever be over Bridget. But he couldn't get the words out. He just nodded and fled as quickly as he could.

Kenzie had suggested that Zachary could conquer his own depression by helping someone else. Zachary decided to put it to the test. Maybe he could head off the rapidly descending darkness by making a difference in some one else's life. After checking with Vera Salter, Zachary sent an instant message to her grandson Rhys, asking whether he would like to go out for a burger.

Following his usual protocol of answering with a gif rather than words, Rhys sent back a picture of a chihuahua nodding eagerly, the bold text "yes!!!" superimposed on top of the picture. Zachary chuckled. That seemed clear enough. He sent back the details and confirmed that Vera had already approved the activity. Rhys returned a thumbs-up, and they were on.

He was at the school waiting when classes let out for the day. He watched the waves of teens leaving the school, some singly and some in groups, feeling that same knot of dread in his stomach that he used to feel whenever he was at school or thinking about being at school. It was hard to fathom that even after so many years, just watching students at school brought back that same anxiety. He was glad not to be a teenager anymore. Glad to be on his own and independent and no longer to have to follow all of the rules of a foster home, school, or other facility. There were still societal rules, but he could live his own life without fear of being beaten, humiliated, or locked up.

His eyes were drawn to a thin black boy with a familiar loping stride, and reached over to unlock the door for Rhys.

Rhys climbed in, giving him a nod and a shy sort of smile.

"Hey, Rhys!" Zachary greeted, holding out his fist for Rhys to bump. Rhys was quick to do so, his smile broadening to show a few teeth. He put on his seatbelt as Zachary backed out of the parking space he had been occupying.

"Find something on the radio if you like," Zachary suggested, not wanting Rhys to feel like he was going to have to hold a conversation while they drove. Rhys ran through Zachary's presets quickly, then scanned for something more acceptable. Zachary let the pounding beat of the station Rhys picked fill him up and block out any worries he had about meeting with Rhys or about the approaching Christmas season. Maybe he should listen to music more often. It wasn't something he usually thought of when he was having a bad turn.

The burger joint was conveniently close to the school, prime real estate for a place that targeted kids as its customer base. It wasn't until they got inside that Zachary realized it might not be the best place for them to meet. Rhys's friends and peers would be there. Would they think it was odd that he was meeting with an older white guy for dinner? Would he be teased and bullied for it?

"Uh… is this okay? Do you want to eat somewhere else?"

Rhys waved the question away with an unconcerned gesture.

"Yeah? You're sure? You aren't going to to get a bunch of questions about what you were doing here with me?"

Rhys shook his head.

Zachary scanned the menu on the wall without much interest. He'd get some kind of small combo. He wasn't really there because of the food, he was there to see if he could help Rhys. Rhys touched Zachary's arm and then tapped the poster beside him.

"Is that what you want? Bacon cheeseburger?"

Rhys nodded.

"Combo, supersize?"

Rhys grinned.

They waited for the teens in line ahead of them to place their orders, and in a few minutes were choosing a table and sitting down to eat. Zachary ate slowly, watching Rhys put away his supersized combo as if he hadn't eaten all day. He was long and lanky, his teenage frame not yet starting to fill in. It would be a few years before he might have to start watching what he ate.

"Do you know these other kids?" Zachary asked, taking a look around the restaurant and classifying which were likely to be the same grade as Rhys. There were not very many non-white students; Rhys would definitely be in the minority.

Rhys gave his hand a side-to-side rocking movement. *So-so.*

Zachary nodded. Knowing who people were wasn't the same as being friends with them. Or actually *knowing* them.

"I guess Christmas is coming." As if Zachary were only casually aware of the fact. "I was wondering if you wanted to do something. It will be kind of different for you, not having your mom around." Or his aunt Robin either. Rhys was probably happy about that.

Rhys nodded.

"Will you be going to see your mom on Christmas Day, do you know?"

Another nod.

"You know what time?"

Rhys shook his head. He made a motion backward over his shoulder, a questioning look on his face. Zachary looked behind Rhys to see if he was motioning to someone. Rhys shook his head and pulled out his iPod. He tapped a couple of words and slid it across the table to Zachary.

Xmas Eve?

Zachary shook his head. He tried not to betray his feelings to Rhys. "I… I can't do anything on Christmas Eve."

Which made him wonder why he was even trying to set something up for Christmas Day. What if he wasn't even around on Christmas Day? What if he slid down that hole and didn't come back up this time? It had been Kenzie's idea to set something up with Rhys, not his, and he should have just left it to her. What kind of service was he doing Rhys if he set something up for Christmas, and then didn't make it? The kid was going to have a bad enough day without that adding to his troubles.

Rhys's eyes were on Zachary, sharp and intelligent. He touched Zachary's arm and again indicated the iPod screen.

Xmas Eve?

"I can't."

Eyebrows up, inquiring. *Why?*

Zachary didn't want to tell Rhys about it. He didn't share the experience with anyone but his closest friends or therapists. Rhys was only a kid. He couldn't understand the full impact of what Zachary had been through.

But Rhys had been through awful experiences of his own. Zachary didn't want to talk about his, but Rhys *couldn't* tell his even if he wanted to. They strangled his voice and kept him from communicating anything but the most rudimentary thoughts.

"I had… some really bad stuff happen to me on Christmas Eve," Zachary explained awkwardly. "There was a fire… my family… the anniversary always gets me… in a really bad place."

Rhys clasped Zachary's hand in a strong handshake, holding it firmly and nodding.

We'll help each other. We'll be strong together.

Zachary gave a little squeeze, then pulled out of Rhys's grip. "I don't think I can."

Rhys studied him for a long moment, his face once again sad.

"We'll figure something out," Zachary promised. "Maybe closer to the time, when our plans have solidified…"

Rhys picked his burger back up and resumed eating. A knot of guilt tightened in Zachary's stomach.

"I'm sorry Rhys. I know it's stupid. I'd change if I could. I've been… it's something I've been working on for a long time."

A shrug. That just made Zachary feel worse. He knew Rhys couldn't understand just how difficult Christmas, and especially Christmas Eve was for him. Zachary concentrated hard on how to explain it.

"It's like with your speech."

Rhys looked up, raising one eyebrow.

"You'd change it if you could, wouldn't you? You'd want to just be able to talk like yours friends can?"

Rhys gave a small nod.

"And you've been working with doctors and therapists since you were little. They've tried helping you in all different ways."

Rhys nodded agreement, his eyes bright and piercing.

"It isn't like you're lazy. It isn't like you just can't be bothered or don't want to talk. It's something inside that's… broken."

Was it offensive for him to suggest that Rhys was broken? Was it too personal for him to compare his psychological problems to Rhys's? He looked away from Rhys's eyes, worried about the anger and insult he'd find there. Rhys held his hands together in front of him as if he were holding a horizontal stick, and then snapped them downward.

Broken.

Zachary breathed out, nodding. "You want to be fixed. You want to fix yourself. But so far... no one has figured out how."

Rhys nodded his agreement. He picked up his iPod and slid it back into his pocket, hiding the offending words away again.

Zachary ate a couple of fries. He wasn't hungry and hadn't even put ketchup on them, but it was something to do, to try to make things more comfortable between them. As if they weren't discussing what messes their lives were, but were just a couple of friends having a meal together.

"Do you remember when you were little, after your Grandpa Clarence died? When you had to go away for awhile, to a hospital?"

Rhys nodded, his eyes downcast. He was ashamed of being in hospital for his trauma and depression. Like he should have been stronger. Should have been *not broken.*

"Well, that's what it was like for me, too. I spent a lot of time in places like that. Hospitals, institutions, therapeutic care centers. Especially around Christmas, but other times too. There were years when I spent more time in crisis than out."

Wide eyes. *Really?*

"Yeah. So... if I can, we'll get together at Christmas. Or maybe New Year's. But not Christmas Eve. I'm not sure where I'll be Christmas Eve."

Rhys nodded and gave Zachary a thumbs-up. *Okay.*

"Okay," Zachary agreed, sighing. He ate another fry, even though his churning stomach did not want anything.

They sat in silence a bit, but it was comfortable. Zachary felt like they had come to an understanding. He no longer felt so guilty. Zachary's phone buzzed in his pocket and he pulled it out to look at the screen. When he put it down on the table to watch for any further text messages, Rhys made a palms-raised query.

What's up?

"It's a client." Zachary hesitated, wondering how much to stay to Rhys. It wasn't like the boy was going to blab it to anyone. He couldn't be much more safe. "She wants to know if I've managed to find out anything else about the man who was stalking her boyfriend."

Rhys's interested eyes begged for more.

"He was killed in an accident, but we're trying to track down this cyberstalker in case it was somehow related."

Rhys nodded.

"They probably weren't. We know who it was who actually hit him—in this accident—and I can't find a connection between him and the stalker." Zachary took a sip of his soda. "The funny thing is, he never even told his girlfriend that he was being stalked. She had no idea what was going on. She knew he was on medication for depression, but she didn't think he was actually depressed. He hadn't told her anything about this guy who was sending him hundreds of harassing messages."

Rhys's mouth formed a circle. *Wow.*

"I don't even know what it was that triggered this harassment. The stalker thought the boyfriend had done something wrong, something terrible, but he never said what it was. Not in any of the messages I read. So I don't know where to look."

Rhys was easy to talk to. Unlike most of Zachary's acquaintances, who would have peppered him with questions, Rhys just listened and let him talk. Zachary shook his head. He thought about his observation to Ashley that someone who was depressed could just as easily appear to be a clown, putting on a happy front while hiding the pain.

"How are *you* doing, Rhys? And I mean for real, not just 'fine, how are you?' For real."

Rhys lifted his hands in a shrug. He gave a pronounced frown, then blinked the expression away. He flicked his hand toward Zachary. *You?*

"You're sad," Zachary deduced, and fished for the words to match Rhys's body language. "But you're okay? You said before, 'it's all going to be okay.'"

Rhys nodded his agreement.

"You still feel like that? That it will all work out and be okay?"

He continued to nod.

"Are you still seeing a therapist? You don't have to answer me, it's private. I just wondered."

A nod.

"Are you on antidepressants? Or something that helps?"

Rhys rocked his hand back and forth. *So-so.*

"You'll tell someone if it gets worse, won't you? It doesn't have to be me. But your grandma or your doctor? A guidance counselor at school? If the depression gets worse, or you start having suicidal thoughts, you'll tell someone?"

Rhys grimaced and nodded. He again flicked his finger back toward Zachary, holding his gaze. *You?*

Zachary sighed. It was hard to pull away from Rhys's intense stare. He looked down at his fries. "I don't know. I've talked to doctors, tried everything already. If I have to check myself in somewhere... I guess I will."

Rhys raised his brows slightly and pointed at Zachary firmly. *You do it. For sure.*

"Okay," Zachary said. "I will. And I told my... *friend*... that I'll talk to my therapist. About Christmas Eve."

Rhys gave a grin and pulled out his phone. Zachary wasn't sure what he was doing, until Rhys slid the phone over to him, and he saw that Rhys had a picture of Kenzie.

"Uh, yeah. Kenzie."

Rhys pursed his lips and made a smacking sound. Zachary's cheeks got warm.

"I wouldn't say she's my girlfriend... not yet. Maybe someday.

We get together... have dinner... consult on cases. But we're not... serious."

Rhys's smirk said he wasn't buying it. Zachary rubbed his chin, trying to hide the flushing of his cheeks. Rhys took the phone back, nodding his approval.

8

Kenzie called shortly after Zachary got back from his dinner with Rhys, and he couldn't help wondering whether Rhys had messaged her, prompting her to call Zachary to check in on him. There was a growing network of people around Zachary who kept in touch with each other, trying to keep watch over Zachary's emotional wellness, and maybe Rhys had added himself as a node. *Check in with Zachary. Make sure he's not going to do anything stupid.*

Of course, Rhys wouldn't use that many words. His communications were much more succinct, but Zachary wouldn't put it past him to shoot Kenzie a brief *Zachary OK?* or to just send her his picture.

"You doing anything tonight?" Kenzie asked.

"I don't have anything planned. Was going to do a bit more work on the Harding case tonight, but there's no urgency."

"Why don't I just come over and we'll watch a movie together? You can do simple stuff while we watch, right?"

He could spend some more time trying to analyze the harassing messages, trying to crack the patterns, to parse the words, to trace IP addresses in case the stalker hadn't always

78

remembered to use an anonymizer service. "Yeah, sure. I'd be up for that."

"Great. I'll bring some munchies. Maybe some soda."

He noted that she did not suggest beer as she often did, which meant she probably already figured he wouldn't be able to have any due to his night meds, which he'd been increasing recently.

"Sounds good. Whenever you want to come by is fine, I'll see you then."

She didn't put the movie on as soon as she arrived, but visited and wandered around the apartment restlessly and asked if he'd gotten any further on the Harding case.

"Not much," Zachary admitted. "Still working on it." He related the finding of the shoe and checking to see whether Harding had filed any complaints against the stalker. Kenzie rolled her eyes at the news that Harding had been on antidepressants. "Well, duh! I think any sane person would be. Who could handle that kind of pressure without some kind of aid?"

"His girlfriend didn't think he was depressed. She though he was just a hypochondriac. But he didn't tell her about the harassment, so..."

"He didn't tell her?"

Zachary shook his head. "No." He narrowed his eyes, looking at Kenzie. Something about the way she asked the question suggested that she had a thought about it.

"Maybe he didn't tell her because he figured she already knew."

"You mean he thought she was the stalker?"

"He might have. Why else wouldn't he say anything about it to her, even just in passing? Maybe he was watching her to see if she was the one cyberstalking him."

Zachary shuddered. "That's horror movie material."

"Psychological thriller," Kenzie corrected. "But really, I wonder."

"I think he just didn't want to look weak. Guys are like that, you know. They want the girls to think they're perfect and don't have any problems. That they're strong enough to take all comers."

Kenzie snickered. "You don't say."

"It could be as simple as that. He was too macho to tell her."

"Could be," Kenzie agreed. "But I like my theory better. It has more... dramatic potential."

Zachary nodded. He clicked through a few more messages on Harding's computer, letting his eyes just skim over the words. They got redundant after a while. The stalker hadn't had a lot of creativity, but tended to use the same words and phrases over and over again. And what stalker sending dozens of messages in a day would have been any different? If he didn't settle on a standard set of half a dozen accusations and threats, he'd wear himself out. He'd have writer's block or a nervous breakdown trying to figure out how to make all of the messages unique.

"Oh, snail mail too?" Kenzie asked, and picked up a paper from beside him.

Zachary was hyperfocused on the screen, and it was a minute before her words reached him, and several more before he realized that he didn't have any hard copy threats from the stalker. By the time he realized what Kenzie was looking at and turned to take it from her, it was too late, she'd already read the message, flipped it over to look at the envelope, and was staring at him with open mouth.

"Where did this come from?"

"It's..." Zachary pulled the plastic bag away from Kenzie gently, taking care not to just snatch it rudely. "That's just a note..."

"From your brother? You told me you had siblings, but I didn't know you were in contact with any of them."

Zachary looked down at the inquiry. *Do you remember me?*

"I'm not. I just got this... a few days ago. It's the first contact I've ever had from any of them."

"That's fantastic, Zachary! How exciting for you!" Her smile was shockingly bright, and Zachary wasn't sure whether it was excitement or dread that welled up in his chest at her exuberance. Her smile remained for only a few seconds, then started to fade.

"But you're not excited."

"I am... and I'm... scared..." He paused, awkward and not sure how she would take his declaration. He remembered Ashley's declaration that it was okay to be sensitive and to have an honest emotional reaction. But he wasn't sure all women felt that way, or that they would still feel that way once they saw their man dissolve in front of them.

Kenzie leaned against the corner of the desk, frowning. "Why would you be afraid? This is your brother! Or are you afraid that it's not? That it could be someone else?"

"I don't know." Zachary's hands had started shaking too much to work the mouse, so he held them in his lap under the desk, squeezing them together. "If it is Tyrrell... I ruined his life. I don't know why he would want to see me again, except to tell me that. Just how much I messed him up."

"Why do you think he would feel that way? What happened when you were kids was just an accident. Kids can't be blamed for things like that. They're not responsible. Whatever happened to your brothers and sisters after that... it probably would have happened anyway. If you hadn't been taken away from your parents that day, it would have been a few days or weeks later. Believe me, they were not going to be ideal parents and raise you right. This didn't happen because you were a bad kid. It's because they were bad parents."

"I burned the house down!"

"I'm aware of that," she said calmly. "And you weren't the first kid to ever light a fire by accident. Do you think every kid who lights a fire by accident should be taken away from his family?"

"No."

"Then why do you think that your parents were justified in doing what they did to you?"

"That wasn't the only thing I did. I was in trouble all the time.

At school, at home, in the neighborhood. I was always getting in trouble for one thing or another."

"Uh-huh." She still didn't sound convinced of anything. Zachary stared at her, trying to figure out a way to impress on her just how bad he had been.

"Zach… those kids that you met at Summit…?"

Zachary blinked and nodded. "Yeah?"

"Those kids were trouble, right?"

"Well… no. They did put some kids in there just for behavioral issues, but mostly it was kids with autism. You know that."

"So they're still pretty bad, right? I mean, they won't follow instructions, they hurt people and cause property damage, they're too disobedient to be able to stay with their parents anymore."

"No. Their brains don't work the same way as other kids' brains do. They learn differently. They express themselves differently. The world can seem very threatening to them. They're just reacting in the only way they know how."

"That's why they need to be zapped. Because they're like animals. They are children who are so wild that they need to be trained like dogs to do what they're told."

Zachary knew she was intentionally pushing his buttons, but he couldn't stop the outrage and anger that welled up in him at her words.

"No!"

"If you can understand that they are wired differently and can't be held responsible like a normal child or an adult, then why are you still blaming yourself and repeating the lies that your mother told you?"

If Zachary hadn't already been sitting, he would have fallen into his seat. As it was, his head spun with blinding speed and he couldn't slow it down enough to allow for logical thought.

"What?"

"Tell me what you know about your own diagnoses."

Zachary cleared his throat. "I don't see…"

"Don't you? Humor me."

"ADHD."

"Impulsivity, difficulty maintaining focus, hyperactivity. Right?"

Zachary nodded.

"That's not something you can just change by deciding to, is it?"

"No."

"You have learning disabilities to go along with that?"

"Dyslexia. Dysgraphia. But that's not—"

"And PTSD, right?"

"Yes."

"Before or after the fire?"

Zachary swallowed. His mouth was like cotton. He looked around for a drink. "They think… before."

"Why?"

"My parents' fighting… and… abuse…"

"If I took one of those kids from Summit and told you that he had ADHD, learning disabilities, PTSD, and a history of abuse, and that he'd knocked over a candle and burned the house down, injuring himself in the process, would you say he was just a bad kid? That he had to be institutionalized because he was irredeemable?"

"No. I'd feel bad for him. But I didn't knock a candle over—"

"No, you just lit them."

"I shouldn't have. I wasn't supposed to be out of bed or to use the matches."

"You were trying to do something nice for your family. Trying to make it so they could all have a nice Christmas Day."

"But I was breaking the rules. My mother said I was incorrigible. I would never follow the rules."

"So any child who can't follow the rules is incorrigible?"

Zachary pressed his lips closed. He didn't need to be told that his feelings were illogical any more than he needed to be told he was broken. Too broken to ever be fixed.

Kenzie's color rose when he refused to engage any further in the debate. Then she covered her eyes and blew out her breath, relaxing her body. She dropped her hands from her face and looked at him.

"I'm not trying to prove you wrong, Zachary. I'm just trying to show you... that *you* wouldn't blame yourself for what happened to your family if it was any other child but you. You are a compassionate person. You try to help people. You get inside and try to understand them. You wouldn't blame yourself, and I don't think your brother would either." She gestured to the letter. "I don't think he'd write to you if he just wanted to blame you for the bad stuff that happened in his life. I don't think he'd reach out just to lash out at you when you answered."

"But you don't know that."

"Of course I don't know that, but you don't know that he will either. Is that the kind of person he was? A mean, angry kid?"

Zachary remembered the sweet, concerned, helpful boy Tyrrell had been. So earnest.

"No. But things can change. I met a lot of kids in foster care and institutions who had turned bad. Bullies and sadists of the worst kind. If he ended up in a bad home... or a few of them... even the sweetest kid can turn into a monster."

"Obviously I'm not going to talk you into anything. You're going to have to work through this yourself. But don't shut him out just because you're scared. Being reunited could be the best thing that could ever happen for both of you. It could be a wonderful experience. You could have family back in your life, and the two of you could help each other and share memories."

Zachary swallowed and nodded. "Yeah. It could be really good."

"So don't block him out. Take a chance."

He looked down at the handwritten note. "I will," he agreed, "just not yet."

"Does that mean not today or not this year?"

Zachary cleared his throat. "Maybe after the holidays. When everything is back to normal."

"Do you think it's a coincidence that he sent that before Christmas? He wants to be with family. Christmas is probably a difficult time for him too, and he's trying to reconnect."

"I just can't deal with it right now."

She opened her mouth to argue.

"I just can't, Kenzie."

She gave a frustrated sigh. "Fine. I'll stop pushing you. You know what's best for you."

9

Having so far run into dead ends identifying the cyberstalker, Zachary decided to change tack and run background on Harding. Sometimes, profiling the victim could provide an investigation with a new direction to go. He wasn't getting anywhere on Rusty Donaldson or the stalker, so he needed a fresh avenue to investigate. Ashley had said Harding didn't have any family, but that didn't mean it was true.

A lot of the background he could run online from the comfort of his own apartment, but the police check required actually going to the police station to fill out request forms. Zachary was pretty sure they would come up clear, since the police would undoubtedly have checked to see if their victim had any prior history, but he wasn't going to assume anything. He would run everything, as if he were just starting the investigation and the police had had no involvement.

Bowen was at the information desk and gave Zachary a big grin, as if Zachary had gone there just to see him.

"Zach, my man! How is the investigation going?"

"Not going very far in any direction," Zachary admitted. "What little I've found hasn't gone anywhere. I thought I'd run police record checks on Harding."

Bowen rolled his eyes. "He was clean."

"Did you do the police checks?"

"I don't remember. Probably. You don't think Campbell and his boys would have forgotten something like that, do you?"

"Not everyone runs background on the victim."

Bowman passed Zachary the requisite forms, still rolling his eyes and griping over the duplication of effort. But he was the one who had suggested that Ashley hire Zachary in the first place, and he knew that meant Zachary going over the same ground as the police had already done.

"How are you and Ashley Morton getting along?" Bowman asked, after he had worn out the topic.

"Alright." Zachary shrugged. "I've certainly had worse clients."

"She's quite the looker, don't you think?"

Zachary focused on filling the search forms out neatly, his printing painfully slow. If Bowman was the one who had done the search, Zachary didn't particularly have to worry about it being legible, as Bowman knew all of the details himself. But if it went to someone else to do the search, they might toss it in the garbage if it was too hard to read. Or misspell Richard's name on the search, even though both names were pretty standard. It was best to get it right the first time.

"Ashley. She's a pretty lady," Bowman persisted, not getting the response he wanted from Zachary.

Zachary looked up from his form, distracted. "What?"

"Where are you, Zach? I was talking about the girlfriend. The client. She seemed like a nice girl."

His words started to filter into Zachary's brain. He frowned. "Her boyfriend just died. You think she's going to want to go on a date with you?"

"With me?" Bowman guffawed. "No, not with me. I thought maybe you and she…"

"Me?" Zachary was getting even more confused. In the past, Bowman had encouraged him to pursue Kenzie, saying that she was interested in him and all he had to do was declare his intentions more clearly. His ears got hot. "But Kenzie and I…"

Bowman raised his brows. "You and Kenzie have been lukewarm for a year. She's a girl who likes to go out and have some fun. I think you're stuck in the friend zone with her, and good luck ever getting out of it."

"Oh." The thought had never occurred to Zachary. They were friends, and he thought that if he just allowed the relationship to unfold naturally, if he and Kenzie were meant to be together, things would work out.

"I told you before you needed to be proactive," Bowman said. "A girl likes to know where she stands."

Zachary looked back at the form that he had come there to complete. "Okay. Good to know." He struggled to focus on filling in the lines on the form. "Is she seeing someone else, then? She hasn't mentioned anyone…"

If he were "just a friend," then she would tell him if she started dating someone, wouldn't she? But she hadn't said so, and when they talked and she was busy and couldn't get together, it was usually because she had friends to meet up with, or work, or she had something to get done. Had those just been excuses? Was she just trying to let him down easy?

"I don't know," Bowman admitted. "No one from here, I don't think. But you have to understand, if you're not meeting her needs…"

"Uh… yeah. Okay. Thanks." Zachary handed Bowman the forms back. "Thanks for that."

Bowman shook his head and pushed the papers back at Zachary. "You didn't sign them."

Embarrassed, Zachary scribbled his signature at the bottom of each page and slid them across to Bowman again. "Just let me know when the results are in."

"Zachary…"

Zachary walked away without another word.

Zachary sat in his car, waiting for his heart to stop pounding and his head to stop spinning. He'd never been good at relationships, but he had thought that he and Kenzie were doing well. They were connecting, they enjoyed doing things together, and they each called the other regularly. It seemed, for the most part, to be a balanced, two-way relationship, with both of them getting something out of it. Even though Bowman had told him he should push harder for a more intimate relationship, it had never felt right to Zachary and he had resisted. Did that mean he'd lost out?

He turned the key in the ignition to warm up the cold car. There was an icy bite in the air. Winter was starting to assert itself. He turned the radio on. It was still on the station Rhys had tuned it to and the heavy beat shook the car. Zachary couldn't help smiling a little as he turned it down. Rhys was a good kid, and Zachary hoped he'd be able to grow and mature and not be kept down by the traumas he had suffered through so young.

Zachary pulled his phone out of his pocket to check for messages. There were no urgent messages. He tapped on the email icon to make sure there wasn't anything in his inbox that he needed to act on. There were a couple more emails from the stalker, which he trashed, and nothing else of importance in the inbox. Everything else could wait until he was at his computer later.

He slid his phone back into his pocket and put the car into reverse to back out of the parking space. He was backed most of the way out when he was hit by a lightning bolt.

Emails from the stalker? In his own inbox?

Stomping on the brake, he pulled his phone back out and quickly navigated to the trash. He opened the first one.

What you did was criminal.

They should have locked you up and thrown away the key.

You should have just died in that fire.

Zachary stared at the words in horror. Of course it wasn't

Harding's cyberstalker, in spite of the similarities between the poisonous messages. Harding's stalker would have no idea of Zachary's past and no reason to start harassing him.

But someone connected to Zachary's past had tried to make contact with him recently. If Tyrrell was able to find Zachary's old address from when he and Bridget were living together, then it followed that he'd be able to find Zachary's email address. Zachary ran a business, he didn't exactly keep it a secret. When Zachary had failed to answer the letter, Tyrrell had gone looking for another way to get ahold of him, and had vented his anger through email.

Zachary closed the first email and opened the second. They were in reverse chronological order with the most recent at the top, so the second email had actually arrived first. Zachary stared at the contents of the email, gobsmacked.

Someone laid on the horn behind him and Zachary realized that he was still sitting in his car in the police visitor parking lot, his car at an angle from pulling out, blocking the aisle completely. He threw the phone on the passenger seat beside him and shifted into drive. Without looking at the car behind him, he drove out of the parking lot and all the way home without picking up his phone again. The radio blasted out music he didn't even hear and he couldn't remember any of the drive home once he found himself sitting in the parking lot of his apartment building.

He picked up his phone, woke it up again, and looked at the screen.

10

It was Pat who answered the door. He stared at Zachary in surprise.

"Zachary! I didn't know you were coming by. Lorne isn't home. Did he know…?"

Zachary had driven for several hours to get to the home of Mr. Peterson, an old foster father, fully believing that he would be there when Zachary arrived. It seemed inconceivable that Mr. Peterson would not be there when Zachary needed him.

"No," he admitted. "I didn't… I just came. Is he coming back? He didn't move, did he?" Already mired in the past, Zachary couldn't help but remember the day he had arrived on the Petersons' doorstep expecting to be able to develop pictures with Mr. Peterson, only to be told by his wife that he had moved out. That had been when Mr. Peterson's relationship with Pat had come to light, predictably ending the marriage.

"Of course he's coming back," Pat assured Zachary. "Come in." He took Zachary by the arm and tugged him inside. "You're white as a sheet, Zachary, what's wrong?"

Zachary leaned on Pat for support. Though a good ten years older than Zachary, Pat was taller and his muscular chest almost twice as broad. With his help, Zachary managed to get to the couch and sit down. He buried his face in his hands, elbows braced on his knees. "He's coming back?"

"I promise, he's coming back. He just went out to pick up some groceries."

Pat didn't tell Zachary that he should have called ahead to arrange something. Mrs. Peterson had always criticized Zachary for showing up unannounced, when he had been told repeatedly that he needed to call and set up appointments ahead of time. In contrast, Pat and Mr. Peterson had always told him that Zachary was welcome anytime, so he hadn't hesitated to go there when everything in his world had suddenly gone sideways.

"Let me give him a call," Pat said. "I'll let him know you're here, see how long he's going to be."

He walked out to the kitchen to make the call out of Zachary's hearing. Zachary couldn't make out his words, but did recognize the low tones of concern. Pat looked back over his shoulder at Zachary once as he talked, then looked back away. After he hung up, he turned back around and stood in the doorway between the living room and the dining room.

"He's on his way. Ten, fifteen minutes."

"Okay." Zachary nodded, his movements feeling awkward and wooden. "Thanks."

"Just relax and make yourself at home. I'll bring you a drink in a minute."

Zachary turned his head to look out the living room window, watching for Mr. Peterson's return. He could hear Pat moving around in the kitchen, but the sounds didn't really enter his conscious thoughts. He was in limbo, drowning in memories, waiting for someone he could share them with to try to get them out of his head.

Pat walked in and placed something on the glass-topped coffee table.

"Zachary."

He tried to travel the long span of time back to the present, but it took a couple more prompts from Pat before Zachary could get there. He turned his head and focused on the older man. Still handsome and fit, looking fashionable even in a t-shirt. Pat motioned to the coffee table.

"Have some tea," he urged. "It will help."

Zachary leaned forward and, with a shaking hand, picked up the white mug with a cat picture on the side and forced himself to drink a few tiny sips of the hot tea. It was an herbal blend Zachary wasn't familiar with, but it was pleasant enough. It had been sweetened with a generous amount of honey. *Good for shock.*

"Thanks."

He put the mug back down. It rattled against the coaster as he set it down.

Pat sat down in one of the upholstered chairs. "It's good to see you. You know Lorne would love to see more of you. Any time you want to make the trip, we'd love to have you. Take a week off and have a real vacation."

Zachary nodded wordlessly. Just a reflex reaction, keeping the flow of the conversation.

"It was nice seeing you at Thanksgiving, but we'd be happy to see more of you."

Zachary turned his head and looked out the front window again, catching a movement out the corner of his eye. But the car continued to drive on past the house. Not Lorne Peterson.

"He'll be coming through the back," Pat advised, following his gaze. At that moment, Zachary heard the grinding of the garage door motor in the attached garage.

Zachary turned toward the kitchen and watched as Mr. Peterson entered with a couple of grocery bags. He put them down on the counter and joined Pat and Zachary in the living room without putting his purchases away.

"Zachary, it's so good to see you!" He sat down on the couch with him. "How are you? Is everything okay?"

"No. I don't know. No." Zachary shook his head, not sure what to say.

"Okay! That's a little confusing. Tell me what's up."

Zachary pulled out his phone and brought it to life. It was still open to the email. He handed it over.

Mr. Peterson looked at the phone screen. He put on a pair of glasses, looked at it again, and took them off. "I really can't see those little phone screens worth a darn. Can you bring it up on my computer? Or just tell me what it says?"

"Uh, yeah." Zachary swallowed and nodded. "Sure. Where's your computer?"

Mr. Peterson led him to a bedroom that was being used as a study, and motioned to the computer on the desk. Certainly not the latest model, but it had a big screen, and it would do. Zachary sat down in the swivel chair and brought up the browser, logging out of Mr. Peterson's email and into his own account. There were several new emails in his inbox, but he didn't look at them, navigating to the deleted mail to open the email with an attachment. He clicked the jpg and it filled the screen.

It was even more disorienting to see it on the big screen than it had been on the phone. Mr. Peterson gazed for a moment at the picture of the family on the screen. Mother, father, and six children, apparently at a Christmas party in the late eighties. Mr. Peterson lifted his hand so fast it made Zachary jump. He pointed at the third child, the oldest boy. "That's you!" He looked at Zachary's face and then back at the screen again. "It is, isn't it?"

"Yes."

"This is your bio family?"

Zachary nodded.

"Where did you find it?"

Zachary closed the picture and pointed with the mouse to the text of the email.

This was your family before you destroyed it.

It's hard to believe that kind of evil can be allowed to exist.

"Oh, Zachary..." Mr. Peterson breathed. "You can't believe that. Who sent you this?"

"Tyrrell." Zachary clicked on the photo again and indicated the smiling six-year-old. "There."

"Are you sure?" The older man shook his head. "I really can't see something like this coming from a member of your family. I know there were issues with your mother, but the other kids…? They wouldn't do this."

"You never even met them. How could you know that?"

"It's just… it doesn't make sense. He was just a little boy. He wouldn't have blamed you. I don't know if they even would have told him any details of what had happened. Social Services wasn't too keen on sharing that information, even with foster parents who needed it."

"He was old enough to remember. He was six."

Zachary had to admit that the little boy in the picture looked closer to three than to six. But he could remember their ages. They had probably all been small for their ages. Zachary knew he had been endlessly teased and bullied for being so small. But that was normal for children who were neglected and malnourished. Then, years of meds that stunted growth had ensured that Zachary would remain shorter than average as an adult too, even though he had been fed better in later years.

"It's not signed. What makes you think it was Tyrrell?"

"He sent me a letter. I didn't answer it, so he sent these."

"He sent you a letter? Snail mail?"

"Yes. I guess I should have answered, like Kenzie said. Maybe he wouldn't have resorted to this."

Mr. Peterson shook his head. "I'm so sorry this happened. The boy obviously has some lasting problems. To blame you for everything thirty years later… maybe he has some kind of psychosis…"

Zachary couldn't envision Tyrrell as a man. In his mind, Tyrrell was forever that six-year-old who had cowered in Zachary's arms as their parents fought. Tyrrell would always be a little boy in his memories.

"But something good did come of this," Mr. Peterson offered.

"Good?"

"You got a picture of your family. You've never had anything to remember them by."

Zachary hadn't. He hadn't had anything after the fire. Had that one picture survived? Had there been anything else that had been saved from the fire? He scrutinized it, looking for any signs of scorching or smoke damage, but it seemed to be in good condition.

"Yeah."

"Why don't you print a copy out?"

"I should adjust it first." Zachary studied the lighting and color in the old photo. "Balance the lighting and fix the color…"

"You can do that later. Just print a copy for now. We'll go sit down and you can tell me about them."

Zachary downloaded the picture and sent it to the printer. He and Mr. Peterson waited while it printed.

"You should report him to the police," Mr. Peterson commented.

"No. I couldn't do that to him."

"He could be unbalanced. He could do something to harm you."

Zachary thought about Richard Harding, getting struck down on the road that night. What had happened? Had his stalker shown up? Had he been running away from someone or chasing after them? From what Ashley had said, he wouldn't have been likely to have chased after the man. Running away, then. Running right into the pathway of a speeding semi? Maybe he had been trying to flag Rusty down for help and had turned away at the last moment to protect himself when he realized the truck wasn't going to stop.

Mr. Peterson put his hand on Zachary's shoulder.

"I'm okay," Zachary told him, his voice hoarse. He leaned forward and plucked the photo from the printer. Holding it in his hands somehow made it more real than just looking at it on the phone and computer screens. He felt like he could reach out and touch each one of them. It was like the fire had just happened the day before. Or like it had never happened.

Mr. Peterson squeezed, then let go of Zachary. "Let's go sit back down."

He shuffled a little when he walked. Mr. Peterson had always seemed so big and solid; it was only in the last couple of years he had started to show some frailty. The fact brought a lump to Zachary's throat. Mr. Peterson was his only family. Zachary had thought that he would be around forever, even though he knew it wasn't true. Maybe his thoughts of the end of his own life had prevented him from seeing that Mr. Peterson would die one day too. Zachary had never been able to see more than a year ahead in his own life. Never past the next Christmas.

Zachary sat back down in the spot he had vacated. He took a sip of the tea, which had cooled enough to drink. He hesitated, then handed Pat the family picture. Pat was family too. He'd been with Mr. Peterson for almost thirty years.

"That's my bio family. Back… before."

Pat handled the picture carefully. He gave a little laugh. "Is that you? Man, look at how young you are!"

Zachary ducked his head. "Yeah."

"How old were you when we first met? Fourteen? You're a lot younger here."

"Ten. Before I went to the Petersons'."

"Wow. Where did you turn this up?"

Zachary looked at Mr. Peterson, not sure he could explain it himself.

"Zachary has been getting… some disturbing letters. This was with one of them. Maybe from one of his brothers."

Pat looked again at the picture and then handed it back to Zachary. "*That's* what happened. That's why you came here."

Zachary nodded. "I just… it's the only place I could think of. I couldn't go to a therapist or group… I needed… somewhere grounding."

"Family," Pat said firmly.

"Yeah."

Zachary held the photo, staring down at it. Mr. Peterson's eyes were on it as well.

"It's hard to believe that's just before you came to us. When the social worker brought you… you were a very sad little boy."

The children in the picture were happy. They were all together and their eyes sparkled with the excitement of the party. There was something else different too; the arm Zachary had around Tyrrell was unscarred. No burns from the fire. No cuts on his wrists. There were a couple of visible bruises, but all active boys had bruises on their arms and legs. And Zachary had been very active.

"No scars."

Mr. Peterson squinted and nodded. "The fire must have been just a few days after this."

Zachary held his breath, waiting for the images to subside. "I guess. I don't remember this party."

"Maybe this is the year before. You don't look ten."

"No, I was."

"How soon did you go to Lorne's?" Pat asked. "Right after?"

"I was in hospital… then Bonnie Brown. It was a few months."

They didn't discuss how long he'd been at the Petersons'. That he'd been too much for them to manage and Mrs. Peterson had insisted that he be reassigned to another foster family within a few short weeks. But even so, Mr. Peterson had become an anchor for Zachary. He had given Zachary his first camera for his birthday and allowed him to keep in contact after he had been moved. They had processed hundreds of photos together and Mr. Peterson had never made him feel unwelcome.

"I want you to tell me about your family," Mr. Peterson said, though of course he'd heard their names and what stories Zachary could remember before. "But first, I want you to tell me what you're going to do. About the letters."

"I don't know."

"It should be reported to the police."

"If I don't respond, he'll stop."

"There's no guarantee of that. Something must have happened to trigger this behavior. You don't know what it was. If he's just been through some kind of breakup or tragedy… you don't know how much it might have affected him."

"I can't report Tyrrell."

"If he starts making threats…"

"He hasn't. Let's just wait and see if it blows over."

11

Zachary had never stayed over at Mr. Peterson's house before. He was close enough that he could drive over in the afternoon for dinner, then drive back home for bed. There had been invitations, but he'd never accepted them. But Mr. Peterson refused to take 'no' for an answer.

"I want to make sure you're okay. This has been very upsetting for you."

Zachary's moods had been all over the map as he'd tried to process both the hate-filled messages from Tyrrell and the precious picture of his family. He'd had several vivid flashbacks, and more than once had excused himself to the bathroom because he didn't want Pat and Mr. Peterson to see him cry. He hadn't been able to touch anything at supper.

In the end, Zachary was too exhausted to argue about it. Mr. Peterson wasn't giving him a choice and it was immensely easier to just accept the edict than to try to fight him on it.

"We have everything you need," Pat assured him, "and we have the space. You're not in the way; you know we've been trying to get you to stay over for years."

"I don't like to impose…"

"Good grief, Zachary. Sleeping on the guest room bed is not imposing. Listen to Lorne."

"Okay." Zachary held up his hands. "Fine. Okay. I'll stay."

And then came the invitations for Christmas. They'd always invited him to join their observance, other than the couple years he'd been with Bridget, but Zachary was always physically unable to accept.

"We might get a visit from my family this year," Pat offered. "Fingers crossed." He held up his hands with this index and middle fingers crossed on both. "One can always hope."

Zachary had rarely heard Pat even acknowledge that he had any family other than Mr. Peterson. He looked at Pat curiously. "Who's coming? Your parents?"

"My dad passed last year. Maybe my mother and sister will come. For years, they've all refused to come anywhere near here."

"They wouldn't have anything to do with me," Mr. Peterson said wryly. "They were fine with Pat going home for a visit, but I'm the person who corrupted him." Mr. Peterson looked at his partner affectionately. "Apparently, I'm very persuasive."

Zachary felt a flush creeping up his neck. He'd never been comfortable talking to them about their romantic relationship; how they had met, what had attracted them to each other, or what other relationships they might have had other than each other.

Pat laughed. "They always hoped I'd decide it was a big mistake. That it was just a phase I was going through. My dad was very religious about this one thing. He was never particularly concerned with any of the other Biblical teachings, but he believed our relationship was unnatural and a sin and he wouldn't do anything that might be taken as condoning it."

"Too bad he missed out on spending time with you," Zachary said. He wanted a family so badly, it was hard to believe anyone would choose to push their child away.

Pat nodded, looking pensive. "We could have had some good years together. But that was his choice."

After a couple of days at Mr. Peterson's house, Zachary was feeling a lot calmer and more stable. Pat and Mr. Peterson repeated their invitations for him to return for Christmas, invitations which, again, were met with fumbling silence.

"You know you're always welcome," Mr. Peterson assured him. "Any time you want to come join us, just do it. I don't need a commitment ahead of time."

Zachary nodded and got back into his car. Heading back home, he had mixed feelings. It would feel good to get back to work and his own apartment and just put the incident behind him.

But he knew that it wasn't over. Tyrrell had demonstrated that he wasn't going to just send one letter and then wait for a response. He had a deep-seated anger and resentment toward Zachary, and he was going to continue to vent it, just the way Harding's stalker had not only continued his harassment, but escalated it. Zachary continued to send the messages to his email trash, but he also found that he couldn't just ignore them and leave them alone. Instead, like picking at a scab, he kept digging back into the trash to read and re-read the messages. Like if he could just figure out what to say to Tyrrell, he could stop the influx of poison pen emails. Even though he knew it was impossible, he couldn't stop himself from obsessing over the contents of the emails and what responses to give.

Probably, there wouldn't even be a way for him to reply if he wanted to. The anonymous email service Tyrrell was employing wouldn't even accept an answer. But knowing that fact logically and being able to stop the obsessive re-reading of the vitriolic emails were two different things. He had put on a mask of dispassion for Mr. Peterson and Pat. *Oh, it's nothing. As long as he's not making threats, I'll just delete them.* But he suspected they didn't believe that for a minute.

As he entered the city limits, work started to call to Zachary.

He could hyperfocus on his files and push everything else out of his mind. That would be a relief, and would bring in some extra cash. His phone rang and Zachary answered it on Bluetooth.

"Zachary, are you okay?"

Zachary took a deep breath. He had answered Kenzie's various messages while he'd been at Mr. Peterson's, but he knew she wouldn't believe he was really okay until she'd had a chance to see him face to face.

"I'm fine, Kenzie. Just got back into town."

"Thought you might want to go over the details of the Harding autopsy."

"Oh!" He hadn't been expecting that, and it was a welcome surprise. "Sure, that would be great. Take you out this time? Buffet?"

"Why is it always buffet when we're reviewing autopsies?"

Zachary thought about it. It wasn't like he had taken that many homicides. But Kenzie might be right. "I didn't realize we did that. Do you want to go somewhere else instead? Somewhere nicer?"

There was a moment of hesitation. "I don't know if it would be kosher to pull out autopsy photos somewhere nicer."

Zachary thought about her response. "We don't have to look at the photos while we're there. We can have a nice dinner and then go back to my place to look at them and go over the results."

"Maybe…"

So perhaps Bowman had been right about Kenzie being interested in a deeper relationship. But maybe it wasn't too late to advance it. As long as she was still calling him, there was a possibility.

"You want to try the Inn? It's been a while since we've been there."

Not since New Year's the previous year. The night that they had been in a serious wreck after someone had cut Zachary's brake lines.

"It was really nice last time, wasn't it? I wouldn't mind that."

"I don't remember much about it," Zachary admitted. His memories of the dinner had been clouded by everything that had happened afterward.

Kenzie laughed. "Then I guess it's about time we went back. And this time, you don't have a psychotic killer stalking you."

Zachary's mouth went dry. He hadn't even thought to check his car for tampering before he'd gotten into it at Mr. Peterson's house. He would have to be sure to check it before and after they ate. He wasn't about to have another accident.

"Zachary?"

"Yeah, I'll make the reservations. Was there anything interesting on the autopsy?"

"I'm afraid not, no. You can look, but I don't think you're going to find much enlightenment in this one."

"He seems to be quite the enigma," Zachary said. "I should be getting the rest of the background reports today, but so far I haven't turned up much of anything."

By the time they met for dinner, Zachary had followed up on the background searches, and not only had they not turned up much of interest, they had come back almost blank. He was used to being able to find at least a few points of interest on a subject, but Harding was different. He didn't seem to have a history. Even his electronic footprint only went back a few years. Before that, he might not even have existed.

"Have you ever had that happen before?" Kenzie asked. "I mean, he could just be a really boring person, right?"

"It's not just that he's boring. Or law-abiding. There's just nothing there."

"So..." She took a polite bite of her salmon. "Are we talking witness protection program?"

"I guess that's a possibility. More likely he was in the country illegally. Or he created a false identity."

"And which do you think it is?"

Zachary poked at his potatoes. "I need to talk to the girlfriend. Ashley. See if she knows anything about it. I know she's been holding back on me. She never could explain *why* she couldn't believe it was an accident."

"She knows, then," Kenzie decided. "How about her? Did you run any background on her?"

"Well…" Zachary was hesitant, wondering whether she would approve or whether she thought it was an invasion of privacy. He didn't usually run background searches on his clients. Not without a good reason. "I did do some preliminary searches on her. Hers come back more normal. Credit history, mentions of awards and scholarships in school, work history on her LinkedIn account. Interests, hobbies, and family on her social media accounts. She comes back as a real person, but he doesn't."

Kenzie pondered this and had a sip of wine. "It's fascinating to hear how it's all done. It really is."

Zachary smiled. Most people, finding out how mind-numbingly boring private investigation could be, were let down. Real private investigators weren't Dick Tracy or Nero Wolfe. Real private investigations work involved a lot of paper, thinking time, and waiting around.

———

Back at Zachary's apartment, Kenzie unpacked her portfolio briefcase while Zachary got out drinks and ducked into the bathroom to take a couple of pills unobserved. When he sat down on the couch with Kenzie, she turned the bottle around to look at the label.

"Sparkling white grape and peach," she read. "Sounds nice." She poured it into the two brand-new champagne flutes and had a taste. "It's good. This is really nice, thank you for a great evening."

"It's not over yet," Zachary pointed out, smiling a little, "there are still autopsy photos."

Kenzie laughed. She pulled the written report out from under one of the pictures and started to tell him the findings, outlining Harding's numerous broken bones. Zachary listened closely.

"Can you tell by the broken bones how fast the vehicle was going when it hit him?"

"Not with any accuracy, no. The breaks are sharper and there is more shattering the faster the vehicle is going, but we can't say 'this was a truck going fifty and this was a truck going sixty.'"

Zachary nodded. "And you can't tell what he was doing— whether he was walking or running, what position he was in when he got hit…?"

"Not much more than that he was standing and he was hit on the left side."

"Is there anything that doesn't make sense? Anything that stands out? Inconsistencies?"

"It's a pretty straightforward MVC."

Zachary nodded. He hadn't really been expecting anything different, but he had hoped that there would be something illuminating. Just one or two little facts that would point him in a different direction. He took a sip of the sparkling juice Kenzie had poured for him. While he would have preferred a Coke, the sparkling juice was to help set a romantic scene. He thought too late about putting on some background music. It might seem awkward to get back up and do it while they were discussing dead bodies. And there were no candles. Never any candles. He had been relieved that the flickering candles on the tables at the Inn had turned out to be little electric lights rather than the real thing.

"How about this…" he said slowly. "You've seen the body. Say it's a John Doe. You don't know anything about him. What does the body tell you about what kind of a person he was? Where he lived, what he did, health issues, medical history…"

"Interesting question." Kenzie considered. She stared up at the ceiling as she thought about it.

Zachary looked through the photos as she thought.

"Caucasian male in his thirties. He was in good shape," Kenzie said, "Body Mass Index put him at a healthy weight for his height. But not really muscular. A bit of stooping in his shoulders and back, which says he was probably sedentary, sitting for long periods of time. Maybe a computer gamer. Hands would suggest some manual work, though. Some dental work that wasn't really up to first-world standards, so maybe he had lived out of the country for a while."

Zachary picked up one of the photos. "He had tattoos." He didn't know why that surprised him. A lot of people had tattoos, even forty-something stay-at-home moms and minor children.

"Yeah, a few of them." Kenzie shuffled through the pictures to pull a couple more out. "I thought this one a little odd." She handed him a picture of a snake tattoo. "It looks like it was applied over broken skin, which is a big no-no. You see how the ink tones are uneven."

"Trying to hide a scar?" Zachary suggested.

"Maybe that was the idea, but any self-respecting tattooist would wait until it was properly healed over, so you don't end up with these color shifts."

"Why put a tattoo over broken skin, then? Wouldn't that be painful?"

"I would expect it to be quite a painful process." Kenzie took a sip of her drink, then suddenly frowned. "Actually, you may be onto something there…"

"What?"

Kenzie looked at her written report, and then tracked down a photo. She handed it to Zachary. He saw an expanse of skin, with a little group of parallel cuts.

"What's this from?"

"We weren't sure when we looked at it to start with. But now I'm wondering… if he was self-harming. You see cutting more often with girls, but some guys still do it. You said he was on meds for depression. Maybe he was cutting too."

"And the tattoos were to cover the areas he'd been cutting? To hide them?"

"Maybe… or maybe to amplify the pain."

Zachary grimaced. "Ouch. You think?"

"Sometimes body modification aficionados are addicted to pain or using it the same way as someone who self-harms. Tattoos or other mods could be socially acceptable ways to harm himself."

"Maybe. He was depressed; if the meds weren't giving him any relief or he was looking for something that would work faster…"

Kenzie looked sideways at Zachary and didn't agree or disagree.

"What about this one?" Zachary held up the initial tattoo picture he had grabbed. "I don't see any scarring in or around this tattoo."

Kenzie studied it. "This one looks different. Like maybe a homemade tattoo instead of a professional one."

"You think he did it himself?"

"I don't think he could have done it alone. He would have needed help, even if he was trying to do it at home."

"Another question to ask Ashley."

"I think you should definitely talk to her. Maybe this is enough ammunition to get her to open up."

Zachary met with Ashley at the police station. He hoped that if he talked to her there, she would be uncomfortable and off-balance, and more likely to talk about what it was she had been keeping a secret. Since he wasn't a police officer himself, it had taken a little finessing to get the use of one of their meeting rooms. In the end, Bowman had reserved it in his own name, and insisted on being present for the interview since his was the name that was on the record.

He started with a disclaimer that Zachary was not the police and that she wasn't required to answer anything he asked. Ashley nodded, but her eyes went back and forth around the room, anxious at the unfamiliar setting.

"Some things have turned up in my investigation," Zachary explained.

"What things?"

"You haven't been completely honest about who Richard was, have you?" Zachary pressed, keeping his language vague. "You thought it didn't make any difference, but I need all of the details if I'm going to sort this out."

She chewed on her lip, uncertain. "I just want you to prove

that the truck driver intended to murder him. You don't need to know every little detail about Richard's life for that."

"I do need to know. Keeping it from me doesn't help."

"What did you find? You said you had turned things up in your investigation."

Zachary studied her, waiting for her to fill the silence. She was sweating and squirming uncomfortably, but she didn't break down. He put down a copy of the photo of the DIY tattoo that Kenzie said Harding would have needed help with. Maybe Ashley had been the one to assist him. If not, he was sure she would at least know the history of such a thing. She wouldn't just see tattoos on her boyfriend's body and not ask about them.

Ashley wiped her forehead and grimaced. "I promised never to tell anyone," she said plaintively.

"I think he would have made an exception for when it would help convict his killer."

"But I don't see—it can't help you. And if you already know, then me telling you would just be betraying him for no reason!"

"I need the details. I need you to explain it to me."

He waited. He had certainly attacked the right weakness on his first try. There were several ways the conversation could have gone and he was happy it had worked right away. There *was* something about that tattoo. Something that had made Richard different. Something that explained it all.

"I told him he should get it removed," Ashley said. "I told him it could come back to bite him if the wrong person saw it. But he said… no one but me was going to see it, because it was covered up normally. He said no one else would ever see it."

"And maybe they didn't. While he was alive. But now we've seen it. I'm still waiting for an explanation."

Ashley sighed. She looked over at Bowman, as if asking whether she really had to tell Zachary. Bowman just lifted his eyebrows and waited, arms folded.

"He got it while he was in prison," Ashley finally admitted.

Bowman shifted. Zachary was careful not to look at him. He

kept his eyes on Ashley. He nodded, showing no surprise, as if she were only confirming what he had already known. And maybe he should have figured it out. A prison tattoo. That's why it was lower quality. That was why it looked homemade.

"How long ago did he get out of prison?"

"Three years."

"Around the time you guys met."

"Yes. I was one of the first people he met when he moved to Vermont. He figured that here, he'd be able to start a new life. He'd be able to be a normal person instead of someone that everyone knew was a convict. You can't live a normal life when everyone knows you've been to prison. They judge you. They don't treat you the same way."

"No," Zachary agreed. And it was true of other facilities as well. A psych hospital, juvie, drug rehab, residential care. People looked at him differently when they knew. They looked at him like he was an alien, a completely different species. "Why didn't you just tell the police that when they started the investigation? Instead, you've had everybody running around not knowing where to look."

"Where to look for what?" Ashley challenged. "You already know who it was that ran him down. You just need to prove that it was intentional instead of accidental."

"How can we do that without being able to tie him to Richard's earlier life? Or even to his original name?"

"He wasn't that person anymore. It was a tragic accident, and he paid for it. He wanted to leave that chapter of his life behind and be able to leave a normal life as Richard Harding."

"But it isn't that easy, is it?"

"No. He was always paranoid someone would recognize him or would be able to track him down in spite of the name change. I told him that was silly. No one was going to be stalking him. Everyone else was just going to go on with their own lives, and he could to."

"Except that it did catch up to him." Zachary thought about

the words in the accusing emails and messages. *People like you. What you did. Unforgivable.* "Someone did run into him or track him down and was sending him those emails."

"He never told me. Did he think I wouldn't believe him? Why wouldn't he trust me with that?"

"Maybe because it was from a part of his life that you hadn't had anything to do with." Zachary thought about how he had instinctively gone to Mr. Peterson when he got the first few messages from Tyrrell, not to Kenzie or Bowman or another of his friends. Zachary had been sent to the Petersons' house after the fire, when he had been put into foster care for the first time. He associated them with that time in his life. Sharing information with Kenzie about his early life wasn't easy. She had not been a part of it. "Is there someone he might have gone to? Someone from his previous life that he would have gone to with his problems?"

"No, he'd completely cut himself off from his former life. His therapist suggested changing his name and moving away. His family didn't really want anything to do with him. So he figured, why not? He didn't want to be punished over and over again for something that wasn't even his fault."

"How much do you know about his life before, when he was —what was his name?"

"Brandon Powers."

Zachary wrote it down in his notepad. "Did he give you his version of what happened when he was Brandon Powers? What it was he went to prison for?" Zachary said it as if he already knew the details, and just wanted to check to see if Ashley did.

Ashley sighed. Zachary could see that even though she had been fighting against telling him, trying to keep the secret she had promised to keep for Harding, she was relieved to have someone to tell it to. She wanted to get it off her chest, to have someone to share the burden of knowledge with.

"It was an accident. He had half his life taken away from him because of a car accident."

Zachary couldn't suppress a shiver. Harding had been convicted because of a car accident and then he had been killed in one? He could already begin to see the parallel that had convinced Ashley that it must have been an intentional homicide.

"Just tell me about it in your own words," he told her. He didn't want to have to drag each individual statement from her. He didn't want to be left with a hodgepodge of unconnected statements and with no overall picture. He wanted to know the story, as if it had happened to him.

"He was in college. He and some of his friends had been out to the bar, and Richard was driving them home. He was the designated driver. But then a girl stepped out in front of the car, coming from nowhere, and he couldn't stop in time."

Vehicle versus pedestrian. Just like Harding's death.

"Did he kill or injure her?" he asked, pushing her to provide the lynch-pin. Everything else would be easier to tell once she had gotten that part off her chest.

"She was killed. Instantly, I guess. Richard… wasn't really clear telling that part."

"Was he arrested at the scene?"

Ashley swallowed. "No. Not exactly."

"Not exactly." He waited for the rest. What, exactly?

"He was woozy. He hit his head during the accident. He couldn't really be responsible for his actions after the accident."

Zachary knew what she was trying to avoid saying before she managed to get it out.

"He sort of… wandered away from the scene. He was disoriented and didn't know what he was doing."

"Hit and run."

"Yes, that's what they called it." She looked straight at Zachary for the first time. "You see? You see why him getting killed in a hit and run just couldn't be an accident? You understand why I'm sure it was intentional?"

"I see your point. It stretches the bounds of plausibility."

"Yes. It does. I don't know what happened out there that

night. I don't know how the trucker is connected. But I know it wasn't an accident."

"I'll do my best to find the connection. But for that, you have to tell me the truth. The whole truth, without covering anything up because you don't think it's relevant."

She nodded, eyes down.

"Good. It's time to hear the real story. Do you know why he was out on the road that night?"

"No. None of that has changed. I still don't know why he went outside and why he'd be out on the road. Like I said, he didn't go outside for walks, he exercised at home on the bike. He didn't spend a lot of time outside the house. He was afraid someone would see him and know who he was."

Zachary thought of what Kenzie had said. At a healthy weight, but not muscular. As if he'd done a lot of sitting, hunched over for long periods of time. The curse of prison life. Free time. Time to sit and think and do nothing else. Waiting for the seconds, minutes, hours, and days to pass. Waiting for the time to tick slowly away, until his release day finally arrived.

Then he'd been released, but he'd been afraid to go out. Whether it was paranoia or agoraphobia, Zachary didn't know. Harding's stint in prison had damaged him. It had affected him for the rest of his life, even though he had tried to put it behind him.

"He was the designated driver the night of the accident." Zachary repeated what Ashley had told him.

"Yes."

"He hadn't had anything to drink?"

Her eyes darted to the side, trying to decide whether to tell him the truth or not.

"He said he'd had a couple of beers. He wasn't drunk, but if the police had tried to test him that night, he would have had some alcohol in his blood. Just a little. It would for sure be below the limit, but it wouldn't be zero."

"Is that why he didn't stick around the accident scene? Because he didn't want to be tested?"

"I told you. He was disoriented."

"I think there might have been more to it than that."

"I know Richard. He wasn't lying about that."

"Even if he'd had no alcohol in his blood, he still killed this pedestrian. He's still responsible."

"And he paid for it. He served his time."

"Which was how much?"

"Eight years in prison."

Zachary nodded. It computed. And the length of time confirmed that the court had convicted him of first degree vehicular homicide, not a misdemeanor. There was more to it than just misjudging the distance of the pedestrian from the car. Leaving the scene of the crime hadn't helped. Neither had drinking, if there had still been alcohol in his system when they caught up with him.

"What was the victim's name?"

"How do you expect me to know that?" Ashley demanded.

Zachary just gazed at her steadily. She turned red.

"Hope Creedy."

Zachary wrote it down. There, at last, were two more names to feed into his searches in trying to find a connection between Richard Harding and Rusty Donaldson. Brandon Powers and Hope Creedy. Hopefully, one of them would lead him to the answer to the puzzle.

"Was there anyone specific Richard didn't want to run into or be tracked down by?"

"What do you mean?"

"Was there anyone from Hope's family who had been threatening him? Anyone sending letters to him at the prison? A specific person that he never wanted to hear from again?"

Ashley's brow wrinkled as she considered the question. "No... I don't think so. He didn't say there was one person, just that he didn't want anyone to know his old name or his history. I wasn't allowed to tell anyone."

"Did you?"

"Did I what?"

"Tell anyone. It's a pretty big secret to keep. Did you tell a girl-friend? Your mother? Your hairdresser? Someone who you thought would keep the secret and would never be a threat to Richard?"

"No!" she looked offended that he would even think such a thing. But in Zachary's experience, people always told someone. A secret just kept itching away and the secret-keeper had to scratch it somehow, by telling at least one person they considered safe and trustworthy.

"A therapist? Someone who was required under law to keep it a secret?"

"No."

But he thought he had seen a shadow cross her face. Who, then? A spiritual confessor? Ashley was keeping tight-lipped. She had no intention of telling him who she had spilled the beans to. Had her indiscretion led someone from Richard's past to him? Or was it just one of those things? People were getting easier and easier to trace. It wasn't just Zachary's growing expertise; there were more tools out there. More electronic trails. Saying one thing online…

"Did Richard ever have any contact with anyone from Hope's family? Did he ever go back to try to apologize?"

"No. He wasn't required to do that. And he hadn't done anything wrong. It was an accident. He didn't see her coming. It was unavoidable."

That hadn't been the court's determination, but Zachary couldn't be sure if she knew that or not. Either way, she was just going to go on repeating Richard's own rhetoric, no matter what Zachary tried to get out of her.

"So as far as you know, he didn't contact them and they didn't contact him."

"No." Ashley looked around the bare-walled meeting room. "So is that it? Can I go now?"

"Did Richard have any papers? Anything from the trial, a legal name change, anything like that?"

"I got rid of it all. Burned it."

Too bad the police hadn't reacted faster than they had. Maybe they would have been able to get their hands on Richard's papers before she'd had the chance. But there would still be public records. She couldn't do anything about those.

N ice job," Bowman commented, as they watched Ashley's departure.

She wasn't happy, but at least she hadn't fired him for doing what she had hired him to do. That just bolstered his opinion that she was relieved to be able to share the burden of Richard's secret. She didn't have to be the only one who knew about it anymore.

"Thanks. I knew from the start she wasn't telling me everything, but I didn't have a clue what it was. Not to start with."

"How did you get that from a tattoo?"

"I didn't… not the whole story. I just knew that it didn't fit. It didn't match the others, and there was no explanation for him having a homemade tattoo. I figured he must have given her some story, even if it wasn't the truth."

"But who would make up something like this? It had the ring of truth, right?"

"Mostly."

"You're saying you don't believe that he was sober?" Bowman gave him a sardonic grin. "Now why would you not take the lady's opinion for that?"

"Because he wouldn't have told her the truth. Maybe he didn't even tell himself the truth about that one. He was the designated driver, but he thought it was okay to have a couple of beers? That's not the way it works."

"Nope."

"And I don't believe the pedestrian jumped out in front of the car, either. I think I'll find a different story when I order the court documents."

"You mean like that he was driving recklessly and under the influence? But that would mean it was his fault, and the lady just told you it was not his fault."

Zachary appreciated Bowman's sense of humor, but at the same time didn't feel it was appropriate for him to be laughing at someone else getting killed. Or even about Richard having to go to jail or Ashley trying to cover for him. It was a tragedy all around. Even a pure accident could change someone's life forever. And one that was Richard's fault because of a stupid choice he had made… Zachary could empathize with that.

***

He didn't have to wait for the court documents to get started on the investigation into Brandon Powers's hit and run in New Hampshire. A few internet searches of Brandon's and Hope's names brought up the old news stories, and Zachary browsed through them for details of the accident and for the names of Hope's family and friends. Enough of them had spoken to the media to get started on his investigation. The news stories had similar details to what Ashley had told him. Harding, aka Powers, had been driving the vehicle with three passengers, college buddies who had been out drinking together. One of his friends had also been killed in the accident, a Kyle Corcoran. He hadn't been wearing a seatbelt and had been ejected through the windshield. The two friends in the back sustained only minor injuries.

Hope Creedy had been waitressing; not at the same bar as the young men had visited. She had finished her shift and was walking back to her apartment just a few blocks away.

The police had determined that speed had been a factor. With Powers having walked away from the accident, they were unable to test his blood alcohol levels. It had taken them a few days to identify and track him down. But they had tested vomit found near the body, which Powers admitted was his, and it did contain alcohol. Powers eventually conceded to having had a couple of beers, but insisted that he was not drunk. The police nevertheless believed that alcohol had been a factor in the accident, and he was charged with manslaughter, conduct after an accident, and DWI.

Zachary made a list of the names of the people he hoped to interview and started to search for their current contact information. When he had everything assembled, he threw some clothes in a bag. While most of his subjects were only a couple of hours away, it would probably take several days to get interviews with them all, and he wouldn't want to be wasting time traveling back and forth every night. He added some toiletries and pills to the bag, his computer, camera, and any electronics that might come in handy. He stopped and considered whether there was anything else he was going to miss. Anything he really needed, he could buy on the way. He had plenty of experience surviving on the bare necessities. He'd already packed more than he normally had going from one foster home to the other.

He waited until he was on the road to make his phone calls. He wasn't sure whether he would be able to catch Kenzie at her desk or not, but she answered after just a couple of rings.

"Zachary. Bowman said you put that tattoo to good use."

"Sure did. Helped us to get a break in the case. He told you it was a prison tattoo?"

"Yeah. That also explains the dentistry and sedentary lifestyle. I don't know why I didn't think of it when I saw the quality of the tattoo. It just didn't click in."

"You can't know everything. You gave me enough to figure it out. Though you shouldn't have had to—the client should have told me everything she knew when she hired me."

"Crazy to expect you to be able to solve a case without giving you the most important details."

Zachary nodded his agreement, not thinking that she couldn't see him.

"So, what's your next step?" Kenzie asked. "I assume you're going to have to look into this old hit and run, see what the parallels are…?"

"The parallels are already pretty obvious. He killed someone else in a hit and run, and then he was killed in a hit and run. If they're not connected, that's a pretty big coincidence. I'm going to see if I can talk to the first victim's friends and family, see if I can figure out if one of them was somehow involved in Harding's death."

"How long will it take you to get that?"

"I'm on my way now."

"On your way… where?"

"To talk to the family. That's why I called you. To let you know that I wouldn't be home. I'll be in New Hampshire. So… don't be worried."

"How are you already on your way?"

Zachary grinned. The expression felt unnatural, like it had been a long time since he had last smiled. "It doesn't take me that long to get a few names and addresses."

"No kidding. You just found out about this other MVC this morning."

"The internet is your friend."

"It must be better friends with you than with me! It takes me time to find the information I want to."

Zachary gazed at the road ahead of him, enjoying the comforting sensation of gliding over the highway. Long-distance driving was one of the few times his thoughts slowed and he felt calm and focused. Maybe he should have become a long haul trucker like Rusty Donaldson, spending most of his days in a rig. It had a certain appeal.

"When will you be back?" Kenzie asked.

Zachary had almost forgotten she was still on the line. "It depends how long the interviews take. If no one will talk to me, it might be a pretty quick trip. But I think it will be a few days."

"Okay. Anything you need? Water the plants? Pick up the mail?"

"I don't have any plants and I only pick up postal mail once a week anyway."

"You should get some plants."

"Why?"

"They improve your environment: clean and oxygenate the air and lower stress levels... and it would give me something I could do for you when you're out of town."

"I don't like to have anybody or anything depending on me. I think it's best that way."

There was no immediate response from Kenzie. The silence grew uncomfortable. Zachary swallowed and licked his lips.

"Why do you say that?" Kenzie asked.

"It's just... I wouldn't want anyone depending on me, because if something happened to me... I would want to know that everyone was okay. That I hadn't left any unfinished business."

"Are you planning on leaving us any time soon?"

"No, I don't mean that..." But Zachary realized too late that that was exactly what he had meant. She'd nailed it. He liked to keep his affairs neat and tidy so that when things got to be too much for him, he wouldn't have to feel guilty about anything he had left undone. He mentally reproached himself for letting it slip out like that. "I'm sorry, Kenz. I really... I just like things to be uncomplicated."

"Yeah." Her tone was hard and biting. "Uncomplicated. Fine. I guess I'll see you when you get back."

She didn't say anything else. When Zachary glanced over at the Bluetooth display, he saw that she had terminated the call.

14

He wasn't sure, to start with, how to approach Hope's family. Whether he should show up in person or call or email them first. Whether to tell them that he was a private investigator, or to suggest that he was a policeman, lawyer, or reporter doing some kind of follow-up on Hope's death.

Eventually, he decided to stick as close to the truth as he felt he could, and that he would make a cold approach. If they had too much time to think about it, they might decide they didn't want to talk to him. If he caught them off-guard, he was more likely to get an honest reaction.

He figured that evening was the best time to catch Hope's parents at home. They were a middle-aged couple who had suffered a terrible tragedy and had been forced to live in the public eye, and he was hoping that meant they wouldn't be out partying, that they would want to relax after work or would be semi-retired.

Their home was a nice brick bungalow. Not the height of luxury, but very comfortable. The home they had raised their children in. Zachary looked at himself in the mirror before getting out of the car. He had shaved carefully before he left the apartment, wanting to look clean-cut and trustworthy, not like some bum who had just wandered in off of the street. His hair was cropped short enough not to have to spend any time worrying about it. He had on a fresh button-up shirt, electing not to go with a tie or blazer. Professional, but not stuffy.

He took a few deep breaths. The anxiety had started to seep back as soon as he got off the highway. He forced himself to get out of the car, go up to the house, and press the doorbell.

It was only a short wait, and then a woman was standing at the open door, looking out at him curiously. Her hair was a sort of dark strawberry blond. It tapered around her face with minimum fuss, but looked polished rather than plain. She was taller than he was, and the step up into the house made Zachary feel even smaller, like he was a kid being dropped off at yet another new foster home.

"Mrs. Creedy? My name in Zachary Goldman." He paused, waiting for her to ask what he was there for, but she didn't. "I am working with the police in Vermont, consulting on a case that has an old connection with your family. I'm wondering if I could come in for a few minutes?"

She frowned slightly, then turned her head to look back into the house, directing her call back over her shoulder. "Mike?"

Her husband didn't show up immediately, and Mrs. Creedy stepped back from the door, motioning Zachary in.

"Mike, can you come here?" She lowered her voice to speak to Zachary. "Just… come have a seat, Mr.…"

"Goldman," he repeated.

He sat down in the living room at her instruction. It was an awkward minute of not speaking to each other before her husband joined them. Mr. Creedy was taller than his wife, dark-haired but balding, with glasses. He was wearing a sweater with a few buttons done up.

"Who was at the door? Oh, excuse me…" He looked at Zachary, raising his brows.

"Zachary Goldman," he introduced himself again, electing not to stand up and shake Creedy's hand. "I'm working with the Vermont police…"

Creedy shook his head, not understanding. But his wife had already invited the unexpected guest in, and there wasn't much he could do about it until he knew why exactly Zachary was there.

"I don't really understand what this is about. Investigating what?"

Zachary studied his hands. "I don't know whether you heard about what happened to Richard Harding."

"Richard Harding?" Mrs. Creedy looked at her husband, but neither of them seemed to make any connection with the name. "Who is that?"

"You would know him by his former name. Brandon Powers."

There was an instant reaction to that name. Anger, pain, and frustration mingled on both of their faces. The anger was stronger in Mike Creedy's face, but that didn't necessarily prove anything. Women tended to be better at controlling their facial expressions.

"Brandon Powers is the monster who killed our daughter," Mr. Creedy spat. "Whatever happened to him, I can assure you it is not enough."

Zachary studied both of their faces, trying to memorize everything he saw, before letting slip the next bit of information.

"He was killed in a hit and run."

Both mouths opened in shock. Mr. Creedy's face drained of all color, making him look like a ghost.

"He's dead," Mrs. Creedy said, a blank statement rather than a question. Repeating the words that she was too shocked to believe.

"Yes," Zachary agreed. "A couple of weeks ago."

"Why didn't anyone tell us? Why didn't we hear about this?"

"Like I say, he was going by the name Richard Harding. No one connected it with his previous name."

"Nobody even knew who he was?"

"I just discovered it myself. His girlfriend knew, but no one else in Vermont, as far as I know."

Mr. Creedy shook his head. "Someone should call the papers. Let everybody know. This is the best news I've heard in years!"

His wife looked at him with wide eyes. "You can't say that

about someone dying. He has a family too. How do you think they're going to feel? How many times have we said we wouldn't wish what we went through on our own enemies?"

"Turns out that wasn't true. I did wish it on my own enemy, and I'm happy it happened. Like I said, he deserved what he got."

Mrs. Creedy wasn't so sure. She was a lot more cautious about her reaction to the news. She looked at Zachary, giving a little grimace to tell him that her husband wasn't always like that. He was a good person, he was just bitter about his daughter. And she wasn't sure how she felt about it. Her eyes were tortured hollows.

"How exactly did it happen?" she asked tentatively. "It's so bizarre that he was killed the same way as Hope."

"That's one thing that we're looking into," Zachary said authoritatively. "It is a big coincidence. That's one of the reasons I wanted to talk to you. To see whether you know of anyone who might have been threatening Brandon or who might have wanted to hurt him."

"It serves him right," Mr. Creedy reasserted. "It's not very often you see real justice done in this world. But that... that might be the exception."

Mrs. Creedy was dabbing at the corners of her eyes. She looked at Zachary, waiting for his answer. Zachary tried to replay the conversation to see what he had missed.

The details. She wanted to know how Harding had died. It wasn't enough for her to know that he was dead, or that he had died in a hit and run like her daughter. That was enough to satisfy her husband, but Mrs. Creedy wanted the details. She wanted the whole story.

"I'm afraid I can't tell you very much. He was walking near his home and he was struck by a semi."

"Just like Hope," Mr. Creedy said with relish. "You see?"

"His body was thrown into the ditch and he wasn't discovered for a couple of days. They had to have scent dogs out to see if they could find him. Search parties. For a couple of days, his girlfriend had no idea what had happened to him; where he had disappeared to, or why."

Mrs. Creedy's eyes were seeking to connect with her husband's. "You see? We didn't have to deal with that. We knew right away what had happened, we didn't have to wait for days to find out."

But Mike Creedy apparently didn't care about that.

"Do you know anyone who might have had reason to harm Brandon?" Zachary pressed. "Or someone who might have threatened to?"

"Besides us, you mean?" Mr. Creedy challenged. "You want to know who other than us wanted to kill him?"

Mrs. Creedy put her hand over his, trying to quiet him. "Mike…"

"It's true and I'm not going to deny it. If I ran into that monster on the street, I would have done my best to kill him. He should not have been out walking free. He should have been behind bars for the rest of his life. He knew what he was doing when he got into that car, and he should never have been given the opportunity to do it again. People like that cannot be allowed to walk around in free society."

"He served his sentence," Mrs. Creedy said.

"His sentence. They could have given him thirty years. Why didn't they? If Hope was still alive today, she would have been thirty-two. She might have been married. She might have had babies, given us grandchildren. She could have been living a happy, fulfilling life with a family and a career. But he took that away from her. He took that away from all of us. And he should have had to pay. Not just eight years. Forever. He should have had to spend the rest of his life behind bars."

Zachary thought about the sentence. Harding had killed two people because he was drinking and driving and stunting. Why had the sentence been so light? He could understand Mike Creedy's bitterness and venom. Brandon Powers might not have planned to kill anyone that night, but he had still caused their deaths. He had chosen to drink when he was supposed to be the designated driver. He had chosen to speed. He had chosen to leave the scene of an accident where two people had been killed, to run away from his dead and injured friends and the stranger he had struck down in the night.

"I imagine that your extended family members probably feel the same way," Zachary suggested, trying to nudge the couple back to the question at hand.

"I'm sure everyone felt the same way," Mrs. Creedy agreed. "We all loved Hope dearly. She was the light of our lives."

"You have another daughter and a son…?"

"Yes. Noelle and Luke. They are twins."

"I imagine this was just as devastating for them as it was for you."

"It was," Mrs. Creedy agreed, eyes filling with tears for her children and the trials they had been through. "They were young teens at the time of the accident and the trial, old enough to understand everything that was going on and to know that they were never going to see Hope again. To be in the public eye all the time, everybody watching them for their reactions, reporters wanting to interview them, and the daily torture of the trial and sentencing… to have to go through that while their brains were still developing…"

Zachary nodded his understanding.

"I can't help but think that it damaged them… that things would be different now if we had been a whole, happy family, instead of having had to go through all of that."

"How are they now? You think it affected them permanently?"

"Oh, they're fine…" Mrs. Creedy looked at her husband, soliciting his opinion. "They're not drug addicts or homeless. But they both struggle with depression, and I think that if Hope had been able to finish college and go on, she would have been such an example for them. They would be motivated to further their educations and to be… more successful in life."

"They've done just fine," Mr. Creedy said. "You don't give

them enough credit. And becoming successful in a career takes years. I didn't get to where I am in a year or two. I had to work at it for a long time."

"Yes. They're doing well, really," she said, retracting her previous comment. "It's so hard for kids to get ahead in today's world."

"They've got their own places?" Zachary suggested, though he already knew this to be the case. "They're not living at home anymore?"

"Oh, yes, of course. Let me get you their information."

Mr. Creedy looked like he would stop her, but then shrugged and let her get her address book to write out the information for Zachary.

"They really are good kids," he said to Zachary, not even looking at him.

"I just need to cover all of the bases," Zachary assured him. "None of you are suspects. Like your wife says, it is a huge coincidence. I don't think I need to tell you, the police don't like coincidences."

Mrs. Creedy focused on writing the addresses, phone numbers, and email addresses down for her two children.

"Did you know that Harding—that is, Brandon—was out of prison?" Zachary asked.

Mr. Creedy nodded. "Of course we knew. We knew the day and the hour they released him. We were doing everything we could to block his release, but there was nothing we could do. We spoke to the review board and everything, but it didn't do any good. They didn't care about us or our family or what damage Powers could do if he was unleashed on the public again. It was all just a sham."

"I suppose they thought he was young and had made a youthful mistake," Zachary suggested. "One that a lot of kids make… but not usually with such devastating consequences."

"He killed our daughter. He should have had to give his life for hers. He should have had to stay in prison for the rest of his life."

So far, Mr. Creedy hadn't repeated the same words as the stalker. He hadn't said that Harding shouldn't have been allowed to live. He didn't say that Harding should have died, or killed himself, or been executed. The stalker had repeated those phrases hundreds of times. If the cyberbully were Mike Creedy, Zachary didn't think he could have avoided saying those things when he was angry. They would have been part of his speech, like an auditory fingerprint.

Mrs. Creedy had kept quieter than her husband, so Zachary couldn't be as sure of her. She might have been saying less and keeping calmer in an effort not to make Zachary suspicious.

They had both seemed genuinely shocked when Zachary had told them about Harding's death. He really didn't think they had been faking it.

He met her eyes briefly as she handed him the addresses, and again Zachary saw the deep wells of sorrow. But he didn't see guilt there. He didn't see the stalker or a killer.

15

Zachary had only just begun his interviews. There were other people to talk to. Noelle and Luke were already on his list, and he added the additional details Mrs. Creedy had provided to his list. Mr. and Mrs. Creedy probably called the children as soon as he left the house, so he decided to give them a chance to talk with each other and decide that it was in their best interests to help Zachary, then he would follow up with them later.

Hope's old best friend, Suzie Markell, would probably be harder to catch in a surprise visit than Mr. and Mrs. Creedy had been. She was younger and more likely to be out, either running children around or spending time with her friends, depending on what direction life had taken her. So Zachary called her to set up a meeting. He was encouraged to be able to meet with her the same day as the Creedys. If all of the interviews could be lined up so quickly, he would not have to spend as much time in New Hampshire and would be home a lot sooner. Maybe with the case laid to rest.

Suzie Markell's house was chaotic. It was not in as nice an area as the Creedys, not as big a house. It looked like it had rolled off the assembly line with all of her neighbors' houses. There were a number of children running around making noise. Zachary wasn't actually sure how many there were. At least four, maybe more. He found it hard to ignore them and to focus on Suzie, distracted by noise and activity around him every few seconds. If he'd had it to do again, he would have topped up his ADHD meds before going to her house. He was used to keeping the dose as low as possible, but that just wasn't sufficient for the Markell house. It was, like some of the homes that Zachary had lived in, a hub of activity, and there wasn't anywhere he and the busy mom could escape to for a quiet word.

"Have a seat," Suzie offered, sweeping toys from the couch to the floor to make space for him. There were cracker crumbs between the cracks of the cushions, and Zachary sat down gingerly, wondering about what else he was going to sit down in.

She made space for herself in an easy chair and flopped into it with a sigh. She straightened up, pulling some more toys from behind her, and leaned forward to talk to Zachary.

"So tell me exactly what this is about? Something to do with Hope Creedy's death all those years ago? Poor Hope. I felt so badly for her family. It was a terrible, terrible thing."

"Yes," Zachary agreed. "I can see that they're still suffering from it. I'm helping the Vermont police with a possibly-related incident. Did you hear anything about the death of Richard Harding?"

"Richard Harding." Suzie shook her head. "That name doesn't ring a bell. Who is he?"

Zachary watched her face for any tells, but there was a crash like a bookcase falling over somewhere above his head, and he nearly jumped out of his seat. Suzie didn't turn a hair.

"Just ignore it," she advised. "If there's no blood, we don't worry about it."

"You're sure it's okay?"

She made a motion to brush it away. "Really. Don't worry."

"I..." Zachary tried to pick up the thread of the conversation.

"Richard Harding," Suzie prompted. "Who is that?"

"Oh. Richard Harding's former name was Brandon Powers."

"Brandon? The guy who hit Hope?" She covered her mouth. "Oh, my goodness. I didn't even know he'd changed his name. I knew he got out, of course, but he just kind of disappeared, so I didn't know whether he had left the area or what. I thought he should go to some South American country and just start a new life. How could you keep living in the same neighborhood when people knew you had done a thing like that?"

"He'd didn't go as far as South America. Just to Vermont."

"I guess if you like snow..." Suzie laughed.

"Mommy!" One of the myriad children rushed into the room and directly for Suzie so fast that Zachary looked around to see who was chasing her. "Mommy, I need to know where the alligator is. I must know where it is *right now!*"

"Later, sweetheart." Suzie kissed the urchin on the forehead. "Mommy's busy right now. Don't you have some homework you should be working on?"

"But I can't do it without the alligator!"

"Then do something else for now. Don't bother Mommy when she has a visitor."

The little girl turned and looked disdainfully at Zachary. "Who are *you?*"

"I'm... er..."

"Leave him alone. Go study your spelling words."

The girl pouted and marched out of the room.

"You said he died?"

Zachary looked back at Suzie in consternation.

"Brandon Powers. You're looking into his death? What happened?"

"He was the victim of a hit and run."

"No!" Suzie's eyes were dramatically wide. Was she putting on an act? Just dramatizing for him? "That has to be the most bizarre coincidence I've heard since... oh, I have no idea. How could he have been in a hit and run? He wasn't the perpetrator again, was he?"

"No. He was the victim. He was walking and was hit by a truck."

"How awful. I remember how sick I felt when I heard about Hope. I just couldn't believe it. I felt like throwing up. It was such a horrible thing."

Another child came into the room. He was Asian, and the rest of the children Zachary had seen had been white. Probably a friend to one of Suzie's own children or someone she was babysitting. He was about four. He walked into the room with a little pair of scissors and a stack of paper. He sat down on Suzie's feet and proceeded to fold and cut a snowflake out of the first piece of paper. Zachary stared at him, mesmerized by the triangular and diamond-shaped bits of paper that fell from the little boy's scissors every few seconds.

"Do you think there is some kind of connection between Hope's death and Brandon's?" Suzie prompted. "I can't see how there could be."

"No… I haven't been able to find a connection either." There was another crash and a squeal from overhead. Zachary felt like his head was going to explode. He closed his eyes, taking deep breaths.

"I mean, the only way they could be connected that I can think of is if someone who knew Hope had tracked Brandon down and then hit him in revenge." Suzie gave a sharp laugh and shook her head. "I don't think that's realistic."

"You can't think of anyone who would be angry enough to do that?" Zachary was forcing the words out, but they sounded wrong in his own ears. Flat and emotionless. Distant.

"No. Unless you mean—no. Nobody would do that!"

"Unless who?"

"I just… I mean, her father… he was so angry. But I know the man and he really is a lovely person. Of course he was angry. Any father would have been. I don't think he was *too* angry. I can't see him doing anything like that. For someone to hunt Brandon down and run him over, that's just… it's sick."

Zachary nodded his agreement. His eyes darted around the room, looking for any other approaching children or disasters. He was perched on the edge of his seat, ready to spring up at the slightest warning. His muscles quivered and adrenaline was surging through his veins, his heartbeat loud to his own ears.

"I really can't think of anyone who would do anything like that," Suzie said. "And I think I've met all the major players."

"Do you know Hope's brother and sister?"

"Yes, but they're just kids."

"They were just kids eleven years ago. They're not anymore."

"No… I guess not. Funny how you think kids don't grow up while you're gone. In your mind, they will always be the same age as they were the last time you saw them. Or when you really knew them well."

A red plastic ball went whipping across the room for Zachary's head, launched with the click of a trigger and the force of a spring somewhere behind Suzie, where Zachary couldn't see. He batted the ball down and jumped to his feet.

"Ari!" Suzie's voice was stern. "What's the rule about throwing balls in the house?"

"I didn't throw it," a disembodied voice replied.

"What is the rule about shooting people?"

"It wasn't a bullet, it was—"

"Okay, Mr. Lawyer. You lose the gun for the rest of the day and your name goes up on the fridge. Go put it up."

The little boy voice groaned, and there was a dragging noise as he scooted out of the room, never becoming visible to Zachary. Zachary stayed on his feet, unwilling to sit down again.

"Can you think of anyone else who was close to Hope at school? Or anyone who organized protests at the court house?"

"It was so long ago now. I tend to have other things on my mind these days! You may not have noticed, but…" She broke off laughing.

"Any names at all?" Zachary prompted, trying hard to stay focused just a few minutes longer.

She thought about it and offered a couple of names, but they were people who were already on Zachary's list, so he just nodded and didn't ask for their details.

"Thanks for taking time to meet with me. I can see you're a busy mom…"

"Oh, any time. I crave adult conversation."

Zachary got out of there as quickly as he could.

The visit at Suzie's had wound up and exhausted him. Zachary decided he'd had enough for the day. He'd compile his notes and follow up with more people on his list the next day.

There was a place near his hotel that sold pizza by the slice, so Zachary bought himself a piece and went back to his room.

So far, he hadn't seen any signs that any of the people he had seen were involved in Harding's death. They had all seemed genuinely surprised. While Mr. Creedy had expressed a lot of anger, Zachary didn't think he was the author of the poison pen messages. With a release valve for his anger, he didn't let the pressure build internally. His wife was a more likely suspect. Did her more calm and empathetic demeanor hide what was actually going on under the surface? Was it all an act?

When he logged on to his computer to write up his notes, Zachary was distracted by the new emails in his own inbox. Adding to the general clutter of messages were several new messages from Tyrrell. Even though he had determined to simply delete any negative messages from Tyrrell, he found he couldn't do so without opening them first, and was again assaulted by the red-hot spewings of hate from his little brother.

How do you think your brothers and sisters felt waking up to fire and smoke and sirens?

If it wasn't for you everybody would have been fine.

You would still have a family if you hadn't destroyed it.

Zachary closed his eyes and tried to push the images back, but he couldn't. He was flooded with the sensations of what Tyrrell described. The fire had started while he slept and he had awakened in a room engulfed in flames. The smoke burned his lungs and made him cough uncontrollably. It burned his eyes, and billowed so thickly through the room that he was disoriented and didn't know which way was out. He had crawled under the couch for shelter, trying to protect himself from the hellfire that burned around him, but it didn't block the heat of the flames from reaching him. His flesh seared and his throat was on fire. Even so, he screamed warnings to his family, trying to raise the alarm and to get them out of the house. He knew he was going to die, and his only thought was to save the other children.

Zachary gasped for breath. He could feel the tears flooding down his cheeks. He tried to tell himself that he wasn't still in the fire, but he couldn't pull himself out of the whirlpool of memories. The hotel room around him morphed into a burning inferno, and he saw Suzie and her multitudes of children.

"You have to get out! There's a fire! Get the children out!" His voice was a croak and he couldn't shout the words to her as the children screamed in terror and huddled and cried for him to save them.

Zachary's phone was in his hand. He fumbled with it, trying to launch the emergency call feature with fingers swollen as fat as sausages. The heat of the fire was so strong his fingers felt like they were going to explode.

Why wasn't the smoke alarm going? Could he get out to the hallway to pull the red fire alarm? It was so far away, and by the time he got there, the children would all be burned. The smoke was so thick, he didn't know which way to go.

"Zachary? Are you there?"

Zachary's hand shook as he held the phone to his ear and tried to croak out an answer.

"Zachary, it's Lorne. Are you okay? What's wrong?"

He sobbed with relief as he tried to answer Mr. Peterson's questions. If Mr. Peterson was there, that meant the fire was over.

The ashes were cold and everybody was out. When he had been taken to the Peterson's house, it had been months later.

"It was—the fire." He tried to croak the words out in an order that made sense.

"Focus on where you are, Zachary. Tell me where you are."

He blinked, trying to see through the tears and orient himself. "Hotel."

"You're in a hotel," Mr. Peterson repeated in a calming voice. "You're not in the fire. Look around the room. Tell me about it. How many beds are there?"

"One. Just one."

"One bed. Can you tell me the color of the carpet?"

Zachary wiped his eyes, looking down at the muddy shades of the carpet, designed not to show the dirt, but looking dingy and worn.

"No. I don't know."

"You're an artist," Mr. Peterson reminded him. "Describe it."

Zachary struggled. "Greeny brown, like goose poop. With flowers… sort of brownish pink."

Mr. Peterson chuckled. "How pleasant. I must have Pat talk to their decorator."

Zachary tried to laugh at that, but it was still all coming out as sobs.

"How's the smell?"

It was musty and stale. He could smell the chemicals they used to clean the bathroom, body odor, and old cigarette smoke. For a few seconds, the cigarette smoke triggered a panic response, but he was able to stay in the present, shifting his focus to the bathroom cleaners.

"The bathroom… bleach and Lysol…"

"At least you know they cleaned it."

"Yeah."

"What hotel are you in?"

Zachary had to look at the receipt he had left on the table, but he could see what was actually in front of him instead of billowing smoke and flames. He instantly recognized the logo of the chain, and when he got that out, knew the name of the city.

"What are you doing in New Hampshire?"

"Interviewing." Zachary sniffled and wiped tears from his face. Hie eyes had stopped streaming. "My hit and run case—the victim used to live here, under another name."

"Got any suspects?"

He cleared his throat and looked around the room again. Everything was perfectly normal. There was no smoke, no fire, no burning children.

"What?"

"Suspects in your hit and run."

"Uh… hard to say. We know who hit him, but not if he was somehow connected to Harding."

"You're sounding better. Are you okay?"

Zachary took a deep breath in and let it out slowly. It didn't hurt to breathe. Everything was returning to normal.

"Yeah. Better, thanks."

"Do you want me to come? I'll stay with you if you need me to."

"No. I'll be okay now."

"Can you talk about what triggered this flashback?"

"An email from Tyrrell." Zachary reached over and closed the laptop without looking at the screen. "An email about the fire."

"I thought you weren't going to read anything from him."

"I know… but… what if he calms down? What if after he's got it all out, he feels better and he just wants to talk?"

"Do you want to have an attack every time you get an email from him? I think it's time to report him to the police. This harassment is causing damage. You don't want to go backward in your treatment."

"No. I can't. You're right, I just won't read them. Like I said to start with. I'll just delete them."

"Can't you report him to his email provider? They could close his account."

"He's using a program that generates unique email addresses for every email. I can't trace him back to his real email account."

"What he's doing is criminal. Cyberstalking is against the law. You can't bully people online and get away with it."

"Tyrrell's just… trying to express himself. He was damaged by the fire too, and by being in the system. He's just trying to heal."

"I don't think so."

Zachary wasn't going to be persuaded. "He's my little brother. He's hurting."

"He probably is," Mr. Peterson agreed. "But that doesn't give him the right to hurt you."

"I'm okay. It was just a stupid flashback. I've had plenty of flashbacks without his help."

Mr. Peterson was quiet for a minute. "You're sure you don't want me to come?"

"No, no. I'm okay now. It's passed."

"Take care of yourself. Make sure to get a good sleep tonight. Have you eaten? Do you need to talk to your therapist?"

"I ate. I'll take a Xanax and go to bed. It will be fine."

"Call me again if you need me. You know I'll be here."

"Yeah, thanks." Zachary blew out his breath. "You really helped."

Zachary's first interview with someone friendly to Richard Harding was with Devon Masters, one of the young men who had been in the car with Harding when Hope Creedy was killed. They met at a coffee shop near the university. Devon was a handsome man, though he looked older than Zachary had expected. He had dark hair and a narrow build. Their eyes met across the shop, and they gravitated toward each other.

"Devon?" Zachary asked.

"You must be Zachary Goldman."

They shook hands briefly. Devon smiled and waited while Zachary got his coffee, then motioned to a table near the window.

"I like to sit in the sun and watch my students walk to class."

"Sure."

They sat, and Devon eyed Zachary curiously. "I have to say, I'm not sure at all what this is about. You said you are investigating… what?"

"I'm investigating the death of Richard Harding."

Devon raised an eyebrow. "And who is Richard Harding when he's home?"

"You knew him as Brandon Powers."

"Brandon?" Devon's eyebrows went up and his eyes widened. "I had no idea! He died? How?"

"It was a hit and run."

"No! I'm guessing you know about… his history."

"I do now, or parts of it, anyway. It took a while for me to get this far, though. He had changed his name, moved out of the state, and started over. But his girlfriend knew who he was."

And did anyone else?

Zachary lifted his coffee cup to his lips, watching Devon's face. Devon stared out the big window. It was a chilly day, so there wasn't a lot of foot traffic. Mostly students running from one place to another, not dressed warmly enough, laughing and rubbing their arms, like it was a big surprise that it was so cold on a winter day.

"Wow." Devon shook his head. "The end of an era. We didn't talk to each other, obviously, but I thought about him sometimes. Wondered how he was getting along."

"He didn't call when he got out of prison?"

"No. We haven't had any contact since the trial. It didn't really… it wasn't a bonding experience, I'll tell you that. I see Fulton every now and then, but we don't really do anything more than nod and wave."

Fulton was the other man who had been in the car. The other survivor.

"It must have been pretty traumatic," Zachary suggested. "First the accident and then the trial."

"And being ostracized. For years, I was identified as one of the boys who had been in that car. One of those boys who had gotten drunk and killed a girl. We were all painted with the same brush, even though Brandon was the one behind the wheel." Devon leaned forward. "He was the one who was supposed to be sober. The rest of us were drinking, but he was the one who had agreed to drive us."

"And you didn't know he had any alcohol while you were together?"

"I guess I was too far gone at that point. I don't remember him having anything to drink. Just Coke."

"So what are your feelings toward Brandon? Do you blame him for that reputation?"

"I've worked hard to dig myself out and overcome that stigma. And I think I'm a better person for it. We had to grow up fast. We were adults, and you would think that we would know better, but we really didn't. They say at that age your brain is still developing… We were still acting like kids, irresponsible, not thinking about the consequences of our actions. I can't put all of the blame on Brandon. I don't remember a whole lot about *that* night, but other nights… we encouraged each other to drink too much, to drive too fast, to do stupid and dangerous stuff. We were an accident looking for a place to happen."

"So you don't resent him."

Devon spread his hands. "How can I resent him if he's dead?"

Zachary's brain echoed the question. If Zachary were dead, Tyrrell couldn't resent him. He would be able accept that Zachary had finally gotten his due and Tyrrell could go on with his life again. Maybe he could let the bitterness go and live the life he'd been meant to. He tried to refocus on the case.

"Did you get any accusatory emails about the accident? Not back then, but recently?"

Devon visibly shrank back. "What?"

"Brandon was getting some pretty awful harassing emails. If you were all painted with the same brush, I'm wondering if you got some too. Did the same person made contact with you?"

"I've had some emails," Devon admitted cautiously.

"Do you think I could see some of them? Maybe you could forward them to me and I can analyze whether they are from the same person?"

"I deleted them."

"You can probably still forward them—"

"No, I nuked them. Permanently deleted. I didn't want to see them again. I didn't want to be tempted to go back and reread them afterward. They were trash. Once I got a few, I set up filters to catch them and permanently delete them before I could even see them."

"That's smart." Zachary wondered for a moment why he and Harding hadn't done the same thing. Zachary was tech savvy enough. But he hadn't, because he wanted to read them all no matter how they hurt. They were the only contact he'd ever had with his family and even if they pierced him to the heart, he couldn't delete them without ever seeing and reading them.

What about Harding? Had he thought to do something like that? Did he even know it was possible? A lot of people didn't bother tweaking their computers to work the way they wanted them to. They didn't know what they could and couldn't do. He hadn't asked Ashley how good Harding's grasp on technology was. Harding had learned to use anonymizers, but someone might have helped him with that.

"Sorry." Devon shrugged. "I didn't want them taking over my life. I have enough to do without having to deal with something like that."

Zachary nodded his agreement. "And the other man who survived the crash—Fulton—you don't talk?"

"Not really, no. We've all gone our different directions. That happens as you get older. All those things that once held you together—school classes, social circles, shared interests—they fade as you grow up and take on different responsibilities."

"Right. And there was another man with you who also passed away."

"Kyle Browne."

"Did you keep in touch with his family at all? There wasn't really anything in the news articles that I read that talked about Kyle. Brandon wasn't charged with manslaughter in his case, which I thought was a bit odd, considering the way they went after him for the rest of the charges."

"You'll have to talk to Fulton about that. I don't remember much... but he said that Brandon made Kyle put his seatbelt on before they started, but at the time of the accident, he wasn't wearing it, so he was…" Devon made a helpless gesture, choking up. "He was thrown from the car. If he'd been wearing his seatbelt, he probably would have been okay, like the rest of us. Fulton clearly remembered Brandon forcing Kyle to put his seatbelt on before leaving. He must have taken it off again after."

Zachary nodded. "Well… one thing in Brandon's favor. You didn't keep in touch with his family?"

"No. I never knew them. I knew Kyle from school. I didn't have any reason to have anything to do with his family, other than to say how sorry I was for what had happened. We didn't have any contact after the funeral. Nothing during or after the trial. I don't know what happened to any of them."

"Do you know of anyone who held a grudge against Brandon? Someone who was still bitter toward him, even though he had served his time?"

"I don't know. Hope Creedy's family, I guess. I did have a confrontation with her brother once."

Zachary's interest was immediately piqued. "Really? When was that?"

"It was a few years ago, I think Brandon was still in prison at the time. The kid was maybe nineteen, twenty."

"And what did he want? He confronted you?"

"Yeah. He was pretty messed up. Wanted a fight. Wanted to punish the guys who had killed his sister. Like it had just happened the day before. It was weird, facing a specter from the past when I had done my best to put all of that behind me."

"So what did he do?"

"Ranted on about it. Told me he was going to kill me. But he couldn't even get one punch in. He was drunk and so agitated… I don't think he could have hit the broad side of a barn."

"What did you do?"

"Bouncers threw him out. I told him I'd call the police if he bugged me again. Or I'd call his mother. He never showed up again. If he remembered it the next day, I suspect he was so embarrassed he never wanted to mention it again."

"You were in a bar?" Zachary wasn't sure why that surprised him so much. He'd half-assumed that after having been in a drunk driving accident, Devon would swear off of drinking. Social drinking, especially.

"A club," Devon said. He looked at Zachary defiantly, like he knew what Zachary was thinking. "It's my life. I didn't die in that accident. I can choose whether to drink or not. That's up to me."

Zachary nodded, not disagreeing. "Luke is on my list of people to follow up with, so I'll see what he has to say. Did you ever have any trouble with his father? Hope's father?"

"No. I mean, the guy was angry, but at Brandon, not us. Brandon was the one who was driving. He couldn't very well blame us for drinking when we weren't driving."

Zachary felt like he was on a see-saw with Devon flipping back and forth between whether they were partially responsible for what had happened or not. He seemed most intent on insisting that he didn't have any responsibility, but had given that little speech about needing to grow up and how they had egged Harding on in the past.

"Is there anyone else you can think of? Ideas of who might have sent those emails?"

Devon shook his head. "No. I never really... there were so many of them to start with, back when the trial was on. Emails, phone calls, people on the street holding signs and trying to tell us how we were going to hell for what we had done. I didn't really attach any particular face or personality to them, I was just... surprised that so long after the trial, anyone still remembered."

There were plenty of people who would never forget what had happened to Hope and that Harding and his friends had been responsible for her death.

Noelle and Luke had obviously been waiting for Zachary's call.

"Mom told us about you," Luke told him. "And about that creep Powers being killed. Good riddance to him, I don't know why you expect us to help you out. He deserved what he got."

"I understand you feeling that way. I'd really appreciate a chance to talk with you, even if it's just for a few minutes. I'm just trying to tie up some loose ends, and then I'll be able to report back to the police that there's no connection between the two deaths. Just coincidence."

"Why should we waste our time?"

"Maybe it will give you some closure on Hope's death. But even if it doesn't, I'd really appreciate your help. This is my job, you know, and if I go back to them saying that no one will talk to me..."

Zachary had gathered from what his mother and Devon had said that Luke's circumstances were not ideal, and he was hoping to trade on Luke having some empathy for someone else who could lose his job if Luke didn't give him just a bit of his time.

There was a moment of silence while Luke considered this. Zachary was afraid it was drawing out too long and Luke was going to come back with the fact that he couldn't care less if Zachary got himself fired, so long as it didn't inconvenience Luke.

"Well, fine," Luke grumped. "You can come see us at two o'clock. At Noelle's apartment." He gave Zachary the address.

"Great, thank you for helping me out. I really appreciate it."

Luke muttered something and hung up.

Zachary hadn't really needed to convince anyone; they had clearly agreed ahead of time on where and when they would meet Zachary.

Since he had a few hours to kill before he'd be able to see anyone else, Zachary decided to visit the scene of the crime. He had no illusions about finding evidence that would somehow shed light on the case. The MVC that had killed Hope had been years before. The police had fully investigated it at the time. Zachary wasn't looking for evidence, he just wanted a feeling for the location. How it would have looked to the boys, to Hope walking home, to the police investigating it. He wanted to see the space himself rather than just relying on the descriptions and diagrams that he had seen and that would be in the court files.

He drove the route that Harding had taken. They had flown along the empty streets, exceeding the speed limit, but Zachary took his time. There was traffic during the day and he wanted a chance to look around. As he approached the intersection where Hope had been killed, he slowed down, drawing irritated honks from the cars behind him. He scanned for a parking space, and pulled over.

Getting out, he walked the intersection, circling through all four crosswalks and taking pictures of the road, the approaching cars, and the light standards. Harding had hit one of them after hitting Hope, perhaps making a last-second attempt to miss her. It was that collision that had thrown Kyle Browne from the car. The news articles reported that Brandon hadn't even seen Kyle after the accident. He knew that his friend had been thrown from the car, yet when he got out of the car, he hadn't seen or looked for him. He had gone to Hope, trying to rouse her, hoping beyond hope that he'd just clipped her. But she was dead, and there was nothing he could do about it. Brandon had done nothing to help his friends sitting unconscious in the back seat, or Kyle, lying broken on the pavement somewhere close by, and had just left the accident scene.

The prosecution had said that Brandon didn't care about anyone else, that he didn't have any concern for anyone but himself, and had left to hide what he had done, to try to escape punishment. Brandon had explained that he was disoriented. He'd hit his head and hadn't known where to go or what to do. He didn't understand what he had done. It never occurred to him to call for help or to give some assistance to his friends. It was all just a blank.

The truth probably lay somewhere in between. He'd been panicked. He was under the influence, had killed at least one person, and he'd hit his head. He wasn't thinking rationally. If he had been, he would have known that the police could trace him from the car he had left behind. They knew exactly who they were looking for and that at some point, he would return home. Where else was he going to go? He was a stupid kid, not a master criminal who had carefully planned an escape route.

"You lost?" demanded a homeless man sitting on a stack of flattened boxes to insulate him from the cold sidewalk. He had apparently been watching Zachary pace around the sides of the intersection.

"Oh. No, I was just taking a look around."

"At what?"

"Just at the intersection. How it's laid out. What it feels like."

"You a surveyor? Planning on building something here?"

"No. A private investigator. Looking into an accident that happened here years ago."

"How long ago? You weren't here."

"No. I wasn't here."

"She was a pretty girl."

"Did you see her? Hope Creedy?"

"No, I never did. You think I was sleeping out here on the road where I could see anything? No one sleeps out here by the traffic."

"No, I guess not. But you might have seen something. Maybe the crash woke you up and you came out for a peek, to see what had happened. The police never identified any eye witnesses."

"That's because there wasn't none. No one saw what happened 'cept those kids in the car."

"So how do you know she was pretty?"

"From her picture."

"In the paper?"

"No!" The man shook his head at Zachary's stupidity. "There!"

Zachary followed his finger and realized that in trying to get a big picture view of the intersection, he had missed the little things. A little homemade wreath strapped to one of the traffic light posts. Inside the circle, a picture of Hope Creedy protected by a plastic bag, the same picture as Zachary had seen in a number of the news stories. A beautiful young lady, struck down in her prime. So full of promise, wiped out by one person's carelessness and disregard.

Looking at the little memorial, Zachary felt anger rise up inside him at Harding. He had been feeling sorry for the man, killed after being stalked relentlessly. A life that had been destroyed by a mistake, by years in prison, and by the person or people who just wouldn't let him carry on. In Zachary's mind, Harding had been the victim. But he *had* killed Hope. Just as certainly as if he'd pulled a gun and shot her. Mike Creedy was right; eight years in prison wasn't nearly long enough for killing both her and Kyle Browne.

"Did you live here then?" he asked the homeless man. "Were you around when it happened? I understand you didn't see it, I'm just wondering if you lived here when it happened."

"I don't know nothing," the man asserted. He spat on the sidewalk. "I ain't the one who put the wreath there. I never knew the girl."

"Who did put the wreath there?"

"A young man."

"So you were here. You saw that."

"I see him when he takes it down and puts a new one up. That one hasn't been around for so many years."

Zachary looked at it again. Of course not. It had been over ten years since the accident, and the wreath was not tattered and stained by the weather. It had been there for a while, but not ten years.

"What does this young man look like?"

"I don't know." The homeless man didn't like being pinned down with more detailed questions and was clamming up. "Young."

"How young? Thirty? Older? Younger?"

"I never asked him how old he was," the man said saucily. "How would I know?"

"Younger than me?"

The man studied him. "You're not so young."

"No, I'm not. So, younger?"

"Yes. Maybe."

"Twenty?"

"No. He wouldn't be old enough to have known her."

Hope would have been thirty-two if she had lived. Her younger siblings in their mid to late twenties. So someone Hope's age. Zachary got close to the wreath and tried to see the back of the photo to see if there was a date or inscription.

"You leave that alone. That's desecration. You can't take it!"

"I'm not taking it. I just wanted to see if it had anything written on it."

"It doesn't."

"No," Zachary agreed, having gotten a good look at it. "It doesn't."

Eventually, it was time to move on. He needed to get back to Noelle's apartment to see her and Luke.

He assumed that they had picked Noelle's apartment because

it was nicer, and that made Zachary wonder just how miserable the place that Luke was living must have been. While he didn't see any evidence of rats, it was small, and it was obvious that Noelle split the rent with other people. There was a communal living room to sit and visit in, but the place smelled like reheated dinners and sweat and uncleaned toilets.

The twins favored their father more than Mrs. Creedy, dark-haired with narrow faces, both of them tall. They looked remarkably alike, more so than most siblings. Zachary knew that fraternal twins didn't share any more genetic material than the average sibling pair, but Noelle and Luke looked like male and female versions of the same person.

When Zachary sat down on the saggy couch, he had the uncomfortable feeling that someone had been sleeping there. His skin crawled as he thought of lice and bedbugs. He wanted to get up and brush off his clothes and wash his hands. Instead, he concentrated hard on giving the twins a pleasant smile, and not being obvious about evaluating and judging the kind of place where Noelle lived.

"Thank you again for agreeing to meet me. I know that you aren't really getting anything out of this, though I hope maybe it helps you to know that your sister's killer isn't out there roaming the streets anymore."

"You think it helps us to know that he's been put out of his misery?" Luke demanded. "He should have had to suffer longer. Just like we have."

Luke's words didn't fit with the stalker's, "Why don't you just die?"

"I'm sorry for what you've had to go through. It couldn't be easy growing up in the shadow of Hope's death and the trial."

"Everything was about her," Noelle agreed. "Not just in the news and every time at school or on the street that someone stopped to talk to us. And not just Mom and Dad being sad and mad about the trial. Everything was about her." Noelle brushed her dark hair back from her face, tucking it behind her ear. "Curfews because we couldn't be out on the street after dark like she had been. Not knowing who really wanted to be our friends and who just wanted to get to know the sister of the dead girl. People watching the news and wanting to talk about it. We didn't just mourn Hope, we had to relive her death. Constantly."

Zachary remembered how it had been for him in the years after the fire. People who were morbidly interested in his burn scars and who wanted to hear his story. Parents and social workers who thought that, given a chance, he would burn another house down, when nothing could be further from the truth. People were fascinated by death and grief. It had kept the pain raw and fresh when he should have been able to put it behind himself long before.

"That must have been very difficult. The two of you were how old when she was killed?"

"Fifteen." It was Luke who answered, his tone still aggrieved.

"And you knew when Brandon got out of prison?"

"Sure everybody knew when he got out. All of the reporters were hounding us again, wanting to get our *reactions* to his release. What did they think our reactions would be? Overjoyed?"

"There was quite a media circus over it?"

"Yeah. It was a circus, alright."

"Did Brandon contact either of you?" Zachary switched his gaze between the twins, looking for any changes in their expressions. They were mirror images, pouting over injustices done years ago.

"Why would he contact us? We didn't want anything to do with him."

"But he might have wanted to make an apology to you, ask for your forgiveness."

"No," Noelle shook her head. "He never contacted us. Or Mom and Dad."

"Did you have any contact with any of the passengers who were in the car?"

There was a quick glance between Noelle and Luke.

"None of them ever contacted us," Luke said.

"And you didn't ever run into any of them and have a conversation?"

Luke stared at Zachary, suspicious. "Why would you ask if you already know the answer?"

"I like to see how people react. Whether they tell the truth."

Noelle was looking at her brother. A warning, telling him to shut up.

"Sure, I ran into that one guy, Devon. Would have beat the hell out of him, too, if it hadn't been for a couple of bouncers. I would have wiped that look right off his face."

"What look?"

"That fake concern. The pity. He helped ruin our family and he thought he could be all sympathetic and I'd think he was a good guy? I would have wiped that smug look right off of his face!"

Zachary nodded. "It bothered you that he never had to serve any time?"

"Well, he wasn't the driver," Noelle put in, before Luke could answer.

Luke looked at her.

"It wasn't his fault," Noelle pointed out. "The only person they could blame for the accident was the person behind the wheel. It wasn't the fault of the passengers."

"They were all out drinking together. If they hadn't been drinking, it wouldn't have happened."

"You don't drink?" Zachary asked. "What were you doing at the club when you met up with Devon?"

"I don't drink and drive," Luke shot back, "and I don't get in the car with a drunk driver. Anyone who let him have his keys and get into that car should have been punished. The bartender, whoever was serving him drinks, all of his friends. They should all have to be punished for letting him drive drunk!"

Noelle gave Zachary a little shrug. "We have issues," she said with a little laugh.

Luke glared at her.

Noelle raised her eyebrows dramatically. "Well, what do you want me to say? That you're a miserable jerk all of the time?"

"I'm glad you know better than to drink and drive," Zachary inserted, trying not to let the conversation degenerate further. "Devon says he doesn't remember Brandon having anything alcoholic that night. His memory of the events of that night seem to be pretty clouded."

"He's lying."

"Maybe he is. Most people will lie to protect themselves even if they consider themselves honest people."

"I'm not sure how any of this is helpful," Noelle said.

"No," Zachary agreed. "Can you tell me whether you know of anyone else who had a grudge against Brandon? Someone who might have stalked and threatened him, even though he had changed his name?"

They looked at each other, but not a covert look this time. Blank faces. Nobody who jumped immediately to mind.

"Anyone who knew Hope," Noelle said. "Who could *not* be outraged by what happened? We didn't know her friends from school. We got to know some people during the trial, but I don't think Mom and Dad have kept in touch with anyone, do you?"

Luke shook his head in response. "Hope wasn't the only one killed, either. It could have been someone who was related to the other victim. His family or friends. His girlfriend."

"Did you meet his girlfriend?"

"No, not that I remember." Another look between the twins, checking in with each other. "No."

"And Hope didn't have a boyfriend?"

Just a fraction of a second too long before Luke and Noelle shook their heads in unison.

"No."

Zachary gave them a few beats to think about it, not jumping in with any accusations, but waiting for them to grow uncomfortable with the lie and either say more to cover it up or to back off.

"No? No boyfriend?"

They didn't admit it.

"Girlfriend?"

Again, a negative response, Luke giving a little grin of amusement at that. Not a girlfriend, then.

"Was she seeing someone your parents didn't like?" 'Seeing someone' instead of 'dating,' to give them a little more wiggle room. 'Seeing someone' could be more casual. Boyfriend made it sound serious, more committed.

Noelle looked at Luke, asking for permission. He shrugged like he didn't care if she spilled it.

18

"She was seeing someone," Noelle admitted. "Mom and Dad didn't disapprove, but only because they didn't know."

"She was afraid to tell them about him? What was wrong with him?"

He was expecting her to say that he was black, or Muslim, or maybe he was unemployed or had been in trouble in the past. People had frequently judged Zachary by his class or social standing, his prospects, or other things he had no control over. Zachary wasn't responsible for his parents' poverty, his learning disabilities, or that there had been no pathway to higher education for him. He was a foster kid, and he'd had to support himself once he'd aged out of foster care, or end up homeless.

"It was… their age difference," Noelle said hesitantly.

Maybe she had gotten together with one of her professors. A May-December romance that she knew her parents would not approve of.

"An older man?" Zachary prompted her for more details.

Luke snorted. "A younger one!"

Zachary *was* surprised by that. He blinked at them. "Younger?"

Noelle nodded, her cheeks getting pink. She looked at Luke,

giggling, and then looked away again. This was apparently something they had laughed about in private before. Their big sister dating a younger man.

"How much younger?" Zachary demanded. Hope had been a young college student herself. How much younger could a boyfriend have been? A year? Two? Did she think that would be scandalous?

"Seventeen."

Not even an adult. No, her parents would not have been happy to hear about such a thing. She should have turned him down and dated someone more suitable.

Zachary gave his head a shake. "Where did she meet this guy?"

Noelle shrugged. "She didn't know at first how young he was. She said he looked a lot more mature. And acted more mature. She didn't see what could be wrong with it and why people made such a big deal when he was more mature than his age."

"She never considered breaking up with him because of it?"

"She wouldn't exactly tell me if she did. We weren't even supposed to know about it, but we had friends who knew him. He was closer to our age than hers!"

"And your parents never found out about it?"

"No."

"And his…?"

"Nothing ever came out after she died. He hung around the courthouse a little. I would see him there, standing out on the sidewalk, with the protesters. But he didn't come into the courtroom. I don't think he could. Or maybe he just didn't want to be seen there and have anyone ask him questions."

"Do you know his name? What became of him?"

Noelle looked at Luke, not sure whether she should tell Zachary or not. He made a little motion. *Go ahead.*

"Roper. Jonathan Roper. He's still around, but I don't know what he does or where he lives."

"You've seen him around?"

"Yeah. I think he does something at the university, but I'm not sure what."

"A teacher?"

"I don't think so. What other kinds of jobs are there at universities? Maybe some kind of counselor. Like, careers or special needs accommodations. I don't know."

Zachary wrote it in his notebook. It was a name that he hadn't picked up from the news or public record. Somebody that maybe the police had never known about. What difference would it have made if they had? They were trying to track down and gather evidence against the man who had killed her. There was no connection between Roper and Harding.

"Harding—that is, Brandon—and his friends. I gathered from what I read that they went to school together. And Hope was going to university, right? Did they know each other at all? Did they have any personal connection with Hope or with Roper?"

"No." They checked in with each other to confirm their responses. "No, nothing ever came out in court. They weren't friends, they didn't share classes. I don't know if they ever saw each other in passing, but they didn't know each other."

"And Roper, he didn't go to university? He wasn't on some kind of accelerated track?"

"No," Luke was definite about this. "He was still in high school, same as us. That was part of what made it so weird."

Zachary was back in his hotel room in the afternoon to do some research on Jonathan Roper. He hadn't heard of the man before, but if what Noelle and Luke said was true, that wasn't particularly surprising. He would have been forced to stay under the radar or risk bringing outrage down on Hope when it was important that she be seen as an innocent victim.

He had forgotten to ask Luke whether he was the one who had put up the wreaths in the intersection, or whether that was Roper. The homeless man had said that it was a young man, not a young man and woman, and Zachary assumed that the twins would have done something like that together; it wouldn't have been Luke alone.

He tracked down Jonathan Roper's contact details pretty quickly and decided to do a quick background on him while he was at it. He wanted to know what kind of a person Roper was or how he had spent the past decade.

He was, as Noelle had suggested, working at the university. If Zachary had known that, he could have gone to see Roper after interviewing Devon. Roper was a "student services counselor," whatever that was. He'd been doing it for several years, maybe since he'd graduated from university himself.

Zachary's phone rang but he kept his eyes on the computer monitor for the first few rings, absorbing what he could, before tearing himself away from it and picking up the phone to see who it was. It was an unexpected name.

"Bridget. What's up?"

"I was just checking to see how you are."

Zachary thought about it for a moment. When he was fully immersed in a case, the time passed quickly and he didn't think as much about himself or his situation. Delving into the background of a new suspect was a good way to leave his own troubles behind for a while.

"I'm having a pretty good day," he offered. He didn't want to mention any of his recent panic attacks or depression to her, so he just focused on the positive. "Making progress on an investigation."

"Good. I know how this time of year… well, it's good that you're having a good day and have something to keep you occupied."

"Yeah." Zachary was silent for a few seconds before he realized he wasn't holding up his part of the conversation. He fished for something to say. "Are you going to Gordon's family's again this year?"

"At some point. Maybe not on Christmas Day, maybe for New

Year's. We're going to have a little party for our friends…"

The Christmases that Zachary had spent with Bridget had been different from any others in his life. He'd actually had something to look forward to and someone to hold on to. That didn't stop the depression, but it made a difference. He'd thought that he might be able to make it through to the other side, instead of seeing nothing but blackness. He'd been very low, but not suicidal.

Nevertheless, his depression had been hard on Bridget. For someone who was used to celebrating the season, to being happy and optimistic and spending time with friends and family, it had been difficult to deal with a husband who just couldn't do all of those social things. The first year, they'd gone to a few quiet events, but then she'd had to explain to friends why he couldn't be in the same room as candles, or why they had to leave when they'd just barely arrived. She told him to get over himself, to cheer up, to quit acting like a baby and embarrassing her.

The next year she'd tried having people over instead of going out, but that had been worse. People didn't know what to do when the host of the party withdrew from the party and took to his bed, unable to deal with anything. She told them he had a migraine and wanted them to go on without him, but people had still left early, marring her plans.

Zachary realized that Bridget had been talking and he'd lost track of the conversation. "What?"

She was silent in response.

"I'm sorry. Just zoned out, thinking about this case. What was the last thing you said?"

"You didn't want to come to the party, did you?" she asked doubtfully. "I mean, there will be a lot of people you know there, and it's just a casual affair, but you…"

"No," Zachary agreed. "You guys have your party. I'll be doing my own thing for Christmas."

"Are you going to see your family?"

"What?"

"Your family. You did get in touch with your bio family, didn't you?"

"Uh… no. Not yet."

"For someone who wants a family so much, you sure aren't doing much to connect with them! Why not?"

"I just… I'm very busy with this case right now, and the Christmas season… I'll connect with them another time. In the new year."

"What exactly *are* your plans for Christmas?" she demanded.

"I'm not sure yet. Kenzie and I are going to have dinner together. And we're trying to set something up with Rhys." Rhys had saved Bridget's life; he didn't have to explain to her who he was, or why he would be having a hard time his first Christmas without his mother home. "Lorne and Pat really want me to come spend it with them. Pat's family might come."

"Really?" Her voice was cautiously interested. It wasn't the answer she'd been expecting. Zachary's Christmas plans were usually solitary. Put on a classic movie and have a drink. Celebrate the fact that he'd survived another Christmas Eve. Telling Bridget he was going to spend it with other people was a surprise.

"Pat's family has never met Lorne. They've never gone to the house. It will be a memorable year for him, if they do."

Bridget *tsked*. "I can't believe that in this day and age people can be so silly about relationships. Pat and Lorne have been together for twenty years. More than that. It's obviously the real deal."

"You would expect them to get used to it before this," Zachary agreed.

"Okay… well… you know how to get me. If you do need someone…"

He knew then just how concerned she was about him dealing with the Christmas season. She never encouraged him to call her. Just the year before, she had torn up one side of him and down the other for still having her listed as his emergency contact when they'd called her after the car accident.

"I'll be fine," Zachary told her. "Don't worry about me."

19

Jonathan Roper might have been a mature-looking seventeen-year-old when Hope had started seeing him, but his boyishly round face and curly hair made him look more like one of the current university students than one of the staff.

Zachary had told him as little as possible about the reason for seeing him, not wanting to scare him off by announcing he knew about his relationship with Hope Creedy.

Roper shook Zachary's hand with an open, friendly manner and motioned him into a chair. His office felt something like a psychologist's office that had been decorated in an attempt to make visitors feel comfortable and relaxed. Just the right furniture, a few books on the shelves, a plant that was real instead of plastic. A picture on Roper's desk that showed him with a young woman and a little girl with a mop of blond hair who was smiling fit to burst. Zachary's background had not turned up a marriage, so the woman and the girl were probably a sister and a niece, just a bit of show to make people think he was actually a family man.

Roper saw Zachary studying the picture and raised his eyebrows questioningly.

"You have a very nice-looking family," Zachary said.

"Thank you," Roper accepted the compliment politely. He

smiled, and just a bit of a flush started at his neck above his collar. This was an implied lie that he was practiced in making, but his body still reacted to it. Not as effective as a lie detector, but his body's psychological reaction would make things a bit easier for Zachary.

"I'm here about Richard Harding," Zachary told him.

"Richard Harding? Is he a student here?"

Zachary couldn't see any change in the flush. He should have made small talk and waited for it disappear before mentioning Harding's name.

"No. It's the name Brandon Powers took after he got out of prison."

The flush rose up Roper's neck. "And who is Brandon Powers?" he asked, choking a little on the words.

"You know who Brandon Powers is. Do you think I would be here if I wasn't sure of that?"

"Maybe I heard his name in the news. It sounds sort of familiar, but I'm really not sure."

"You were dating the woman he killed."

Roper opened his mouth to deny it again.

"Isn't it obvious that I know?" Zachary challenged. There was no point in Roper wasting time in denials. They needed to get past the lies and have a real conversation.

Roper swallowed. His eyes rolled up toward the ceiling, either searching for another lie or trying to hold back tears. Maybe both.

"Okay," Roper said in an unsteady voice. "I knew Hope Creedy. I know who Brandon Powers is."

"You were more than a casual acquaintance."

"We were... close."

"How close?"

"I don't see how that's any of your business."

"Maybe not. I guess I'll just have to imagine."

"There was nothing wrong with us dating. We were only four years apart. Plenty of people who are further apart than that in age have long, successful marriages."

"Yes. But not usually the ones that start while the younger partner is still a minor. Hope shouldn't have been dating you."

"There was nothing wrong with us dating."

Zachary let it go. He said nothing for a minute, considering the possibilities. If Roper had been forced to keep their relationship a secret for all of those years, it was certainly possible that the pressure had built too much and he had turned his anger and resentment outward, taking it out on Richard Harding and the other men who had been in the car.

"It must have been very hard on you to mourn her passing when you couldn't tell anyone about your relationship. All these years, you've had to keep it from your family and friends in case it was to get out in the public and damage Hope's reputation. You didn't want anyone to think less of her for falling in love with you." Zachary looked at the picture on the desk. "Does your wife know about her?"

Roper sighed, looking at the girl in the photograph. "That's my sister and her little girl."

Zachary had been right on the money. "And I'm guessing she probably doesn't know."

"She was a few years younger than me. I don't know if she even remembers the accident and the trial. It was big news around here, but news fades fast. A few years in prison and they can let a murderer go free."

"You know it wasn't intentional murder."

"No. But he still killed her."

"Not like Brandon's death."

Roper shook his head. "I don't know anything about it. I didn't even know he was dead."

"He was killed in a hit and run. Just like your girlfriend. Only the driver wasn't drunk, was he?"

"How do you expect me to know anything about it?"

"You're used to keeping secrets."

"I've kept them quiet for a lot of years, yes… but that doesn't have anything to do with Brandon Powers, or whatever else you called him. I never knew the guy. Never spoke to him. Didn't keep track of what happened to him after he got out of prison."

"Someone did."

"Who?"

"Someone was stalking him."

"If you know anything about it, then you know it wasn't me. I haven't had any contact with the guy ever."

"How about the other men who were in the car?"

"The other men?" Roper looked puzzled for a moment. "I remember... there was a passenger who was killed, wasn't there? Were there others?"

"They testified in the court case."

"I couldn't go to that. I couldn't do anything that would suggest that I knew Hope. I had to pretend that nothing had happened. I had to just go to school and pursue my normal activities and not give away that she had meant anything to me. It was awful. You can't know what it did to me."

"You were seen at the courthouse. Outside, where the protesters were."

Roper looked stunned. "By who?"

"By people who knew who you were and that you were in a relationship with Hope."

"But nobody knew. I didn't tell anybody. Hope didn't tell anybody."

"Maybe you mentioned it to a best friend. Or maybe someone saw the two of you together. Maybe Hope told one of her friends. But the two of you didn't keep it quite as quiet as you thought you did."

Roper sat back in his chair, shaking his head in disbelief. "All these years... I never thought anyone else knew." He tilted his head thoughtfully. "Whoever it was... they didn't leak it. I never had anyone approach me about it. Not a single reporter."

"Maybe they had reason not to tarnish Hope's reputation either."

There was a flash of understanding across Roper's face, and Zachary thought he might have figured out who had known.

"Just why are you bringing all of this up now?" Roper asked. "Why not just let sleeping dogs lie?"

"Because I'm investigating Brandon's death."

"What does that have to do with me?"

"There are a lot of people who had reason to want him dead."

"And you think I'm one of them?" Roper shook his head. "I'm not some psychopath who thinks that I can bring Hope back by taking revenge on her killer. What good would that do anyone? Like you said, Brandon never intended to kill her. He made stupid choices. Choices he could never take back or make amends for. The court decided what the penalty for that was, and he paid it."

"And you're not at all bitter about him walking away from prison eight years later."

"On one hand, it seems like it happened just yesterday. But on the other hand... it feels like it was a whole lifetime ago. I was a different person then than I am now. I can't live my life being bitter about what happened over a decade ago. It would be a waste."

Zachary studied him for any sign that he was just putting up a smokescreen. He had to assume that Hope had been Roper's first girlfriend. The first person he had ever fallen in love with and maybe been intimate with. It wasn't so easy to forget a relationship like that. But Roper sounded sincere.

Zachary's eye was drawn back to the photo of Roper and his sister again.

"You never married."

"Not yet. That doesn't mean that I never will."

"Do you have a girlfriend? Are you dating?"

Roper's eyes slid to his computer. "I have a pretty busy life. Not a lot of time left for socializing."

Zachary rolled his eyes. "Plenty of busy people have time for a private life and relationships. People get married, have kids, raise families while they're pursuing busy careers. It isn't like you're a surgeon or working eighteen-hour days. Unless you choose to."

"Then maybe I'm just not ready yet."

Zachary took a deep breath and let it out slowly. "Can you think of anyone who is still bitter toward Brandon? Bitter enough to want him dead?"

"I wasn't in touch with anyone involved in the case. Look at Hope's family and close friends. I don't know what any of them are thinking and feeling now."

"Well, if you think of anyone… if anything comes up that you think might be worth looking into, give me a call." Zachary slid a business card across the table.

"Don't count on it. I've moved on with my life."

Max Fulton was the fourth man in the car the night that Brandon Powers had mowed Hope down, killing her in the middle of the street. Zachary had been expecting a clone of Devon Masters. They had been friends back in the day. They had drunk together, had been sitting in the back of the car together. They could have died together, if they hadn't been wearing seatbelts or if Brandon had driven into the river or been hit by a train instead of hitting Hope Creedy. But Fulton was not like Devon. He was quiet and reticent, a contemplative man. He took his time in answering Zachary's questions and kept the inner workings of his brain hidden from observers. Zachary had a feeling that people didn't know much more about Fulton than he was willing to let people see.

"Explain to me what it is you wanted to see me about?" he asked Zachary. "I don't like this. I don't like being kept in the dark about people's motives."

"I'm investigating the death of Richard Harding."

"Richard Harding," Fulton repeated with a frown. He didn't

say it in that same blank way as everybody else had. It seemed to mean something to him. "When did he die?"

Zachary was surprised. "You know who that is, then?"

"I assume that's why you want to talk to me. There wouldn't be much point in questioning people who'd never heard of him."

"Most people have disclaimed knowing Harding's name."

"He told me before he moved. Said he was hoping to make a fresh start. I thought he deserved that. He'd suffered through a lot. I didn't know if he'd ever be able to put it behind him, but why not try? I didn't begrudge him that."

"I'm sure the accident made your life harder too. He wasn't the only one in the car, and I imagine people partially blamed you as well."

Fulton was quiet for a while. "I had my fair share," he agreed eventually. "But I wasn't the one who was driving. I didn't have to live with that on my conscience. Brandon did. When he got out of prison, he was a different person than he had been when it happened. That guilt over having killed an innocent person through his own carelessness and poor choices... he had to live with that for the rest of his life. However short that might have ended up being." He scratched his ear, staring off into the distance. "He didn't contact me again after he moved to Vermont. Did it happen right away? Or was it just recent?"

"It was more recent. He had a few years to try to start a new life."

"Did he find any peace?"

"I haven't looked too deeply into his history... but I would say no. He did his best. He was dating. He was working. He hadn't been in any trouble. But someone had been stalking him, and he was very agitated and depressed over it."

"Stalking him?" Fulton's voice went up several notes.

"Yes, I'm afraid so."

"In person? Or on the computer?"

Zachary watched Fulton's face for what he was thinking, but

he wore a mask, keeping it to himself. But he had brought up the cyberstalking immediately.

"On the computer and phone. Emails, texts, messages. Devon said he's had a few messages as well. Have you?"

Fulton nodded slowly. "It's been very disturbing. I've done my best just to ignore it, but those times when things are quiet and my mind is looking for things to think about... when I'm going to bed at night or having a quiet drink... I can't stop thinking about it."

"Do you know who is sending the messages?"

"No. It's all fake addresses. Nothing that you can respond to or trace back to the sender."

"Have you talked to anyone about it?"

"No... I don't really want to remind people about that part of my past. I'd rather not bring all of that up again."

"You didn't mention it to Devon?"

Fulton's eyes flicked to the side. "I might have."

"He set up his mail so that the messages are automatically deleted and he doesn't even have to see them."

"That would be smart. I'll have to see if someone can help me set that up..."

Zachary noticed he didn't say he'd get Devon to help him set it up. Obviously, as Devon had said, the two of them were not close friends. Fulton didn't think to ask Devon to help him set up the same thing.

"That might be a good idea; help ease your mind a little."

"You don't think that Brandon's death and the stalking are related, do you? I mean... I don't have to worry about this guy coming after me next?"

Zachary had wondered that briefly himself. He didn't want to tell Fulton that there was no danger, in case there was and Zachary's advice made him less cautious. But he didn't want to scare Fulton unnecessarily either.

"I've been looking for a connection between the stalker and the motorist who killed Brandon, but I haven't been able to find anything. None of the messages were overtly threatening. Nothing that said 'I'm coming after you' or 'I'm going to kill you.' It looks like a coincidence, but I can't tell you for sure."

"I appreciate that." Fulton sighed. "I didn't report it to the police. I don't really want to bring myself to their attention. Do you think I should?"

"Cyberstalking is a crime. I'd like to catch this guy, and if law enforcement can help to track him down…"

Mr. Peterson's words came back to him. His repeated advice for Zachary to report Tyrrell to the police for his similar activities. But like Fulton, he was reluctant to take it to the police. Not because he was worried it would tarnish his reputation, but because he didn't want to hurt Tyrrell. Not when he had already ruined his life. It was Zachary's own fault Tyrrell was sending those messages, and they were all true, however painful it was to admit it.

He realized that Fulton was saying something, looking at him with a pronounced frown.

"Oh, sorry. What was that…?"

"Something more important on your mind?" Fulton asked sarcastically.

"Not more important. Just… distracting. I'm sorry. I didn't mean to zone out like that."

"I guess… I'll report it. But are they going to want my computer? I can't really function without it."

"They might want to look at it, but I think mostly they'll want your login information for your email address, so that they can examine the messages and try to trace them."

"I hate the idea of someone going through my email…"

Did he have something to hide? Some other secret that he would rather they didn't know about?

"I know," he assured Fulton. "We don't like people poking around in our private lives. But if you want to help them to find this guy, to get him off your case…"

"I don't suppose I'm the only one he's doing this to. There are other people out there who are more vulnerable. People who would take it more seriously or are more suggestible. Children. If he's harassed all three of us, what are the chances that he's never done this before and would never do it again?"

"If it's someone who was hurt by Hope's death, they wouldn't be targeting anyone else, I don't think. The three of you were the only ones in the car."

"Do you really think so? They could decide to go after our families. If they're unstable enough to go over the deep end about an accident that happened over a decade ago, what's to say that they won't flip out over something else? Especially if they are getting satisfaction out of it? I don't think this is someone who is going to be stopped by logic."

He was right. An obsessive personality didn't just go away. It would find a new direction. Was the same true for Tyrrell? Was there any danger he would start harassing someone else too? Zachary knew Tyrrell. He wasn't that kind of a person. He'd always been a very sweet and sensitive boy. His anger toward Zachary was justified. He wouldn't carry that over to someone who was innocent. Tyrrell understood the difference between right and wrong. He wouldn't hurt someone else.

"So you think I should go to the police?" Fulton pressed.

"Uh… yes. I think it would be a good idea. You want to stop this guy. I don't see any way for them to stop him without the evidence. I have some idea of who it could be… but we don't have any proof connecting them yet."

"I hesitate to do anything that would harm anyone from Hope's family. They've gone through so much already. Do you think it's one of them?"

Zachary thought of the people he had interviewed. Mike Creedy, with his vitriol for the person who had killed his daughter. Mrs. Creedy's suppressed emotions, kept carefully under wraps. The twins, Luke trying to keep Noelle from saying too much to Zachary, with an explosive temper when he'd been drinking. Suzie didn't seem like a viable suspect. Zachary couldn't even imagine her finding the time to send that many emails. And Jonathan Roper, the boyfriend who could never be acknowledged, forever excluded from Hope's circle of mourners, looking in from the outside.

"I suspect it probably is," Zachary admitted. "I'm going to have to spend some more time on it, now that I've had a chance to meet everyone. And I should probably meet Kyle Browne's family as well."

Fulton looked surprised at the mention of Kyle's name. "I don't think he has anyone left around here. His parents have passed away. There was a sister, but she moved years ago. Even before the trial concluded. She just couldn't handle being in the spotlight."

"Do you know where she went?"

"No… I really have no idea. It wasn't the same for them as it was for Hope's family. They didn't get much public sympathy, and Brandon wasn't even charged in connection with Kyle's death."

Which could have left them feeling very bitter toward the man who had taken Kyle away from them. If Kyle's parents were dead, then it wasn't them, but it could be the sister.

Zachary decided he'd done all that he could in New Hampshire. He was feeling increasingly anxious in the hotel room and wanted to be back home in familiar surroundings, so rather than stay one more night, he checked out and hit the road, pointing the nose of the car west. He could have sworn that it knew they were going home and was as eager to get there as he was. Traffic was good and the trip uneventful.

At home, he showered off the dust of the trail as if he'd been riding in an open coach. After so many years without a permanent residence, it felt good to have a place of his own. He plugged the computer in and opened it up. He had more notes to compile, research to do, and theories to think about. He was distracted by the email notifications counter and clicked through to see what was awaiting him.

Of course, he knew in the back of his mind that there would be another email or two there from Tyrrell. Should he make contact with him, like Bridget said he should? Should he turn the matter over to the police like Mr. Peterson suggested and like he had advised Fulton? He hated to do that. Tyrrell was hurting. Maybe venting all of the poison would get it out of his system, and he'd be able to move on, if he just thought someone was listening to him.

He clicked on the latest message from Tyrrell, trying to brace himself mentally. He was just there to listen, to hear what it was Tyrrell had to say. He didn't have to take it personally and let it affect his mood.

You have done nothing but cause pain to everyone who knows you.

Why don't you just kill yourself?

Zachary swallowed. A pain started in the center of his chest and radiated outward, making it hard to breathe. He knew it was true. He'd brought pain and suffering to his family. To other families he had lived with. He had brought it into his marriage with Bridget and into other relationships. He brought it to the Creedys and other families he had questioned in the cases he investigated. Everywhere he went, he dragged his own pain and sorrow with him and infected everyone around him.

His head throbbed with the heavy beats of his heart.

Why don't you just kill yourself?

He rubbed his eyes and looked at the words again. He'd seen the same phrase repeated a number of times in the cyberstalker's messages to Richard Harding. It was hardly a unique phrase; he had seen it in other incidents of cyberbullying before. He read through the other recent messages, analyzing the language and repeated phrases clinically instead of reading them as personal attacks. He did a search and looked at the list of results.

The pattern of send times was similar to what he'd observed in the messages from Harding's stalker. Most of them before nine, over the lunch hour, after three or four. Like someone fitting them in around a work or school schedule. That didn't mean anything by itself; a high percentage of the population followed a similar schedule. It wasn't the same person just because he used a few of the same stock phrases and worked a similar schedule.

Zachary *knew* that his emails were coming from Tyrrell. No one but someone in his family could have had that picture. They were not from Harding's stalker. There was no connection between Tyrrell and the cyberstalker, other than their style and the timing of the messages.

That twigged another thought for Zachary. He logged in to Harding's account and looked at the messages the cyberstalker had been sending Harding. He double-checked the dates.

For a few minutes, he just sat there, thinking things through. Then he called Campbell.

Zachary," Campbell greeted cheerfully. "How goes the battle?"

"I don't know how much progress I'm making with this, but I had another thought."

"Yeah?"

"When Harding died, he stopped getting emails from the stalker."

"Well, yes, that makes sense."

"No, it doesn't."

"What do you mean?"

"How did the stalker know that he was dead?"

There was silence while Campbell thought this through. It was a more complex question than it sounded like.

"When, exactly, did the emails stop coming?" Campbell asked.

"The last one was the night he died. Nothing after that."

"And he'd been getting them pretty regularly up until then. There weren't any other gaps in the timeline when the stalker took a break and stopped sending them for a day or two?"

"No. They were coming in several times a day, faithfully."

"The stalker knew there was no point in sending any more messages. That means that he knew Harding was dead. But no one else knew Harding was dead. Not the truck driver, not his girlfriend, not the police."

"No."

"Does that mean he was there? Does that mean that Rusty Donaldson was somehow involved and could report back to the stalker, or was the stalker himself?"

"You might want to get him back in and look into it further."

Campbell grumbled. "This was supposed to be an open-and-shut case, Zachary. What are you doing to me?"

"Sorry. I didn't expect to find anything, but…"

"First you find out he was being cyberstalked. Then you find out he'd been in prison for killing someone in a hit and run himself. Then that the stalker knew almost the instant he died. This is turning into a much more complex case than it was supposed to be."

"I know. There's more going on under the surface than I would ever have expected."

"It could all be coincidence. His stalker might have just decided to give up at that point. He might have had enough. Or something else came up in his life and he couldn't keep it up. Maybe his computer died."

"I don't like coincidences. I'll see if I can find any connections between the people I interviewed in New Hampshire and Rusty Donaldson. Another possibility is Ashley herself."

"You think the girlfriend is the stalker?"

"She could be. Kenzie suggested it. Ashley is the only one who knew that he was missing the morning after he died. Did she tell someone else? Or was she the one who had been sending him the messages all along?"

"You have a devious mind, Zach. That's very… disturbing."

"I know. But it had to be someone close to him. I just don't know how to explain it otherwise. Either the stalker has a connection with Rusty Donaldson, or he was out there to see the accident, or it was Ashley or someone she talked to that morning. I can't think of any other scenarios, can you?"

"No… that's all I can think of. Would she give you access to her phone records if you asked?"

"I might be able to get them out of her. See who she called that morning. And the night before."

"Get her to show you whatever you can get out of her, it will be easier than us trying to get a warrant for them. If she is the stalker… then I'm guessing she won't show you everything. Or she'll have an alternative phone or email that she won't show you."

Zachary grunted his agreement. He couldn't quite wrap his mind around why Ashley would stalk and harass her own boyfriend, but that didn't mean she hadn't done it. She might have a motive buried deep beneath the surface. She might have gone to school with Hope, she might have had a sister who had been killed in a hit and run, or she might be mentally unbalanced. There was no telling what her motives were. But Zachary didn't have to know the motive, not initially. If he had proof, or at least strong evidence, that she had been the one harassing Harding, that would be a start. Enough, at least, for the police to question her and look into it further. As things stood, they didn't have any reason to insist she submit to further questioning.

"I'll find out what I can."

"Thanks, Zach. Appreciate you keeping me apprised—"

"Actually, there was something else I wanted to mention." Zachary raised his voice, trying to grab Campbell's attention before he could hang up.

"What?" Campbell questioned from farther away, then held the phone to his mouth again. "I didn't catch that?"

"There was one other thing."

"Oh, boy. Am I going to like it?"

Zachary thought of the news that Hope had been dating a younger man, and a minor at that, carefully keeping it a secret from his parents and their friends. But that wasn't what he had stopped Campbell for.

"Around the time I took this case… I started getting some nasty emails."

"You don't think they're from the same guy, do you? Harding's stalker?"

"No, I was pretty sure they were from… a family member I've been estranged from. But the similarities between them are marked. I don't know what to think. I can't see how they could be related."

"Can't you?" Campbell was amused. "If it's Ashley…"

Ashley knew when Zachary had taken the case. She knew his email address and phone number and other details of how to contact him. Had she seen him as a replacement target for her boyfriend? Harding was gone and she couldn't tease and taunt him anymore, so she had needed a new victim?

"But the things that she—he—has said to me have been very personal, things that someone outside of my family wouldn't know."

"Things that you've never told anyone else about? Can you be sure that your estranged family members have never told them to anyone else? Once you put something out there, you lose control of it."

Zachary considered. The accusations that had come to him from Tyrrell or the anonymous stalker were not actually that specific. The mentions of what he had done were vague, sometimes focused on the fire and sometimes not. While he had not shared the story of the fire with many people, there were others who knew not only that he had been in a fire when he was young, but that he had been the cause of it, and that his family had broken apart after that. Dozens of doctors, therapists, social workers, foster parents, foster kids, teachers and school administrators. And the few people he had told the details to, like Bridget and Kenzie. Someone running background on him could have found out from many different sources. Despite the fact that his privacy was supposed to be protected by social services, Zachary knew of plenty of cases where confidentiality had been breached. Foster parents gossiped with each other. Professionals discussed difficult cases among themselves. The foster brothers and sisters he had lived with hadn't been under any legal requirement to keep his story to themselves. They were taught to respect each other's privacy, but that didn't mean they did.

"Zachary?"

"Just thinking about it. I guess… there were people who knew, alright. But he sent me a photograph. One of my family, right before… that had to come from someone else in my family. No one else could have had it."

"Maybe someone in your family posted it online somewhere. Have you done a search to see if you could find it? Asked your family about it?"

"No. Not yet."

"Someone in your extended family could have shared it. It might have been placed in a public archive for some reason. Hell, you know all this, Zachary. You're a photographer. You're a private investigator. You know what happens once a picture is circulated. It never goes away."

"Then…" Zachary's mood lifted a little. "Maybe it wasn't Tyrrell. But he did send me a letter, to our old address. It ended up being forwarded to Bridget's."

"How do you know it was him? Did you contact him?"

"Well… no. Not yet. I thought that maybe—" Zachary cut himself off. He didn't need to share any more details than that. He didn't need to say where or when he thought he was going to see Tyrrell, or if he was really going to follow through. "No. But it was before I took the case…" Zachary trailed off. "Actually… I don't think it was. It arrived after our first meeting."

"After being forwarded in the mail? Forwarding tends to add a day or two to delivery time."

"Wait… I still have the envelope." Zachary shuffled through the papers on his desk and pulled out the letter and envelope that had come from Tyrrell. He studied the postmark, trying to make out where and when it had been mailed. He was relieved to see that it had been mailed from Vermont, not New Hampshire, and the mailing date was several weeks back, before he'd been hired to investigate Harding's death. "Yeah. It was mailed before I took the case. So this one is from Tyrrell..."

"But you're right, the emails might not be. They follow the same patterns as the ones to Harding?"

"Same phrasing in a lot of places. Same distribution of times, like the person has an office job or goes to school."

"And Ashley Morton, what is her schedule like?"

"I'm not sure... I think she's been on leave since Harding died. But the emails I've been getting are still in the same distribution pattern. So either she's very careful to follow the same schedule as before, or it's not the same person."

"Right," Campbell agreed. "I want you to send them to me anyway. We have someone working on the communications with Harding. They can look at your emails too and see if there is anything comparing them side-by-side can reveal. Maybe if they have two reference points, it will help to triangulate this guy's location. I don't know if that's something they can do with emails."

"Uh... I don't really like the idea of someone else reading these. There's personal stuff..."

"You want me to get a warrant for your whole email account or your computer? If there's a couple you don't want anyone to see, then hold them back, but we need a stack of them to do a proper analysis. These guys aren't going to be reading them for their own entertainment or to hold over you. They're trying to solve a case, that's all. The point is to learn everything they can about the stalker, not about you."

"Yeah. Okay." If he could hold back the ones with the more personal references, that helped. He didn't want Campbell's department having full access to everything in his email or on his computer.

"That's more like it. We're on the same side here. We both want to find out who the stalker is. Or who they are."

"Thanks. I appreciate your help."

"Is there anything else?"

Zachary thought about Jonathan Roper. "N-no."

Campbell heard his hesitation. "On the case or personally. It sounds like there's something else."

"I don't know whether it's relevant or not yet. I have to process my New Hampshire interview notes."

"Is it time sensitive? Are we going to miss something if we put it off?"

"No. I don't see him going anywhere."

"Alright. We both have plenty to look at, then. Let me know if you find anything in Ashley's records and I'll tell you if we can get anything from the email comparison."

In spite of being back in his own bed for the night, Zachary found he couldn't sleep. He tried lying down a few times, but each time his brain started chattering, processing all of the disparate clues, and he'd think of something he had to get up and check, or to write down so he wouldn't forget it in the morning. Eventually, he gave up and went back to his computer, carefully sorting through everything he knew and trying to make sense of it. He ran deeper background on the suspects in New Hampshire, looking for any clues in their past and trying to tie them to Rusty Donaldson or Ashley Morton.

It struck him that while he had tried to find a connection between the stalker and Rusty Donaldson, he hadn't spent much time trying to find a connection between Donaldson and Ashley. Maybe Ashley was the stalker and maybe she wasn't, but what if she knew Donaldson? What if she put him up to killing Harding?

The trouble with that was that he couldn't think of a motive. They hadn't found any evidence that Harding was abusive or that Ashley would benefit from killing him. He was a blue collar working stiff without any money, without even a life insurance policy. She wouldn't get anything material from his death. There wasn't any sign that he'd been cheating on her. Despite having changed his email address and phone number, there was nothing on the old accounts to incriminate him. Zachary was an expert at spotting signs of infidelity.

By the time it was what could be considered a decent hour to call Ashley to see if he could meet with her, his eyes burned from staring at the computer screen for too long. He rubbed them and showered and put in eyedrops, then made himself a cup of coffee and sat down. Ashley still sounded like he had dragged her out of bed. Zachary explained that he wanted to get together to talk, to follow up with her on what he had learned in New Hampshire.

Ashley yawned unenthusiastically. "Couldn't you just make a report to me over the phone? I really didn't want to have to deal with anyone today."

"There are things I don't like to discuss over the phone. I'd like to come see you at your house. Would that be okay?"

"At Richard's, you mean?"

"No, no. There's no need to drive out there. I'll just come to your house. Why don't you give me the address, and I'll be there as soon as I can? Then you're free to do what you want the rest of the day."

She gave a noisy sigh. "Did you find something?"

"I need to talk face to face," he insisted. "I'd like it to be today, if possible… do you have work or another commitment?"

"Fine." She gave him the address that he already had for her and advised that she would need to shower and dress before he arrived. "So don't get here too fast."

"An hour?"

"I suppose."

Zachary did his best to soften her up, stopping at the donut shop to pick up some pastries and some good coffee before swinging by her house. Her hair was still wet from her shower, but she did manage a smile when she saw that he had brought her breakfast.

"Well, at least I get something out of this," she grumbled. As if Zachary weren't doing anything else for her.

They went into the kitchen to put the pastries and coffee on the table. Zachary had thought through his approach with Ashley, so he had his story all prepared. "I'm sorry I couldn't really say anything to you over the phone, but I'm concerned that someone might be monitoring your communications."

"Monitoring… you mean someone has my phone tapped?"

"I don't know whether it's your phone or your computer, but I'd like to look at both of them. And what about in here or your car? Have you had anyone out of the ordinary in your house lately?"

Ashley looked around her eyes wide. "You think the house is bugged?"

"It's a possibility, but probably not. It's easy to tap a phone or computer remotely. Not so easy to arrange to have a bug physically planted in a house or car that's in a different state."

"You think one of these people you saw in New Hampshire might have bugged me?"

"I can't say they did without looking at your equipment. And if you could get me a printout from your phone company of all of your call and text logs that they give you access to, that might be helpful."

"Why?"

"Chances are, if someone bugged you remotely, they sent you a trojan. I'll look at what I can find on the phone and computer, but if it was attached to a text that was since deleted, or if the stalker called you first to make sure that your phone was turned on…"

Wide-eyed, Ashley unlocked her phone and handed it to him without a word. She grabbed one of the pastries from the box and ate it as she walked into the living room to retrieve her laptop, scattering crumbs along the way.

"I'll print out what I can while you look at the phone," she said. "Then you can look at it. Unless… should I not be doing that?"

"If there's a key-logger installed, you'll need to go through your various online accounts and change the passwords after I clean it off anyway. I don't think it will hurt to print out those logs."

They sat down. Zachary went to Ashley's texts, and started flicking through them. "You don't recall getting any strange texts lately? From someone you didn't know or who normally wouldn't be sending you something? A video or gif or song?"

"Uh… maybe, I don't know."

Zachary went through each sender, scrolling back to when Richard Harding had died. If she had any brains, she would have deleted any incriminating texts she had sent; but criminals made mistakes all the time. That was how they got caught.

He stopped when he got to a sender that had sent only one text, apparently a video of a cat. Zachary turned the phone around to show her the screen.

"Who sent this?"

"Uh… I don't know. I thought maybe it was a school friend of mine. I ran into her at the store, and she said she would connect with me. But I don't know," Ashley shook her head, looking at that one lonely message. "She never sent anything else or responded to my texts…"

Zachary turned the phone back around to investigate further.

"Do you think that's it?" Ashley asked in a low, nervous voice. She looked around. "Do you think that's some kind of virus that bugs my phone?"

One of the problems with phones was that they were always on. Even when she turned off the screen, that didn't turn off the phone or its broadcasting abilities. A clever hacker could use it like a baby monitor, to listen to anything that was going on, even when she wasn't making a phone call. Zachary held his finger to his lips to silence Ashley. He turned the phone to airplane mode and removed the SIM card. He put the tiny black chip on the table.

"I'll need to spend some more time with it, but for now, no one can monitor you through the phone. If that was a trojan, I would suggest getting a new phone. I can't be sure he hasn't done something that will give him permanent access whenever it is online. Even with a system wipe… I can't give you any guarantees. You might have backed up the trojan. It may have attached itself to some other app or file that you've saved to the cloud. You should probably do like Richard did, get a new phone and a new email address. Don't try to retrieve anything from this account."

Her eyes were wide. "But my whole life is on that little thing! All of my contacts, my plans…"

"I can convert contacts and calendars to CSV files and reimport them on a clean phone. That should be safe."

She just continued to shake her head. "How could this happen? I thought phones couldn't get viruses?"

"People can hijack them. This wasn't just a random virus."

Ashley stared at her computer for a long time, then logged in. "Do you still want this log, or do you not need it anymore because you already found it?"

"Uh…" Zachary thought it through. The reason he had asked for the logs had not been to track down spyware, but to see if Ashley had any connections with anyone else on his list. He hadn't actually expected to find spyware. "Yes, to be safe, if you could still print them out. We want to be thorough."

Ashley nodded and went to work. Zachary focused his attention on the phone, seeing if he could track down a suspicious program in the app list. It was probably lurking in the operating system, not visible to the user, but sometimes they still left traces in the visible interface.

As Ashley printed off pages of phone and text logs, he found a calculator app that seemed to be more than it appeared to be on the surface. It wasn't the built-in calculator app, though it was certainly intended to mimic it. But Zachary's keen eye picked out a few discrepancies. He pulled out his own computer and, being sure to tether it to his phone rather than to Ashley's potentially insecure network, he searched up the app and confirmed that it was spyware.

"It is infected," he confirmed to Ashley.

She looked at him with wide eyes and said nothing. She left the room, and came back a few minutes later with a thick stack of print outs.

"Can you do anything with it?"

"I'll do my best, but like I say, if it's sophisticated… that might not be enough."

"And my computer?"

Zachary reached across the table and turned her computer around. "That may take longer."

But it didn't. The malware seemed to be fairly unsophisticated. Checking for open ports, it was quickly obvious that Ashley's computer had been infected as well. He blocked each of the spyware programs and downloaded his preferred app to clean it. While he was working on it, his mind was churning through all of the possibilities and implications. He had told Campbell that the stalker was quite possibly Ashley or someone she had told that Harding was missing. That was no longer the case. Whoever had had access to her phone and computer via the spyware knew about all of her phone calls and messages. They had read and listened in on her increasingly worried messages to Harding, and then to the police. They knew everything that she knew in real time. It was back to square one, unless they could figure out who had been monitoring her.

The chances that Ashley was the stalker had gone down considerably. But they hadn't been eliminated. She still might have infected herself as a cover, or someone else might have infected her for some other reason. Maybe a friend of Harding's had been suspicious of her and had investigated her. For that matter, maybe Harding himself had suspected her.

"How long had you and Richard been dating?"

Ashley looked at him, eyes narrowed. "What?"

"I don't even know how long you had been together. You met him when he got out of prison. I assume you had been dating for a while. But you were not living together, so maybe that was a wrong assumption."

She considered him for a minute before answering. "Two years," she said finally. "But I don't see what living together has to do with it. Plenty of people know each other for years and years and never move in together. You have different kinds of relationships. Some people don't want to give up their own independence."

"Was it your decision or Richard's? Were *you* someone who didn't want to give up your own independence?"

Again, Ashley weighed her answer carefully before saying anything. Zachary didn't like how cautious she was. Her answers were not natural, unplanned replies. They could easily be lies.

"I admit I didn't want to give up my own place," she said, looking around. "I don't like to be… subsumed in a relationship. I don't like the idea of only being a part of a couple, instead of an individual. I don't like how at the end of a relationship, someone has to move out, and all of the belongings that you had together have to be divided. You give up some of your own stuff to combine households, and then when you break up again, you don't have it anymore. Unless you left it in a storage locker or your parents' house."

As a foster kid, Zachary understood the loss of status that went along with losing his home and his material possessions. While he was at a foster home, he had stuff. He had a bed and clothes and books and toys. He had access to a TV and fridge and closet space. When it was time to go, he would get his toothbrush and a change of clothes in a plastic bag, and the camera he kept on his person at all times, and everything else was stripped away.

But as far as relationships went, his experience with the dynamics of two people becoming one couple was the opposite. He had loved the feeling of being a part of a completed whole. He had felt like for once he was a full person instead of one that was damaged and missing vital parts. He had been absorbed into Bridget's life. Her full, engaged life. He wasn't just Zachary anymore, but Zachary, Bridget's husband.

Her name was like a password that had opened up a magical world he could never had been a part of before. People knew her, admired her, and wanted to please her. Everywhere she went, she made friends. Even in places that were previously Zachary's domain, like the police department, Bridget quickly knew and was friends with more people than Zachary. And while they had been together, he had been a part of that.

Zachary forced himself back into the conversation with Ashley. "That makes sense." He saw her shoulders dip, her body language relaxing. "So you didn't know Richard in New Hampshire."

"No. I never met him until he moved to Vermont."

"When did he tell you about his past? That he had been in prison and had unintentionally killed someone in a hit and run?"

"I don't know when, exactly. We started getting serious. I knew that he avoided some topics, social situations, that he had problems with his health and with sleeping. It didn't all come out at once. Little revelations that he'd lived in New Hampshire, that he'd been involved in an accident, that he'd served time for his fault in it… it was difficult for him to talk about, so I didn't push to know everything at once. Just a little bit more every now and then, until I had the whole story."

"So you know everything?"

She pursed her lips, looking at him. "What do you classify as 'everything'? He was driving, he'd had a couple of drinks, he hit and killed a girl. He was disoriented and left the scene."

"There were others in the car."

Ashley nodded. "Yeah. He was driving the others."

"Did you know that one of them died too?"

No indication of surprise on her face. "Well… yes."

"Did he ever have any contact with anyone else involved in the case? Hope's family or friends? The other guys who survived the collision?"

"No. Except, I guess, whoever was stalking him. But I didn't know that before he died."

"So he might have had contact with any of them without you knowing it."

"Yes. But you've looked at all of his phone records and emails, right? So you'd know if he'd had contact with them."

"In the last couple of months, yes. We haven't gone three years back in phone records. Where did you live before?"

She raised her eyebrows. "Before what? I live here."

"Before you moved here."

She obviously hadn't lived there forever. It wasn't her family home. She complained about losing her home during a previous relationship or relationships. She must therefore have had several addresses before the current one. The fact that she wasn't answering automatically made him wonder why she wanted to hide it. Had she lived in New Hampshire? Did she have connections she didn't want him to know about?

"I'm not sure what you mean. I grew up in Burlington."

"And you came here from Burlington?"

"No… I've had a few other residences. But I've been here for three years."

About the same time that Harding had gotten out of prison. Zachary pretended to be occupied with Ashley's computer, clicking through a few screens to see how the virus scan was progressing and giving her time to relax between questions.

"You like it here?"

"Sure. It's a nice town. I've got a good job. No reason to leave any time soon."

"It has a nice atmosphere," Zachary agreed. It had felt like a good place for him to settle down too. After spending his life moving around, it had seemed like a good place to put down his roots. Big enough for there to be plenty of work for him, but small enough that it felt like a community instead of a big metropolis. "How about Richard, what did he think of it?"

"Well, he lived where it was more rural… I don't know if he

really liked it, though. Most people choose to live on rural properties because they want gardens, or animals, or to be out in nature. But I think Richard just wanted to be away from people. He got anxious when he had to be in the city. He was... I'm not sure what the best word for it is. He was always watching, like something was going to happen. And in the city, he had to watch everything at once, all the different directions at the same time."

"Hypervigilance," Zachary supplied. That was something he knew plenty about.

Ashley's expression cleared. "Yes, that's the perfect word. When he had to be in the city, whether it was out on the street or in a grocery store, he was hypervigilant. He was okay for a while if he was here, in a house, but after a while, he'd get... jittery and want to go back home."

"Was he afraid of being in another accident?"

"Yes... but I don't think that was the only thing. He didn't like being around a lot of people. I don't know if he thought people were going to recognize him, or maybe bad things had happened to him in prison that had affected him... he was happier when he was at home, or just with a small group of friends."

"Did the two of you have shared interests? How did you spend your time together?"

"Like I said before. Just watching TV together, talking, relaxing. Maybe it doesn't sound like much, but it worked for us."

Zachary nodded. "And you weren't aware of it when the stalker started harassing him?"

"Thinking back... maybe... he said he was depressed. He started shutting down different accounts, saying that he needed to spend more time IRL—in real life—instead of so much of it online. I didn't really think anything of it. I thought he was exaggerating about being depressed. Maybe he was a bit down about things, but not really depressed."

Harding was probably just good at hiding his feelings. His time in prison had probably taught him that. Like Zachary's time in Bonnie Brown had taught him to mask his anger and pain, to keep anyone from thinking he was weak and a good target. If Harding's feelings about the cyberstalker's messages had been anything like Zachary's, he had probably been seriously depressed. The cutting and antidepressants were pretty big signs that he hadn't just been trying to get attention.

"So you couldn't narrow down the timeframe when the stalker first made contact."

"You can tell from his emails, can't you?"

"He deleted them and emptied his trash, so I can't be sure exactly when he started getting them." He watched Ashley's expression closely. "You don't know when the stalker started to send them?"

She shook her head. "So, sorry. And I don't understand why it's important."

"Don't you want the cyberstalker to be caught and punished?"

"Yes, of course…" her voice was uncertain.

"I would think you would want his stalker punished just as much as the person who killed him. After all, the person who killed him didn't cause any suffering. The person who stalked and harassed him did."

She didn't offer anything up. If she was the stalker, she didn't seem to be experiencing any regret or sorrow for it. If she wasn't, she didn't seem to have any comprehension of how much pain those words could cause. She acted as if it were nothing, instead of something that could have led to Harding's death just as surely as being hit by a truck.

2 2

As he got back into his car to return home, Zachary called Campbell to give him a heads-up on the latest developments, aware that it unraveled all of the progress they thought they had made with the realization that the stalker had stopped harassing Harding immediately after his death. Campbell wasn't as dismayed about it as Zachary was. Zachary could practically hear his heavy shoulder-shrug over the phone. "That's one mystery solved, anyway. You got the number that sent this suspected malware? We'll see if we can chase it down."

"He'll have thrown it out."

"Undoubtedly. But we still might be able to figure something out."

Zachary gave him the number. Campbell didn't hang up immediately. "And you're okay? You sound discouraged."

"I'll be fine. Just tired. Haven't slept much the last few days."

"Make sure you get it tonight, then. You need to get enough sleep for optimum brain function. If we're going to close this case, we need you at your best."

"Thanks." Zachary wasn't sure anymore there was any chance in bringing it to a successful conclusion. He hadn't been able to provide anything that showed that Rusty Donaldson hadn't just killed Harding by accident, just as the police had initially determined. "I'll try."

"Take care of yourself. We're going to need you on other cases. Got to have someone keeping us honest."

Zachary tried to laugh at the suggestion of him keeping the police in line. "I don't think this was anything other than an accident," he admitted.

"No. Neither do I. But at least we'll have independent confirmation of that."

Zachary grunted. After a bit more casual conversation, they hung up. Zachary put the car in gear and drove for a few minutes before calling Kenzie.

"Thought I'd let you know I'm back in town. Got back last night."

"Oh, good! How did it go?"

"Well… there are still a lot of bad feelings for Harding. No one was too sorry to hear he'd died. But I haven't been able to connect any of them to Rusty Donaldson or the cyberstalker."

"Maybe it just was a coincidence."

"That's what I'm thinking."

"Well, maybe you'll be able to close this case before Christmas."

"Yeah." And then what? He had plenty of little jobs to keep him busy, but they wouldn't occupy his attention like the Harding case had. And he needed something to distract him from the poisonous email messages. If they were from Harding's stalker, would they just go away when he had closed the case? Or had the stalker transferred his obsessive interest to Zachary, and would just keep taunting him? And if it wasn't Harding's stalker, if it was Tyrrell like Zachary had originally thought… then what was Zachary going to do about it?

"Still there, Zachary?"

"Yeah. Just thinking. Sorry. What are your Christmas plans again?" He was pretty sure she had told him, but he tended to withdraw from any conversation about Christmas.

"I thought we were going to have dinner together and go see Rhys."

"Rhys. Right. Did you manage to get something set up with Vera? Rhys said he was going to see his mom on Christmas Day."

"You were supposed to talk to Vera to hammer out the details."

"I was?" Zachary searched his memory, but couldn't remember anything of the sort. Had Kenzie told him to do that? Had he offered? Did Kenzie just think she had mentioned it? "I… guess I forgot."

"You'd better call her and find out. It's just a few days away, Zach."

"Uh, yeah. I will. I'm sorry."

"Are you going to do it?" She gave him a few seconds to answer, in which Zachary tried to formulate an answer, but failed to find the right words. "Don't tell me you're going to if you're not."

Zachary swallowed. "I don't think I can."

"Fine. I'll call her. But that means you'll have to abide by whatever plans I make."

"Yeah. Sure. No problem."

"You are nothing *but* problems," Kenzie complained, blowing her breath out in a sigh. But she didn't say it in a mean way. It was lighthearted, just a bit of teasing between friends.

Zachary pulled into the parking lot of his apartment building and headed toward his parking space. He hit the brake and swore.

"You okay?" Kenzie asked. "Did something happen?"

"Uh—fine. Everything is fine."

"It sounded like something was wrong."

Zachary tried to breathe long and slow. If he breathed slowly and calmed his body, then his heart would stop racing like it was going to drill right through his chest and everything really would be fine. There was a beep behind him. Zachary glanced into the rearview mirror and saw one of the other tenants trying to navigate to his own parking space. Zachary was stopped right in the middle of the lane, blocking him from entering. He eased his foot off the brake and crept forward, steering slowly, driving like he was a hundred and three and half blind. He managed to get into his spot and put the car into park. He was okay. There was nothing to worry about.

"What's going on? Should I hang up so you can focus?"

"No. I'm here. Just got home."

A few seconds of silence passed. "What happened? A black cat cross your path?"

Something just as ominous for Zachary. He swallowed.

"Apparently… the manager of my new building decorates."

"Decorates… for Christmas?"

"Yeah."

"That's nice. I like it when businesses take part in the festivities of the season. It's nice to look around and see everything looking Christmas-y."

Zachary's mouth and throat were too dry to agree.

"Okay, well, if you're back home, I'll let you go. Have a good night."

Zachary whispered a hoarse goodbye and hung up the call.

He took the key out of the ignition, gathered his things together, and got out of the car. He stared at the Christmas display inside the lobby apartment. Twinkle lights, a couple of decorated Christmas trees with fake presents underneath, and garlands around the windows.

He could deal with it. Every year, there was no avoiding Christmas decorations completely. He stuck to the stores and restaurants that did not usually decorate, didn't accept Christmas invitations, and was generally a Scrooge. But there would always be a few times when he had to walk past decorated trees or window displays or when he couldn't avoid Christmas music piped into a store. He still managed to do it.

The longer he took, the harder it would get, so Zachary forced himself to walk down the sidewalk to the building's doors, to push them open, and to use his security card to unlock the inside door.

There was no one else in the lobby. He aimed his body toward the elevator doors, closed his eyes, and started walking, hands held slightly in front of him so he wouldn't walk right into the wall.

But his brain knew where the trees were and the fact that he was focused on them meant that he course-corrected to walk into them instead of past them. He felt the prickly needles and stopped. He didn't want to open his eyes, but he wasn't going to be able to get back on track without looking. The sharp smell of pine filled his nose. He opened his eyes and it was like he was inside the tree. His face was only inches from the upward-reaching branches, lights, and decorations. Zachary backed up, found the elevators again, and shuffled toward them, hands still held out in front of him in spite of the fact that he could see the trees and the walls and wasn't going to walk into anything. When he reached the wall, he put his hands flat against it. He bent his head forward slightly and rested his forehead against the cool wall.

He heard the lock on the lobby doors beep and then swoosh open. Trying to avoid looking like a complete idiot, Zachary managed to find the up button and push it. One of his neighbors fell in behind him to wait and didn't ask him what he was doing worshiping the wall.

When the elevator bell dinged, Zachary peeled himself away from the wall and shuffled into the elevator. He didn't turn around immediately.

"Floor?" the neighbor asked helpfully.

Zachary cleared his throat and gave it hoarsely, turning himself around as the elevator started up with a stomach-dropping lurch. The other man's eyes flicked over him.

"A bit too much Christmas cheer?" he suggested.

Zachary nodded, his head swimming. Definitely too much Christmas cheer.

"Do you need a hand or can you get there yourself?"

Zachary held to one of the hand rails inside the elevator. "I'm okay."

"You're sure? It would only take a minute. I don't mind."

"No. No, I'm good. Thanks."

He took a few deep breaths. Out of sight of the Christmas trees and decorations, the panic was starting to subside. He'd touched one of those trees. Actually touched it. It had been years since he'd done that. It hadn't been on purpose, but he hadn't fainted or thrown up in response. It had just been prickly.

The elevator stopped. Zachary checked the number to make sure it was his floor, and moved forward. The other man reached his hand out, tracking Zachary, making sure he wasn't going to topple over. His other hand pressed the 'open' button, making sure Zachary had lots of time to navigate through them without a problem.

"Thanks," Zachary told him, stepping over the gap into the corridor. He kept moving, showing the other tenant that he was able to manage on his own and didn't need to be physically escorted to his door.

The doors swooshed closed. Zachary stopped and stood still, one hand on the wall, waiting for the nausea the elevator had induced to calm back down. Then he walked slowly down the hallway to his door and let himself in. No lurching, no need to hold on to the wall, just a normal walk like it was any other day. He closed and locked the door and sat down in a chair in his kitchen, the closest piece of available furniture. He put his shoulder bag with his laptop and other items on the floor and took a few more breaths.

His phone buzzed, and Zachary took it out to look at it. A text message from Kenzie.

I just remembered how Christmas decorations bother you. Sorry. U ok?

Zachary blew out his breath. He was fine. He'd made it on his own with no ill effects. Just like a normal person.

Fine. Thanks for checking.

He watched the screen for a few minutes, waiting for her response.

Good. Call if you need to talk.

He texted back a thumbs-up emoji and turned the screen off.

The rest of the evening should have been fine. He was winding-up the file. Write out his conclusions. Put them together in a coherent report. Collect the rest of his fee.

His mind kept going back to the Christmas decorations in the lobby. He was going to have to walk by them every time he went out and returned. Unless there was an alternate route out of the building. Freight elevator? Stairs? Loading dock or emergency door? He'd never explored the building; he just walked in and out the same way every day like anybody else. But surely there was another way out. There had to be emergency exits in the event of… any sort of emergency. He'd figure it out. Then he wouldn't have to look like a fool every time he had to get through the lobby.

But the decision to find another way in and out of the building didn't help him to write his notes. He got hung up on the twins' names. Noelle and Luke. They must have been Christmas babies, with Mrs. Creedy marking the occasion by giving them Christmas names.

He was glad that Kenzie had agreed to take over the arrangements with Rhys and Vera. Zachary just couldn't manage it on his own. One day, maybe. After all, he'd touched a Christmas tree without any ill effects. But he wasn't ready for it yet.

Around and around his brain went, like a hamster on a wheel. While he'd been aware that Christmas was getting closer and closer, he'd been avoiding focusing on the exact date. When Kenzie had said it was only a few days away, it had sent his brain into overdrive. It was all coming back. The blackness and despair that he had to swim through every year never seemed to get any easier. Knowing ahead of time that the depression would worsen was no help at all.

He finally put his notes and unfinished report aside. If he

couldn't distract himself with work, then maybe it was time to just veg out in front of the TV. While the networks were full of seasonal offerings, he had a streaming account that was full of non-Christmas shows and movies. He could start on a new series and binge watch until he fell asleep or Christmas Eve was over, whichever came first.

But he couldn't settle on anything to watch. That hamster kept running and running around the wheel. Kenzie was going to talk to Vera and set something up. Rhys had already said he wanted to do Christmas Eve instead of Christmas Day, and what if Kenzie set that up instead? She said that Zachary had to go with whatever she set up. Or what if she set it up for Christmas Day and Zachary was no longer around? It wouldn't be fair to put Rhys through something like that, especially on his first Christmas without his mother. If something happened to Zachary, it would be on Christmas Eve. Just like the fire.

The previous year, he had been in the emergency room. Not for himself, but for Isabella, waiting to see if she would pull through after her own suicide attempt. It was ironic that her attempted suicide had pulled Zachary away from his own contemplations. Without knowing it, she had saved his life.

Zachary went to the bathroom and opened the medicine cabinet. While he tried to keep things in his life neat and orderly to combat his distractibility and anxiety, the medicine cabinet was one area that he could never seem to tame. Maybe because he was so often at the end of his rope when he finally decided to take something, the bottles never got put away in proper order.

He started to turn each pill bottle around to read the prescription label and see how many pills he had left. His doctors thought it best not to dispense too many pills at one time, to try to discourage an overdose, but the different prescriptions could still be combined.

Zachary's hand brushed against something on the back of the mirrored door that hadn't been there before. He opened it farther and looked at the index card taped to the inside of the door. At the top of the card was the stern instruction "Call somebody!" And on each line was a name and number. Emergency hotline. His therapist. Bridget, Kenzie, and Bowman. Mr. Peterson. Hospital.

There was a lump in his throat. The printing, he knew, was Kenzie's. She must have put it there the last time they had gotten together, and he hadn't even noticed.

He closed the medicine cabinet. It snicked softly into place against the magnetic latch. Zachary went back out to the living room and picked up his phone. He launched the phone app and tapped on Kenzie's name.

"Zachary." Kenzie was mid-yawn as she said his name. "How's it going?"

"Can you come over?"

Her yawn cut off in a tiny squeak. "What?"

"Could you come over. Now."

"It's kind of late."

"I know. If it's too late for you… I can call someone else."

"Wait." She no longer sounded sleepy. "Are you saying you need help? Are you having a bad night?"

"I was just in the medicine cabinet… counting pills."

She swore. "You're having suicidal thoughts?"

"I just can't… shut it all off."

"I'll be right over. Do you need me to stay on the line with you?"

"No. I'll be okay for that long."

"Are you sure? Don't play the macho card here. I'm not going to get there and find out that you couldn't wait?"

"I won't do anything. I'm sitting on the couch. I'm going to stay here, right where I am, until you get here."

"Okay. I'll be right over. Hang in there."

Zachary was true to his word and sat there on the couch, browsing again through the options on the TV, trying a game of solitaire on his phone, and staring out the window at the lights of the city, streetlights mixed with traffic lights and multicolored

Christmas lights. No matter what he did, Christmas would keep coming every year, plunging him into the unwanted memories.

Kenzie knocked at the door, calling out his name right away, as if afraid he wouldn't be there anymore. But he had told her he would be. He got up and went to the door to unlock it. She looked at him, relief flooding her features. She wrapped her arms around him and pulled herself tightly against him. He squeezed her gently, but she didn't release him. She kissed him urgently, and Zachary wriggled out of her grasp, overwhelmed.

"I'm sorry," Kenzie apologized. "I'm just so relieved to see… that you're okay."

"I know. I don't mind." Zachary's ears got hot. "I just… we're in the doorway… and I can't breathe…"

Kenzie gave a flustered laugh. She stepped the rest of the way into the apartment and shut and locked the door behind her.

"Yeah. Well. Let's go sit down. Do you want to sit down? Or should we… go somewhere?"

Zachary made a gesture toward the living room and the couch. "Yeah, come in."

Kenzie put her hand on his arm as they moved into the room, comforting him or reassuring herself that he was really there and was still okay. When they sat down, he noticed she sat closer to him than was usual.

"Should we go somewhere?" she asked again. "Do you want me to take you to the emergency room? What can I do to help you?"

"No. I don't want to go out." Especially not if he had to go past the Christmas display in the lobby. And whatever decorations they had at the hospital, though emergency room decorations were usually pretty sparse. Going to the emergency room would mean sitting and waiting for hours on end, just to have some young intern advise him that he should have his doctor do a thorough med review and send him home with a brochure on available services. Or if he wanted, he could admit himself for an evaluation, and he would be there for at least three days, taking him into the black hole of Christmas Eve.

"You want to just talk?"

"I don't know." Zachary rubbed his temples, his head pounding. He wasn't sure how long it had been since had had slept more than a couple of hours.

Kenzie studied him, her expression earnest and concerned. They were both turned toward each other on the couch. She put her hand on his knee. "Did you take anything before I came here?"

"No."

"Are you sure? You don't look good. If you did take something, you need to tell me, so we can deal with it."

"No. I was thinking about it… but I saw your note… and I called."

"I'm glad you did. And you haven't hurt yourself?" her eyes searched his face. "When we were talking about Richard Harding cutting, I got the feeling…"

"No." Zachary shook his head. "I didn't. I just called you."

"Do you want to talk about the case? You haven't told me any details of what you discovered in New Hampshire."

Zachary's thoughts were scattered. He gave her a disjointed account of the people he had interviewed. She was more interested in his description of what he had found on Ashley's phone and computer.

"So this stalker had been spying on them? Watching them, listening in on conversations?"

"Looks like it. I passed the details on to Campbell. The more data they have, from Harding's and my emails, the phone number that possibly sent the trojan to Ashley, and any numbers that repeat in the call and text logs… the better the chances that they'll actually be able to find who did this."

Kenzie nodded slowly. Her brows were down and Zachary wondered if the words were coming out differently from what he had composed in his head. Sometimes they did.

"Your emails?" Kenzie asked.

"What?"

"You had emails with this cyberstalker as well? Did he answer you, or…?"

Zachary tried to sort through his memories. He had told Mr. Peterson about the emails when he'd been so shocked by the picture of his family. He had told Campbell about them in case they had been from Harding's stalker instead of Tyrrell. He couldn't remember whether he had told Bridget or whether she only knew about the initial letter. He apparently had not told Kenzie.

He cleared his throat. "I've been getting emails like Harding was. I thought… that they were from my brother. Tyrrell. But it's possible they came from Harding's stalker."

Her eyes got wide. "Why didn't you tell me about that before?"

"I thought they were from Tyrrell… until recently."

"How would Harding's stalker get your email address? How would he even know you were on the case?"

Up until then, Zachary had been puzzled by that point. But knowing the stalker had the ability to monitor Ashley's phone, the answer was obvious. He'd been able to hear their conversations. He knew that Ashley had hired Zachary. A two-second search on the internet was all it would take to find his email address.

"He could hear anything that happened in earshot of Ashley's phone. We don't know when he was listening and when he wasn't. From the arrival times of the emails he sends, he's busy during the day, but when we initially met, it was for supper, in the evening."

"So what was in these emails? How bad are they?"

Zachary swallowed. He couldn't repeat out loud the things that the anonymous emailer had sent to him. He picked up his phone from the side table and went into his email app. He tapped a couple of times to find one of the more recent emails.

Nobody wants you after the horrible things you've done. Why don't you just kill yourself?

Kenzie took it when he handed it to her and only took a couple of seconds to read it. She swore under her breath.

"Oh, this is just what you need right now. Is that why you're having such trouble tonight? Because of this pile of crap?"

The corner of Zachary's mouth twitched at her words. Even in the dark place he was in, she could still almost bring a smile to his face.

"I probably would be anyway… but it doesn't help. I can't get his words out of my mind. And they keep coming…" He should have set up a filter like Devon had. Permanently delete the messages before he ever saw them. But even knowing they might have come from Harding's stalker instead of Tyrrell, he couldn't bring himself to do that. He needed to read them. He needed to be sure. If they were Tyrrell's words, he couldn't just discount them. He needed to hear them even if they hurt.

Kenzie shook her head. "It's horrible. You know it's not true, don't you? People do care about you. People would be hurt if something happened to you, especially if you harmed yourself. You haven't been as efficient about avoiding *complications* as you would like to be."

I just like things to be uncomplicated. He had admitted to her that he tried to avoid letting anyone get too involved in his life because he didn't want to leave anyone behind to mourn him if he did someday take the path from which he could never return. He had broken that rule with Bridget. He had tried to keep friends like Kenzie and Bowman from getting too close. But they had become a part of his life. Complications.

"I'm sorry. That was a thoughtless thing to say." He shrugged uncomfortably. "Poor impulse control gets the better of me…"

"But it was the truth."

"Part of the truth."

"Do I want to hear the other part?"

Zachary swallowed. He wasn't able to look her in the eye, staring down at his hands instead. "Yeah… the other part is… I need you."

There was only silence in return. Zachary shifted uncomfortably, looking around for something else to focus on or to keep his hands busy. Kenzie took his hands in hers.

"Life is complicated."

"Yeah," he agreed. "It definitely is."

She moved in closer, until she was snuggled up against him. Her body felt good against his. He tried to store that feeling away, to take a snapshot of it to remember during the lonely nights. She moved in and kissed him, not so desperate and insistent this time. He wasn't sure how much time passed while they sat there on the couch, wrapped up in each other, exploring a new level of intimacy. But Zachary's exhausted body and agitated brain couldn't advance any further. Eventually, Kenzie withdrew. She gazed at him.

"You look like a zombie."

"It's been… a while since I've slept."

"Then let's get you to bed."

She got to her feet. Zachary didn't rise immediately. His arms and legs felt leaden. He knew he should jump at the suggestion, but he was incapable of jumping at anything, physically or emotionally. Kenzie reached down and took his hand, giving him a little tug. Zachary rose to his feet slowly and, at her insistence, he dragged himself to the bedroom. He looked at the bed, his stomach writhing with guilt and dread.

"I'm sorry," he said. "But some of the meds… and the way I feel… I don't think I can…"

"Shush." She gave him a little push. "You need sleep. I promise I won't take advantage of you."

Zachary felt removed from the situation, watching from a safe distance. Kenzie encouraged him to get comfortable and lie down. She kicked off her shoes and peeled off her socks. After shutting off the lights, she lay down behind him, wrapping her arms around him and holding him as he had held Tyrrell or one of the other children when they'd had a nightmare or were frightened by the yelling and fighting, helping them to calm down and feel safe enough to sleep. He could feel her warm breath on his neck. He tried to match his breath to hers, slow and deep instead of the quick, shallow breaths his anxiety-tightened diaphragm produced.

"Do you need to take something?" Kenzie asked after a while, obviously able to tell that he was still awake, still too rigid and agitated to convince his brain it was time for sleep.

"Yeah." He tensed to get up to go to the medicine cabinet, but Kenzie pressed his shoulder down.

"Stay put. Let me get it. What do you want?"

"Xanax and Ambien."

"Both?"

"If I'm going to get to sleep."

"Okay. Stay here, I'll be right back."

She brought him the pills and a glass of cold water. Zachary propped himself up on his elbow to wash them down, then lay down again in the warm pocket his body had created. Kenzie put the cup away and climbed into bed, again snuggling up behind him and putting comforting arms around him.

"Just relax," she whispered. "It doesn't matter whether you really sleep. Just let your body and brain rest for a few hours."

He tried to do as he was told, and some time in the early

hours of the morning, his consciousness released its hold and he dropped off to sleep.

***

Zachary was groggy and disoriented on waking, conscious thoughts coming to him slowly as his brain sorted itself out. He was alive. He had been asleep and had awakened. He must have taken something to sleep or he wouldn't have such a heavy, groggy feeling.

He shifted his position and rubbed his eyes. It was light out. Not a filmy dawn light, but the full light of day, well into the morning. The movement he made was echoed by another body, and a hand landed on his shoulder, molding to it.

Bridget?

"Hey, how are you doing?"

Kenzie. Zachary was still trying to catch up to the present. He lay still, feeling her breathing and trying to recall all that had happened. He'd been feeling dangerously low. He'd called Kenzie. She'd spent the night watching over him and making sure he slept.

"Kenzie?"

"Yes, Zachary?" her tone was slightly mocking, good-humored.

"Nothing. Just… thanks."

"Of course." Her hand left his shoulder and she turned and stretched. "You want coffee?"

"Sure."

She got out of bed. He listened to the whisper of her bare feet over the floor. It was nice to have someone else there. It felt like she belonged there. She opened and closed cupboards in the kitchen. She knew where everything was and moved around confidently. Before long, he could smell coffee brewing. He rubbed his eyes. They didn't ache as much as they had, and were not scratchy and gritty like they were after a long sleepless night. He knew he wouldn't be caught up on sleep after just a few hours, but even just part of one night helped. His brain wasn't chattering quite so frantically and the anxiety was a notch lower than it had been.

Kenzie returned to the bedroom and handed him a cup of coffee. She sat on the edge of the bed. They both sipped, knowing the coffee was going to be too hot, but savoring the ritual anyway, each watching the other to make sure they were comfortable.

"You think you can get in to see your doctor today?" Kenzie asked.

Zachary hesitated. "I don't really know if…"

"You should talk to him about seasonal shifts. Have a plan for this. Take something stronger in anticipation to see if you can head it off. Have a safety plan. Maybe arrange for inpatient treatment ahead of time." She raised her eyebrows at him. "For next year. It's too late this year to bother raising your doses; by the time your blood levels are up, you'll be past the crisis. But you need to see him, to make sure you're safe for the next few days. I know you'd rather stay home, but if a professional says it's not safe…"

"He'll say I'm the best judge."

"Fine. But I want him to know about this."

Zachary shrugged.

"And your therapist? You've been seeing him? He knows about Christmas and then this email harassment?"

Zachary took another sip of his coffee, hiding his face from her. "Um… I've been busy with this case… I haven't seen him for a while."

She raised an eyebrow. Zachary cleared his throat and looked away uncomfortably.

"You know that when you are having issues, you should be seeing him more often, not skipping sessions."

Zachary nodded.

"So you need to see him too."

"I don't know if I can get appointments for today. They'll already be booked up or off for the holidays. I usually have to schedule at least a couple of weeks out…"

"Call and see."

"I…"

"You need to. I want to make sure you're taken care of properly. I'm glad that you called me last night. I don't want you stepping in front of a bus or something next time."

Zachary frowned.

"Zachary…" Kenzie said insistently.

"I wouldn't do that."

"That's what you say, but if you're not well and you had the impulse…"

Zachary didn't say anything, his mind working through possibilities, fitting pieces of the puzzle together. Kenzie cocked her head to the side.

"What's going on in there?"

"Richard Harding."

"Harding? What about him…?"

"Ashley said it couldn't be a coincidence that Harding was killed in a hit and run after what he had done. She was right. It wasn't."

Kenzie's eyes sparkled. "You figured it out?"

"It wasn't homicide. It was suicide."

F or a minute, Kenzie was quiet, considering this. She nodded slowly.

"He was depressed, he was being stalked and harassed. He felt guilty about what he had done."

"We kept wondering what he was doing out there on the road. If he had seen or heard something. The fact that it was a hit and run. Why he would be outside wearing dark clothing, no lights or anything reflective. Why he wasn't walking on the left side of the road, where he'd be able to see oncoming vehicles. It explains all of that. It was suicide by truck. He was walking in the dark, waiting for a vehicle to come along. And then he stepped in front of it."

"And that's why the driver didn't see him ahead of time," Kenzie agreed. "He didn't want to be seen. It didn't just happen to clip him. It didn't steer into him. He waited until the last minute and jumped in front of it."

Zachary was sure they were right. Everything fit. There hadn't been a note, but that wasn't unusual. A lot of suicides never left notes. Richard Harding had wanted out. He'd tried changing his name and moving away, but his troubles followed him. He'd been stalked relentlessly, and Zachary knew what kind of feelings those poisonous words stirred up. The stalker piled on the guilt and suggested suicide as the way out. After enough repetition, Harding couldn't get it out of his mind. It wormed its way down, burrowing into his brain, until he couldn't think of any other way to relieve the guilt and pain.

Kenzie touched his knee, but didn't say anything. Zachary swallowed and nodded. He put his hand over hers briefly. He looked around for his phone. "I should call Campbell."

"I think it's still out in the living room. Hang on."

When she came back and handed it to Zachary, she had a grin on her face. The phone was ringing, and Campbell's name was on the screen. Zachary swiped it on.

"Hey, I was just going to call you."

"You must be psychic."

"Richard Harding's death wasn't an accident. Ashley was right."

"Are you sure?" Campbell's voice was surprised. "You found a connection?"

"Not to Donaldson. It was suicide. He was depressed. He stepped in front of the truck on purpose."

Campbell hummed for a moment, thinking about it. "It fits, but there isn't a way to prove it."

"It's circumstantial," Zachary agreed. "But…"

"It's not going anywhere. If it was suicide, there's nothing more we can do on *that* front."

Zachary heard the implied "but."

"What did you find out?"

"Looks like we—meaning the feds—have a lead on the stalker's phone. It was a throwaway purchased at a shop in New Hampshire, like you figured. Near the university."

Jonathan Roper.

"It's her boyfriend. Hope Creedy's secret boyfriend. Got to be."

"The distribution pattern is suggestive of a school schedule."

"He would have been meeting with students the rest of the time. He's young, a technology native, probably knows his way around computers. I'm sure there are plenty of people at the university who could help him out if he needed any advice. Maybe even some of the kids he mentored."

"It will take a while for the feds to gather enough evidence to get a warrant on the guy for computer fraud and cyberstalking. They've got to have evidence that he was the one who bought the phone and sent the spyware, and that he was the one who sent the harassing messages."

"What if he happened to confess to a private citizen who happened to record him?"

Campbell chuckled. "That might help law enforcement along a little, if it's legally recorded. You don't know any private citizens who might happen to have a chat with him, do you?"

"I might."

Zachary and Kenzie made the trip back to New Hampshire together. Kenzie seemed to be concerned Zachary might do something impulsive if left to himself, and he couldn't really argue her logic. As he got closer to D-day, he grew more reckless, less likely to take precautions for his own safety. He might not intentionally step in front of a truck as Harding had done, but he might do something less overt, tempting fate, telling himself that if he was meant to die, it would happen anyway.

Kenzie had called Dr. Wiltshire to tell him she was taking a couple of days extra for her holiday, not explaining that it was to babysit Zachary, and promised to be back to work after Christmas to help with the influx of holiday homicides.

Though Kenzie loved to drive her car out on the highway, Zachary insisted on driving his own, needing to be the one in control of the ton of metal hurtling down that interstate.

"We need something less identifiable," he told her. "Yours stands out too much."

"You're just going to go see this guy in his office, aren't you? He's never going to see what we're driving."

"I can't predict what is going to happen. We should take precautions. And yours is too cold. Mine holds the heat better."

Kenzie shrugged irritably and gave in. So Zachary drove, the stereo playing summer songs from his phone rather than the holiday songs on all the radio stations, Zachary pretending that it wasn't snowy and almost Christmas outside the toasty-warm car. Kenzie kept him distracted with interesting stories from the morgue when he wasn't too zoned out to hear them.

They drove directly to the university. Zachary remembered where Roper's office was. He tried out different scripts in his head, trying to determine what approach was most likely to get a confession out of Roper. He didn't have much time to plan, but sometimes the unplanned, reaction-driven conversations were the most effective.

"You really think he'll confess to you?" Kenzie asked.

"With a little nudging… I think so. I didn't have anything to challenge him with before. This time, I have the phone that he bought and I can use the emails against him."

"You can't prove he was the one who sent the emails or bought the phone."

"That doesn't mean I can't tell him I have proof."

They reached Roper's office door.

"You stay here," Zachary advised. "I don't know how long I'll be… but I think he's more likely to confess if it's just me."

He rapped sharply on Roper's door, reached for the handle, and stepped forward smack into the door when the handle didn't turn.

Kenzie snickered. Zachary tried the handle again, as if he might have been wrong the first time and just not turned it hard enough or in the right direction. He turned and looked at Kenzie.

"Locked?" she inquired sweetly.

Zachary knocked a few times on the door, loudly, hoping that Roper was just inside with a student and would open the door to see what the racket was. But everything was quiet. No one came to the door.

"Maybe he's gone for the holidays?" Kenzie suggested.

"Maybe."

There was no schedule or sign up on Roper's door to indicate where he had gone or when he would be back.

With a sigh, Zachary headed back toward the car. Down the hall, a young woman was walking the other direction. She gave Zachary a warm smile.

"Are you looking for Professor Devon?"

Professor Devon. Zachary blinked at her, thrown for a loop. *Professor* Devon? He had done background on each of the people who he interviewed in connection with Hope's death, but he hadn't remembered Devon Masters being identified as a teacher.

He remembered Devon's words when he and Zachary had sat down at the coffee shop. "I like to watch my students." Not *the* students, but *my* students. He was a university professor. But Zachary's initial background had listed Devon as a lawyer. That was why it was important to verify everything.

"I saw you at the coffee shop with him," the young woman confessed. "I memorized your face."

Zachary forced his head to bob up and down in a nod. "Yes, that's right. Could you show me where his office is?"

"Sure. This way."

He followed her through a few turns in the corridor, until they stood in front of a closed door.

Professor Devon Masters, Criminal Investigation.

Posted on his door below the name plate were the class marks for an exam or class. Cyber Investigations.

The girl pointed to one of the top marks. "That's me," she said proudly.

She was a good student, bringing in a ninety-five percent.

"Good job!" Zachary told her. He tried the door handle, but found it locked as well. "Has everyone gone for the holidays?"

"Yeah, pretty much. Just a few of us floating around, getting the last few things done."

"I wonder if he left me a message," Zachary bluffed, taking out his phone as if to check. "I thought he said he would be here." He looked at the number on the door. "Room 232. That's just what he said, isn't it?" he asked Kenzie.

She nodded helpfully. "Yes, 232."

"Huh."

The student hovered, wanting to help, but not sure what she could do.

"He didn't say where he was going, did he?" Zachary prompted. "He didn't mention to you…?"

"No. I saw him at his car. He was loading some boxes into it. But he didn't say where he was off to."

Zachary tapped at his phone. Bluffing, he brought his email up and studied it as if looking for Devon's name among the senders.

His eyes were drawn to the subject of one of the bolded, unread messages.

You're too late, detective.

The email address it had come from was a random string of alphanumeric characters like the ones he had been getting from the cyberstalker.

Kenzie looked down at Zachary's phone when she saw his expression. "Too late for what?"

Zachary's hands started to shake. The criminology student looked at him, concerned.

"Is there something wrong? What is it?"

"Do you have any idea how I can get in touch with Professor Devon?"

"I have his phone number and email address…" she offered tentatively. Of course she would have. He would give all of his students his phone number and email so that they could get in contact with him when they had questions or concerns. When they needed to submit assignments.

While she pulled out her phone to look up the information, Zachary tapped the email message to open it, dread forming a tight knot in his stomach. Kenzie peered over his shoulder.

For the crime of accessory after the fact and harboring a fugitive.

There was a picture below the words. It was a high-resolution image that took a minute to load, signals blocked by all of the brick and concrete in the university walls. Zachary saw a pixelated image to start with, a couple of faces close together, before they resolved into something recognizable. Lorne Peterson and Pat, with an X through Mr. Peterson's face.

Zachary swore. "Back to the car," he told Kenzie urgently.

"Wait," the student stopped them as they turned to hurry back to the parking lot. "Don't you want his number?"

Zachary fumbled with his phone to open up the contact app to add the details. He had to erase and re-key the information again several times before getting it right.

"Thank you. This is really helpful," he told her quickly, and he and Kenzie raced to get back to the car.

Zachary tried to dial and run at the same time. He was sure it would go through to voicemail, but in a moment, he heard a familiar voice.

"Don't tell me you got it already?" Campbell's cheerful voice inquired.

"No. It's not Roper, it's Devon Master. He's in the wind. I have a phone number. You need to get the feds to find him. He's... he's threatened my family."

"What?"

"I'll get Kenzie to forward you the email. But here's the number." Zachary read it out. His voice was cracking. "You can't let him hurt them."

They raced for the car. Zachary's gait was awkward. His heart was pounding hard and he was out of breath. But he pushed through, made it back to the car and jumped in. Zachary passed the phone to Kenzie when they were both in. Kenzie said a few more words to Campbell and promised to send him the email, then hung up.

"Seatbelt," Zachary told her as he pulled his across his body and snapped the buckle into place, getting the car started out almost out of the stall by the time he was done.

"I will," Kenzie said irritably, "let me just forward this first."

"No. We're going to be moving fast."

Kenzie looked at him, and seeing his face, didn't argue any further but put the phone down for a second to get her seatbelt on. Zachary hit the gas. She hung on to the door for a moment as he accelerated and rocketed around a corner.

"Sheesh! Where did you learn to drive like that?"

"This is nothing. Wait until we get to the highway."

Kenzie shook her head. She tried to hold the phone steady in front of her face while she forwarded all of the pertinent information on to Campbell.

"Where are we going?"

"To make sure they're safe."

"But Devon's ahead of you. Maybe by an hour or two."

"Or maybe not. I don't plan on him being ahead of me by the time we get there."

He made sure the Bluetooth was connected and told the in-car system to dial Lorne Peterson. It went to voicemail.

"Lorne. It's Zachary. Call me back right away. It's urgent."

He tried calling Pat, but with the same results.

"Give those numbers to Campbell. Have them located too. We need to know where they are. Devon might already have them." His heart pounded so hard he felt like he was going to have a heart attack. Surely Devon wouldn't hurt an innocent person. He pressed the gas pedal down farther, swerving around slower-moving vehicles and getting angry honks in response.

"You don't think they're at home? They might just be occupied."

"They'd answer. Mr. Peterson knows… about Christmas. He wouldn't ignore a call from me this time of year."

"Okay." Kenzie complied with his order, calling Campbell back again to give him the two numbers to track. Zachary couldn't hear what Campbell was saying back to Kenzie, but she cut her eyes toward Zachary, and said, "We're on our way there making due haste… let me know as soon as you locate them, and we'll adjust our course if they're somewhere else." She held on to the door as they careened down the exit ramp to the interstate. "You're going to get pulled over for speeding, Zach!"

"They'll have to catch me first."

But he took her point. Getting stopped by the police was the last thing he needed. It would take time for Campbell to get what he needed from the FBI. Zachary didn't know how long it would take for them to figure out where Devon and Mr. Peterson and Pat were. He eased his foot off of the gas and let the car slow to the speed of traffic. As usual, the flow of traffic was somewhat over the speed limit, but not fast enough to soothe his nerves. He pressed the gas again, until he was going just fast enough to overtake the cars in front of him and pass them, but not fast enough for anyone to take notice and call 9-1-1 with reports of some crazy driver speeding down the highway at a breakneck pace. Kenzie settled back into her seat, blowing her breath out through pursed lips, like a whistle.

"You don't think he'd really do anything to Lorne, do you? He didn't kill Harding, just sent him messages. I think that words are his only weapon. He's trying to drive you crazy with worry, but he wouldn't actually do anything."

Zachary bit the inside of his cheek. He couldn't point to anything that suggested that Devon was a violent person. He wasn't the one who had been driving the night Hope was killed. He hadn't, as far as they knew, done anything physically violent toward Harding. He hadn't been the truck driver and hadn't hired Donaldson to do his dirty work.

There was nothing wrong with Kenzie's logic. Devon was a university professor. Not a killer. He could have been going home for the holidays, like everyone else. His taunt to Zachary could have just been hot air, intended to goad Zachary into doing something stupid like getting into a crash on the interstate or humiliating himself in front of someone he loved. Just a bluff to see how far he could push Zachary.

"I don't know. There's no way to know, so I have to assume it's true."

"I agree," Kenzie said, "I know you have to do something; I'm just saying, he probably won't actually do anything. We probably don't really have to worry."

Zachary nodded. She might be able to choose not to be worried, but he certainly couldn't. His heart was pounding as hard as if Devon were holding a knife to Mr. Peterson's throat. What if he got to their house and found them dead? What if Zachary were responsible for destroying the one long-term relationship he had managed to maintain?

He tasted blood and didn't care, switching to chewing the cheek on the other side instead. He stayed focused on the road, carefully snaking his way through the traffic, doing the best he could to get to his friends before anything could happen to them.

His phone rang. Kenzie answered it rather than letting him take it on Bluetooth, probably figuring he had enough to concentrate on with his driving. She spoke few words, mostly listening to what Campbell had to report, then hung up.

"What did he find out?" Zachary asked, when Kenzie sat there without a word to him.

"They're still working on it."

He navigated around a slower-moving SUV. "They couldn't get a location?"

"Apparently, his phone is turned off. So they only have his call history to go by, and his most recent calls were made from the university."

"We already know he's not there. What about Mr. Peterson? Where is he?"

"Campbell is still trying to talk them into tracking his phone.

They're being cautious, not convinced there is any real danger to Lorne and Pat."

"Can't they track them anyway? Just to make sure they're safe?"

Kenzie shook her head. "Apparently not. Privacy concerns. Campbell's working on it. I think he'll convince them sooner or later. He just hasn't yet."

Zachary thumped the steering wheel with the heel of his hand, frustrated.

Kenzie didn't say anything else, but she took a sidelong look at him that communicated she was holding something back. Zachary gripped the steering wheel, breathing slowly.

"What else?"

She didn't answer.

"Kenzie. What else did he say?"

"I don't think I should get you any more upset while you're driving. You have enough to focus on."

"Holding something back is going to distract me more than telling me what it is. I need to know everything Campbell found out."

"Zachary…"

"Tell me."

Kenzie rested her head back against the headrest, giving in. "He has a concealed carry permit."

Zachary felt sick. It took all of his willpower not to stamp the gas pedal to the floor. It would do Mr. Peterson no good if he ended up having an accident or getting pulled over because he was driving recklessly. Kenzie was watching him, waiting for him to explode or melt down. Eventually, she looked away. Neither of them said anything about what it meant. So much for Kenzie's evaluation that Devon wouldn't do anything violent. Mr. Peterson didn't carry a gun. Zachary didn't carry a gun. They were going to rush into a confrontation where the only one with a gun would be Devon. Zachary had no idea how they were going to handle it.

Campbell would make sure they had police and FBI backup as

soon as they located Lorne and Pat. Now that they knew Devon was likely to be armed, they wouldn't fool around.

But that wasn't true, because even knowing that Devon had a permit for a concealed weapon, they were still reluctant to track the phones of two citizens who might be in danger.

With anxiety and anger burning a hole in his stomach, Zachary narrowed his focus to a fine point. He could do only one thing, and that was to get to Lorne.

25

He didn't even hear Kenzie talking on the phone again. He was so narrowly focused on driving, shutting the rest of the world out, that it took Kenzie's persistent nudging and calling him to get his attention.

Zachary startled and glanced over at her. "What? What is it?"

"They tracked Lorne's and Pat's phones. They're okay, Zachary, they're just not at home."

He found he could barely breathe for a minute or two, like he'd been kicked in the gut and had the wind knocked out of him. He rubbed his eyes.

"Really? You're sure?"

"They're at some kind of spa. Probably one of these places where they have a rule about leaving their phones in their lockers so that they can relax properly."

"Someone talked to them?"

"No, just located the phones. If they're not at home, they're not in danger, Zachary. We'll just keep calling them, and we'll warn them when they answer. We'll tell them not to go home until Devon is found."

"We have to go there. Can't the FBI send someone just in case?"

"There's no danger. They won't waste the manpower."

"What about Campbell? He believes me, doesn't he? This guy's got a gun."

"But Devon doesn't know where Pat and Lorne are. They're safe where they are."

Zachary glanced over at Kenzie. She really believed it. She wasn't just trying to calm his anxiety, she truly believed they were safe.

"Didn't you see the paper on his door? Cyber Investigations. You know what that is, don't you?"

She sighed in exasperation. "Yes, of course I do. Computer research. Online and all that."

"And using other technology. Like the spyware on Ashley's phone and computer."

"Right."

"Don't you think he could tell exactly where Ashley's phone was once he had the spyware on it?"

Kenzie's irritation changed into uncertainty. She frowned. "Well… I suppose. But how would he have gotten something onto Lorne's or Pat's phone?"

"The same way as he got it onto Ashley's. Send them something that looks legitimate and wait for them to open it."

"But how would he even know their phone number or email address to send it to them?"

"How did he know Ashley's?"

Kenzie was stumped. She looked for a way to argue his logic.

"Did you get the name and address of the spa?"

"I got the name. Let me look it up."

She used his phone to look up the address and directions. "There's an exit in a couple of miles. We're about half an hour away."

That was better than Zachary had hoped. The spa was closer than Mr. Peterson's house, instead of farther away. For once, things were working in his favor.

"Can Campbell send someone? Just in case?"

"It's out of his jurisdiction."

Of course it was. Zachary knew that. "And he can't talk to the local police department? Or get the FBI to send someone?"

Kenzie bit her lip. "I'll see… but don't count on it."

She wiggled her own phone out of her pocket instead of using Zachary's, which still had the GPS program running to direct him to the spa. Zachary listened to the half-conversation, Kenzie presenting his arguments and pushing for them to please send someone, anyone, who had some authority and could back them up.

When she hung up, she wiped her arm across her forehead. Zachary turned the car heater down, though he knew that wasn't why she was sweating.

"Well…?"

"He's going to make some calls, see what he can do."

"He's never going to get someone out there in time."

Kenzie shook her head. "Probably not. But hopefully, he doesn't need to. We're assuming an awful lot. That it was Devon and not the boyfriend. That he would actually approach Lorne. That he would do him any harm. We don't have any proof, just conjecture."

"We'll have proof when we see him."

"He won't be there."

"Then why are you nervous?"

She looked like she was going to try to argue that she wasn't nervous, then abandoned that plan. "Okay. I'm nervous because of the possibility. I'm nervous because you are so sure. But I don't really *think* he'll be there."

Zachary nodded and followed the instructions of his phone GPS. It wasn't smart, walking in there unarmed against a possibly armed threat. Maybe there would be security guards who could help. Maybe an off-duty police officer there with his wife for a little pre-Christmas cleanse. A spa just wasn't the sort of place that a person took a gun to.

"It will be okay," Kenzie assured Zachary as they pulled into the parking lot and scanned around it for any sign of disruption or trouble. It was, Zachary thought, more to reassure herself than him. He already knew it wasn't going to be okay. Things didn't turn out okay in his life. He ended up burning down houses, getting electrocuted, or putting friends in danger.

There was no sign of trouble. If Devon was there, he hadn't driven his car up onto the sidewalk or left it parked in a driving lane. If he was there, he had parked it neatly in its slot and walked in, acting as if nothing was wrong.

Zachary also parked his car, though he picked a handicapped parking slot right in front of the building. He knew it was wrong, but if Pat's and Lorne's lives hung in the balance, he wasn't going to waste time parking farther away in a legitimate space. He got out of the car, wiping his hands on his pants. The cold air was a shock, but a welcome one. It sharpened his senses and helped to wake him up. His adrenaline had been running too long to be effective anymore. It had sapped his energy while sitting in the car, unable to use it constructively.

They walked into a warm, humid lobby that was full of light, green plants, and trickling waterfalls. A complete change from the frigid weather outside. Zachary took a second to acclimatize himself, looking around to be sure that Devon was nowhere to be seen, and then walked up to the smiling, fresh-faced blond woman at the reception desk.

"Hi," he forced a smile that he hoped was at least a shade as warm as hers. "I'm supposed to be meeting my friends here. I don't know if they'll be finished yet. Lorne Peterson?"

"Oh, yes." She gave him another smile, as if she had been expecting him. "Let me just see…"

She tapped the keys of her computer. Zachary looked around, taking a few calming breaths. It was a peaceful, relaxing place. No indication of any threat. Maybe he could relax.

"It looks like they should be finished with their treatments," the receptionist told him. "So they're probably at the juice bar." She pointed a tapered index finger to a set of glass doors. "Just through there, and follow the blue signs."

Zachary looked at Kenzie. She smiled back, clearly comforted by their surroundings. But Zachary didn't like it. The place was wide open. Anyone could walk in. There was no security, no attempt made to screen visitors.

"Let's go." He clutched at Kenzie's elbow and walked more quickly than was comfortable. Since the car accident of a year ago, his physiotherapist had mostly focused on walking, but walking faster than his normal pace felt awkward and out of sync. He scanned the signs as they moved through the broad, brightly-lit halls with inspiring words painted on them and gorgeous landscapes on display.

"Nice place," Kenzie commented, as if they were there on a tour.

"Yeah."

They eventually made it to the juice bar. Spacious and well-lit, just like the rest of the facility. Zachary bypassed the service counter and looked around at the tables for his former foster father. They were almost safe. They were almost to the end of the journey.

With relief, he saw Lorne and Pat sitting at a table by the patio. They were partially blocked from view by a waiter with his back to them. Zachary hurried across the room toward them. The waiter turned slightly and Zachary saw his profile.

It was Devon.

26

Zachary swore. His foot slipped on the tiled floor, and the resulting lurch as he caught his balance attracted the attention of Mr. Peterson. When he focused on Zachary coming across the room toward them, Pat and Devon both followed his gaze.

"You can stop right there," Devon warned.

Zachary did. Devon stood with one hand in the large pocket of the apron he was wearing. He must have taken it off of a hook or a shelf on his arrival in order to blend in while he watched for Mr. Peterson and Pat. It was impossible to tell whether there was anything in the apron pocket, or whether the threat was only implied.

"Zachary?" Mr. Peterson said, "What's going on?"

Zachary bit his lip. Keeping his eyes on the three of them, he tried to scope out the room peripherally. There were too many people there, coming and going. But he hadn't seen any kind of security staff. No one appeared to be aware that anything untoward was going on. Would Devon dare to do something around so many other people? There was a big difference between sending someone bullying emails from an anonymous address and overtly committing violence in full view of a dozen people.

"Kenzie," Zachary murmured, very low so that only she would be able to hear him, trying not to move his lips as he spoke. "Get cops here *now*."

She gave no sign of having heard him, fiddling with her phone and then turning around to look at the densely written columns of ingredients over the juice bar.

"This is a pretty cool place," she said. "Really relaxing atmosphere. We should come back here, you know? I should ask them about packages. You should ask Pat and Lorne which package they got."

He wasn't sure whether she really didn't understand the danger they were in, or was just acting for Devon's sake. But he couldn't repeat the instruction and draw attention to it. He kept his gaze trained on Devon.

"I don't understand why you're doing this. Explain to me… why you are even here. Mr. Peterson never did anything wrong."

"You're the one who needs to be punished. You're the one who thought he could get away with it without having to pay the piper," Devon growled.

"Get away with what? I'm not the one who killed Hope."

"Not that. This isn't about Hope. This is about you, burning down the house, putting all of those people in danger. They could have all died in the house because you were so stupid and reckless. Society has to weed out people like you. You shouldn't be allowed to hurt other people with your stupidity."

Zachary resisted the flashbacks. He had to stay present to help Mr. Peterson. He couldn't let Devon and the memories sweep him away.

"What does that have to do with Mr. Peterson? If you want to punish me for what I did, then punish me. Not him. I didn't even meet him until after that."

"He took you in. Instead of letting you rot in some institution somewhere, he was an accessory. He sheltered you and kept you from having to pay for what you had done."

Mr. Peterson sat there with his mouth open, shock on his features.

Devon sneered at him. "People who protect murderers and arsonists should be thrown in prison themselves. They should have to pay the price!"

Mr. Peterson closed his mouth, still staring at Devon. "Zachary wasn't a murderer or arsonist," he finally said. His voice was quiet and even, his most soothing, calming voice. Used to calm dozens of foster kids over the years. Used to calm Zachary himself during the weeks he had lived there and when he had returned for help over the years as a troubled child, panicked teen, and confused adult, always trying to escape a past he could never forget. "He was a scared child in need of a home. I was sorry he wasn't able to stay with us for longer, but he turned out to be more than we were able to handle."

"He should never have been in foster care. Don't you know what he did? He ruined their lives! All of their lives!"

"No. He made a mistake that he's paid for a hundred times over. Are you…" Mr. Peterson looked at Zachary and mouthed the words, asking Zachary rather than Devon, "your brother?"

Zachary gave a tiny shake of his head. He wished he could explain to Mr. Peterson more clearly what was going on, but he wasn't sure what would set Devon off. He needed to understand what was going on in Devon's head, but he couldn't quite wrap his mind around it.

"Are you friends with Zachary? I don't understand how he hurt you."

"People like him ruin lives. They ruin the lives of everyone around them."

"Like Brandon?" Zachary asked. "Is that what you mean? Brandon ruined your life when he hit Hope? He prejudiced people against you and treated you like it was your fault?"

Devon nodded his agreement. "He killed Hope and he messed up our lives forever. He should have just killed himself."

"He did."

"Not until it was too late. He should have done it long before then. People who do things like that should die. Why are they allowed to pollute our population? They should *all* die."

"You can't kill everyone who makes a stupid choice," Mr. Peterson pointed out. "Everyone makes stupid choices at some point."

"It wasn't my fault!" Devon protested, his voice going up a note. "It wasn't Fulton's or Kyle's fault. It was Brandon's. You can't paint us all with the same brush!"

"I didn't say it was your fault." Mr. Peterson considered for a moment. "But maybe you're feeling guilty about it."

The light went on in Zachary's brain and he knew Mr. Peterson had hit the nail on the head.

"Maybe you feel like you should have been punished for what happened," Zachary said. "Maybe you feel like you never had to pay for your mistakes, and it's eaten away at you all of these years. You went into law, hoping to bring criminals to justice, but it didn't make you feel better the way you expected it to, and all you ever saw was your own guilt."

"For what? Because we rode with him? Because we were drinking and he wasn't supposed to? How could we control that?"

"You call a cab," Mr. Peterson said. "You take away his keys. You make sure everyone gets home safely."

"He didn't seem drunk. He only had a couple of beers. He wasn't staggering or slurring. They called it a DUI, but he wasn't drunk. He'd barely had anything."

"You still shouldn't have let your designated driver have anything," Zachary pointed out. "When you saw him drinking, you should have made new plans."

"I didn't remember anything afterward. I don't know if I saw him drinking. I don't remember him drinking." Devon gave a little shake of his head. His eyes were haunted.

"You said that other nights, you had egged him on. Encouraged him to speed or stunt."

"Not *that* night."

"You can't remember. Or was that a lie? Are you just afraid to tell anyone the truth about what really happened that night?"

"Brandon was driving!" Devon's hand moved in his apron pocket. "He's the only one who is responsible for what happened!"

Zachary took a tentative step forward, seeing if he could close the distance between them. "You feel awful about what happened. Whatever it was, you are sorry. You feel the guilt all the time, weighing down on you." Zachary knew what that felt like. "It's there all the time and you just want it to go away. You'd do anything to make it go away."

A nod from Devon. Zachary took a couple more slow steps forward. "You want it to end. You want someone to stop the pain. You think that maybe if you were punished properly, it would go away."

"I wasn't at fault," Devon whined. But Zachary knew better. Criminally liable or not, Devon was still guilty. He had taken that on himself. It wasn't something that any outside force could wipe away.

"You wanted Brandon to pay. You thought that if he had to pay more, you would feel better. Justice would be served."

Devon looked at him, his expression frozen.

"But when Brandon killed himself, you didn't feel better, you felt worse."

"It was his choice. I never touched him. We weren't even in the same state. I'm not responsible for him killing himself."

He had stalked and bullied Brandon relentlessly. Brandon had served his time. He had a new name and a new relationship. He had been on the way to healing and a new life. But Devon had refused to let him off. What Devon had done contributed to Brandon's death, as surely as if he'd put a gun into his hand and then badgered him to use it.

"You felt so guilty over what you had done to Brandon, you needed a new target. You needed someone else you could blame for what you were feeling. You wanted to punish someone else, but you're the one you think needs to be punished."

Zachary was almost within arm's reach of Devon. Devon startled suddenly, jamming his hand deeper into the apron pocket. "Stop it. Stay there. Don't you say another word."

Zachary swallowed. He had almost been there. He had almost reached Devon both physically and emotionally. He looked at Mr. Peterson, not knowing what to do. He couldn't open his mouth again without endangering their lives.

"Have a seat," Mr. Peterson invited. "It's been a long day. Why don't you have a drink?" He nudged his own drink toward Devon. "I haven't even touched it. Pat's always trying to get me to eat healthier, but I'm really just not a wheatgrass kind of guy."

Devon looked at the cup. Zachary wasn't sure he was even seeing it.

"You need to let it go," Lorne continued softly. "You've been holding onto this for too long. Hanging on to pain doesn't help anything. It festers and gets deeper over time. You need to forgive yourself. You and Brandon didn't intend to kill anyone that night. It was a horrible mistake. But hanging on to it all this time hasn't made things better."

Devon put his hands on the back of one of the other chairs at the table, hesitating about whether to pull it out.

"You can forgive yourself and let it go. Just let the guilt and the pain go. You were young and you made a choice that would impact your life forever. You couldn't have known how it was going to turn out."

Zachary eyed Devon's apron and the big pocket he had taken his hand out of. Did he have the gun or not? If Zachary tackled him, was he fast enough and skilled enough to get the gun away from Devon? Without hurting anyone else? The wrong choice could have an impact on both of their lives, just like the fire and Brandon's MVC. Make the wrong choice, and someone in the room could be dead.

"Sit down," Mr. Peterson coaxed. "Come tell me about it."

Devon drew the chair out. Zachary took another step closer while Devon was looking away from him. Devon looked back, but didn't catch Zachary moving. He hesitated for a moment before lowering himself into the chair. In his new position, Zachary could see down into the gaping pocket. He could see the gleam of the pistol inside.

Zachary swallowed, mouth as dry as cotton. He must have made some change in expression that Mr. Peterson caught. He looked at Zachary for a moment, then focused all of his attention on the young man who sat across from him. Elbows on the table, Devon covered his eyes and cradled his head.

"How could anyone forgive me?" he demanded in a choked voice. "I can't forgive myself, how could anyone else? That girl died. I saw her family in court every day. Her parents and her little brother and sister. They had to grow up without her. I knew I was responsible for what happened to her. I had to take some of the responsibility."

"It takes time, but don't you think it will be easier to forgive yourself than it has been to beat up on yourself all of these years?"

It was like Mr. Peterson was speaking to Zachary. They rarely spoken of the fire and Zachary's part in it. Mr. Peterson knew what the social worker had told him before bringing Zachary to them, and little else. But Mr. Peterson knew how guilty Zachary felt. He knew the pain that Zachary carried around with him and how he beat up on himself. Zachary had no idea how to begin to forgive himself. He didn't deserve forgiveness.

There was a buzz in his pocket. Zachary had picked up his

phone and put it back in his pocket as he got out of the car. He stayed still, moving only his eyes to look around. Where was Kenzie? Had she managed to talk the police into getting them some backup? Kenzie was right at the edge of his vision. When his eyes met hers, she made a small motion, tapping her own pocket, then indicating Devon with her eyes.

Zachary curled up the pinky and fourth finger of the hand that Kenzie could see hanging at his side, forming a gun shape with his index and middle finger and thumb.

Her eyebrows went up. *Are you sure?* Zachary gave a nod, just a fraction of an inch.

Kenzie moved silently out of Zachary's vision, too far back for him to see.

"You need help. You need to talk to someone," Mr. Peterson told Devon. "A licensed therapist would be better, but since I'm the only one here, why don't you tell me what happened?"

Devon rubbed his eyes. He started to talk, telling Mr. Peterson the now-familiar story of the hit and run. Zachary looked down at the gun in Devon's pocket. While he'd learned some pickpocketing, figuring it was a useful skill for an investigator to have from time to time, he hadn't practiced enough to become skilled at it. The gun was heavy and Devon was likely to notice a shift in its weight if Zachary lifted it.

He caught a glimpse of Kenzie again, approaching an older couple several tables away and speaking to them quietly. They got up and moved out of Zachary's vision, toward the door they had come in. Zachary turned his head toward her. She gave him a tiny motion. *Back up.* Zachary slid one foot back, then the other, as silently and slowly as possible. Devon didn't take his head out of his hands to see what was going on.

A dark figure slid by Kenzie like a ghost. A black-uniformed cop. He crouched down behind the table Kenzie had just vacated. She moved back the direction she had come. The cop had everyone's attention but Devon's. He made a motion to indicate Mr.

Peterson and Pat, and pointed to the floor. *Get down.* He held up three fingers, then two, then one.

Mr. Peterson wasn't as spry as he had once been, but getting down was easier than getting up, and Zachary was surprised at how quickly the two men hit the floor.

"Devon Masters!" an authoritative voice boomed.

Devon dropped his hands from his face and looked around, pale and wide-eyed. His face was wet with tears.

"Put your hands on your head!"

He didn't obey immediately. His hands hovered as he tried to decide whether to go for the gun. Zachary was still close enough to grab him. If Devon went for the gun, Zachary could grab him, wrestle and hold on to him until the cops could get close enough to get the gun away from him and get him under control.

Then Devon did the smart thing and put his hands on his head. Zachary breathed a sigh of relief. He made a motion toward Devon's apron pocket. "Do you want me to—"

"Just stay where you are, Goldman," the voice barked. "Don't move."

Zachary froze. He looked at the cop that he could see, sheltering behind a table, gun trained on Devon. He didn't know how many others there were behind him and around the room. He didn't want to step into the line of fire, so he stayed where he was, as motionless as possible.

"Masters, lace your fingers together!"

Devon did as he was told. In another moment, he was stretched out on the floor, belly down, as he was instructed. Finally, the police moved in, securing his hands and removing the gun.

"I have a permit," Devon protested. "You don't have any cause to arrest me or to take my gun. I'll sue you for false arrest."

"We're responding to a call placed by a citizen. We'll get all of the pertinent details now. If there's no evidence of wrongdoing, you'll be allowed to go," the officer who handcuffed him said reasonably.

He was removed from the room to be interviewed separately from the witnesses. The cop who appeared to be in charge turned to Zachary.

"You're Zachary Goldman?"

"Yes."

"Mind if I check you for weapons?"

Zachary raised his hands. "I don't carry."

They patted him down just to be sure. At the cop's request, Zachary showed him the email message from Devon with Mr. Peterson's face x-ed out. The cop compared it to Mr. Peterson's face when he'd managed to get up from the hard tiled floor and back into a chair.

"Well, that's the first spa day I've ever had end that way," he said cheerfully.

"It's your first spa day ever," Pat pointed out.

Zachary grimaced, thinking about how it could have been Lorne's first and last spa day, if things had gone differently. He slid into the chair that Devon had vacated, across from his ex-foster father and longtime friend. It wasn't until then that he realized how much his legs were shaking.

"You're okay?" Zachary asked Mr. Peterson.

"The old ticker is apparently still working." He was all smiles, as if the whole thing had been nothing more than an interesting diversion.

"What did he say to you before I got here?" Zachary asked. "Did he threaten you?"

"He wasn't here much before you. Said he recognized me, was I Lorne Peterson, did I used to take in foster kids. I was trying to figure out if he was one of ours, but the face didn't seem familiar. I take it... this is the guy who was emailing you? Harassing you?"

Zachary nodded. "Yeah, I guess so."

"But he's not your brother."

"No." Zachary frowned, looking in the direction they had taken Devon. "So... where did he get the picture?"

"Maybe from the photographer. I don't know how he would

track it down, but…"

"He was teaching criminal investigation at the university, so he's had some experience… and with a concealed carry permit, maybe he's been a private investigator. I ran an initial background on him, but I thought he was just a lawyer."

"If he's been an investigator himself, he knows how to cover his tracks. Do you remember where that picture of your family was taken?"

Zachary steadied himself on the table. Thinking back was dangerous. It could open a whole floodgate of memories that would quickly whirl out of his control. He tried to keep narrowly focused on the night of the Christmas party and not let his mind slip to Christmas Eve, a few nights later.

"I think it was a company Christmas party. For my dad's work."

"They might have kept a historical archive of some kind."

Zachary nodded. "Yeah… I guess they must have."

He'd never gone looking himself. If he had, maybe he'd already have had that picture. Maybe others. Maybe even social network pictures his siblings had posted of their growing-up years, so he could find out how they had done and whether their lives had been as traumatic has his, or whether they'd had good lives and grown up happy in stable foster homes.

"That was really amazing," Pat told Mr. Peterson. "I've always known you could talk to anyone, but it was really something to see you connecting with him." He smiled proudly.

"I dealt with a lot of damaged kids when we were fostering." Mr. Peterson met Zachary's eyes and gave a sad smile. "Deep down, they all want the same thing."

Zachary tried to swallow the lump in his throat. Mr. Peterson had been the one constant through his rocky growing-up years. The one place he could go for acceptance and a shared interest. When he was with Mr. Peterson, he wasn't a broken kid anymore. He was a photographer. A friend. Mr. Peterson was someone he didn't have to prove anything to or be anyone but who he was.

"You were sad when you had to stop fostering," he said. "You should get back into it… or Boys and Girls Club or another organization that mentors kids. You're so good at it."

"Unfortunately… I still don't think we're to the point where gay men are accepted in organizations with access to children. Even an old guy like me is still seen as a potential pedophile, just looking for my next victim."

Anger flared in Zachary's chest. He'd experienced his share of predators in foster homes and institutions, but Mr. Peterson had never been like that. "That's not fair. You're really good with kids and you'd never hurt one of them."

"In today's world, even a pat on the back is interpreted as a sexual advance. You're not allowed to touch kids. Hugs are out of the question. Kids with disrupted lives *need* physical touch and reassurance, but they're barred from getting it."

Kenzie was allowed to join them at the table. There were still police everywhere, but without any actual drama going on, the other spa customers and employees were going back to their own conversations.

"Hey," Kenzie smiled. "Everyone okay?"

"Kenzie," Zachary motioned for her to sit in the fourth chair. "This is Lorne and Pat."

Everyone nodded and exchanged handshakes.

"I've heard so much about you," Kenzie said. "I'm glad to finally meet you."

Mr. Peterson smiled. "I could say the same. Good to actually meet one of Zachary's friends."

Zachary's face heated. While Mr. Peterson had always made it clear he was welcome to bring anyone along with him on visits, Zachary never had. Except for Bridget. Lorne had met Bridget at the wedding, and there had been one or two visits in the time they'd been married. But in spite of Bridget being polite and friendly to his surrogate father, Zachary hadn't felt comfortable mixing those two lives.

"So…" Pat looked at Zachary and Kenzie, his brows down

slightly. "How did you two happen to come here? For that matter, how did your friend know that we would be here? It wasn't just chance, was it?"

Zachary scratched his ear. "Uh… no." He turned his phone back on and slid it over to the space on the table between Pat and Mr. Peterson so they could both see the threatening email with Mr. Peterson's face crossed out.

Pat shook his head. "He's more than a little unbalanced. How does he know you? And I still don't understand how either of you knew where we were."

"Zachary *is* a private investigator," Mr. Peterson pointed out.

"We had help. When I got this," Zachary gestured to the phone, "and I couldn't get ahold of you, we got the police and FBI involved. Kenzie managed to convince them to track your phone locations. I'm sorry. I was worried he might have already done something… that you might be in real danger."

"Don't apologize," Mr. Peterson said, smiling and shaking his head. "You didn't do anything wrong."

"I invaded your privacy…"

"You did the right thing," he said firmly. "Pat's not accusing you of doing anything wrong."

Pat shook his head. "Just trying to understand how it all went down. I'm pretty good with technology, but I don't understand how someone goes from being a cyberbully to actually finding us in real life. When we're somewhere like this, away from home. You went through the police, with legitimate concerns, but that's obviously not what he did."

"Did either of you get any strange emails or texts recently? Something with an attachment?"

They looked at each other.

"No, I don't think so," Mr. Peterson said. "The most unusual thing I got recently was that new social networking site you sent me."

Zachary shook his head. "I didn't send you anything."

"It was some professional referrals network. 'Click here if you would recommend Zachary Goldman Investigations.' So I did, of course."

"Well… thank you… but I didn't send that and I haven't joined any networking sites lately. That must have been it. You clicked on the link, and it installed a tracking program on your phone. Told Devon exactly where to find you at any time."

"They can do that?" Mr. Peterson sat back in his chair, shaking his head. "Well. Isn't that something."

"I'm so sorry he targeted you. I never thought that anyone would ever try to use you to get to me."

"Not to worry. No harm done." The man shrugged.

"But he came here to punish you. He brought his gun. He wanted to hurt you."

"Maybe, but deep down, I don't think he could. He couldn't make the leap from anonymous bullying to actually meting out punishment face-to-face."

"He killed Richard Harding."

"Physically? Face-to-face?"

"Well… no. Bullied him until he committed suicide."

Mr. Peterson made a gesture that indicated Zachary had just confirmed his point.

The cop in charge approached the table. His name bar said Buck, and he had heavy jowls like a bulldog.

"I need a little move information from you folks, if I could." Though his words were deferential, his manner was aggressive. Clearly indicating he was in charge. They all nodded they would cooperate.

"When Devon approached you," he directed the question to Pat and Mr. Peterson, "did he threaten you? Did he tell you he had a weapon on him?"

Mr. Peterson shook his head. "No, he never made any threats. I didn't know there was any danger until I saw Zachary's reaction to him. When he said to stop, and Zachary froze there… I knew this wasn't just an old foster kid trying to reconnect."

"And to you?" Buck looked at Zachary. "Did he tell you he had a gun? Did he tell you he was going to shoot someone?"

"No. Just the email I showed you, with Mr. Peterson's face crossed out. I found out when I talked to the police that he had a concealed carry permit, and when I got here and he confronted me, he had his hand in the apron pocket, where the gun was."

"But he didn't tell you he was going to shoot or hold you at gunpoint."

"No. But he's involved in a homicide in Vermont. A man he was harassing online."

"He was involved how?"

"He was stalking him and sending him harassing emails, telling him that he should kill himself... until he eventually did."

"Well, that's not exactly homicide, is it?"

Zachary opened his mouth to argue, then closed it again. He looked at Kenzie. She was obviously reading the same thing in Buck's manner as Zachary—that as far as he was concerned, Devon hadn't broken the law.

"He's been stalking me too. Sending harassing emails and messages... telling me that I should die..."

"Anything related to stalking, you'll need to take that up with the police in your jurisdiction, which I understand is Vermont...?'"

"Yes."

"File with the local police. Because it's a cross-border thing, they'll get the FBI involved, and they'll decide whether any laws have been broken."

"He threatened to kill Lorne. I showed you the email."

"It's ambiguous. It doesn't actually say he's going to do anything. I doubt it would ever hold up in court as a death threat."

Zachary swallowed. "You're not going to arrest him for anything?"

"I don't see anything I *can* arrest him for. The fact that we've detained him will be enough for him to launch a suit against us already. It wouldn't go anywhere, but it would be an annoyance."

Zachary looked at Kenzie. He looked at Mr. Peterson and Pat. No one had anything to offer. Kenzie gave a shrug and shook her head.

"I don't know, Zachary. We can call Campbell, but… I can't think of anything else we can do."

"So he stalks my—my—friend, threatens to kill him, brings a gun, and it isn't anything? There's nothing to charge him with? He can just go?"

"They're going to let him go. Let's take some time to relax and calm down, and then we'll call Campbell and see if there is anything he can do. Okay?"

Zachary buried his face in his hands, unable to let them see his fury and grief at the injustice of it.

For a while he just swam in the darkness, the quiet conversation of the others going on around him.

When he finally got control of himself and pulled his hands away from his face, determined to remain cool and aloof, Buck was gone. All of the police were gone. Pat's and Mr. Peterson's drinks were finished. Kenzie sat with one foot up on her chair, knee bent. She turned her head to look at him, but didn't say anything or make a big deal of his meltdown.

After a while, Zachary cleared his throat. "Guess we should be getting on our way. We've probably already kept you here longer than you meant to be."

Mr. Peterson shrugged, looking around at their surroundings. "It's a nice peaceful place—at least most of the time we were here. It's not exactly a hardship."

"I never pictured you as a spa sort of guy." Even in his drained emotional state, Zachary couldn't help the little tug at the corner of his mouth. Mr. Peterson had never had the exaggerated effeminate mannerisms popularized by gay characters on television.

"It took some talking to get him to agree," Pat advised. "But I told him this was what I wanted for Christmas and I finally managed to talk him into it."

"It was actually okay, though." Mr. Peterson put his hand over Pat's on the table briefly. "Next time you won't have to work quite so hard to convince me."

"I hope not. Though, don't expect the floor show next time."

They both laughed. Zachary wasn't quite up to seeing the humor in the situation. He shook his head, worrying it over in his mind. If the police wouldn't arrest Devon, how could Zachary ever be sure that the people around him would be safe?

"Zachary, why don't you and Kenzie come back to the house for supper? It's much closer than going home," Pat suggested.

"I wouldn't want to put you out."

"It's not. We'll put a couple of frozen pizzas in the oven and use disposable plates. No fuss. Give you some time to relax and recover."

"That sounds good," Kenzie agreed. She nodded to Zachary to encourage him to accept the invitation. "I don't want you driving all the way back yet. You must be exhausted, I know I am."

Zachary's body ached from holding every muscle tense and his brain felt wrung out. He could drive, but maybe it wasn't the best idea. If he had something to eat and some more time to relax before going any distance, that might be better.

"You really want to eat something like pizza after a spa day?" he asked. "Isn't the whole point to cleanse your systems or detox or whatever? Are you allowed to eat pizza?"

"We're allowed," Mr. Peterson said, so firmly it made them all laugh. He might give in to going to the spa at his partner's insistence, but he wasn't giving up his pizza.

"It's settled, then," Pat said. He glanced toward the juice bar. "You need something to boost your blood sugar before hitting the road, Zachary?"

2 8

The three of them talked Zachary into a strawberry mango smoothie to replenish the calories he had burned off with the adrenaline-fueled rush to get there and facing down his opponent over a gun. Zachary put it into the cupholder in his car and sipped it occasionally along the way. He wasn't hungry, but it was sweet and refreshing and everybody insisted he needed something. Zachary hadn't heard what was in the dark purple concoction Kenzie had chosen, but she seemed to enjoy it. It was all gone before they reached Mr. Peterson's house.

Kenzie looked over the brick bungalow and smiled. "What a nice little place. It suits them."

"You should see it during the spring when the flowers are out. Pat has pink tulips in the borders."

"That's great. They're a really nice couple, I can see why you get along so well."

Pizza suited everyone. Mr. Peterson, Pat, and Kenzie seemed to be completely relaxed and unworried, not even thinking about Devon, but Zachary found himself unable to sit still. He prowled around the house, looking out the windows and rechecking the locks on the doors.

"You should sit down and relax," Kenzie said. "What are you so worried about?"

"They just let Devon go. He could come here. He could be here now. If he decides he wants to do something to Mr. Peterson... he'll be a sitting duck."

"Devon is not going to come here. Not now, when everybody knows his identity. He met Lorne face-to-face and knows what a nice guy he is. Devon couldn't do anything to hurt him. You don't need to worry. It's over."

Zachary looked out the dark windows. There were Christmas lights on all sides of the house, which didn't help calm his anxiety at all.

"He could be out there now."

"He isn't."

Zachary paced the house, looking out each window. When he returned to the living room, Kenzie and Mr. Peterson were talking in low voices, and their glances toward Zachary told him they had been discussing him.

"I'm not being paranoid," he asserted.

"You're the expert," Mr. Peterson said, no hint of sarcasm in his voice. "I was wondering whether we could persuade you to stay overnight. I thought maybe you would feel better if you could stay and see that everything was okay."

Zachary considered. He thought initially that they were just trying to placate him, but he could detect no eye-rolling or false front. The last time, he had felt better after staying over, rather than being anxious at being away from his own bed. He paced restlessly into the kitchen and looked out at the back yard, but there was no sign of trouble.

"I guess we could stay, if Kenzie is okay with it." He looked at her with eyebrows raised. Kenzie nodded.

"Sure. I've already let Dr. Wiltshire know I'm taking a couple of extra days for my holidays. I'm game."

"Then... just one other thing..."

"If you think there's a problem, we'll listen to you," Mr.

Peterson promised, trying to anticipate what the condition would be.

Zachary rubbed his forehead, trying to disguise his embarrassment. "Could you put the candles away?"

"Oh!" Pat looked around at the various decorative groupings, which included a number of red and white Christmas candles. They weren't lit, but they were still ratcheting up Zachary's anxiety. "Sorry, Zach! If I'd known you were coming, I would have had those cleared away earlier." He got up and immediately started removing the candles and readjusting the spacing of the decorations to make up for their lack. "What about all the rest? The tree…?"

Zachary eyed the brightly-lit tree. He'd been doing his best to ignore it, focusing on keeping everyone safe from Devon. But it was one of the reasons he couldn't sit down and be comfortable in the living room.

He folded his arms across his chest, the best he could do to put a barrier between himself and the tree.

"It's okay. But if we could… turn off the lights before bed. Just in case."

Mr. Peterson was the closest to the tree. He leaned over and fished around until he caught the cord for the lights. He pulled the plug. The tree went dark. Zachary breathed out a slow sigh of relief. A cold, dark tree was infinitely better than one all lit up, with hundreds of ignition points around the tinder-dry needles and branches.

"You could have said something earlier," Mr. Peterson admonished.

Zachary's cheeks warmed. "I don't like to ruin things for everyone else just because of my issues. I can still enjoy myself around a Christmas tree."

As long as it was after Christmas Eve. Or clear of all sources of ignition.

"You're okay to stay over?" Kenzie asked.

"Yes. Sure. That would be good."

He carried an emergency supply of pills with him just in case he ended up in a situation where he could not get back to his apartment to get them. The second fire, his apartment fire, had taught him that. If he had a panic attack or couldn't get home for some reason, he needed to have a few things with him, to make sure he could get through the night.

But he didn't take anything to help him sleep. He was too worried about Devon breaking in during the night. Mr. Peterson needed a burglar alarm. He didn't have anything, not even a door chime or broken glass detectors. Zachary would have to see to it that the situation was remedied. That could be his gift to Mr. Peterson. A security system that would help to keep him safe from lowlifes who might target him because of Zachary.

"You need to get some sleep," Kenzie urged. She had borrowed a t-shirt from Pat to wear as a nightshirt and was reading in bed, waiting for Zachary to settle down and join her. He had told her several times to just go to sleep without him, but she seemed to think she could outlast him.

"I can go one night without," Zachary countered. "It's not going to hurt me."

"I thought one of the reasons to come here and to sleep over was to make sure that you could get some rest. Prowling around the house isn't going to help."

"I need to be sure."

"You're planning on staying up all night?"

Zachary nodded. He waited for her to tell him that he was being ridiculous and nothing would happen if he went to sleep.

"Do you want to take turns, so you can at least get a few hours?"

He was pleasantly surprised. "I'd say yes, but... I don't think I'd be able to sleep anyway, so you may as well get yours. No point in both of us being short. I'll sleep during the day tomorrow when everyone is up."

But he knew he wouldn't. It was too late in the year. He was too close to the edge of the abyss.

Kenzie shook her head. "Are you sure it isn't just because you don't trust me to do a good enough job? You're afraid that I'll miss something or fall asleep during my shift?"

"No. There just isn't any point, when I'm going to be awake anyway."

"Okay." Kenzie gave a big yawn. "I guess I'd better knock off. If something worries you, will you wake me up? Or if you start feeling... bad."

"If it gets too bad," Zachary said, not quite confessing that he was already feeling pretty desperate. But he had purpose. He needed to stay awake and alive to look after his family. He couldn't let Mr. Peterson suffer because he was too self-absorbed.

Kenzie looked at him steadily for a minute.

"Why don't you leave your pills in here?" She motioned to the side table on her side of the bed. Zachary didn't bother to argue. He retrieved them from the bathroom, and put them beside Kenzie.

"Is there anything else I should be concerned about?" she asked.

"No. I need to keep Mr. Peterson safe. I'm not going to do anything."

"Your brain can do strange things when you get overtired. You come and wake me up, got it? If you start hallucinating or having suicidal thoughts or anything unexpected, you come wake me up."

"Okay."

"And stay off of the computer and email."

He nodded his agreement. He didn't need any extra nudges toward the edge. "My computer is in here." He gestured to it. "I'll leave my phone here... no. I'm going to keep my phone with me. If I need to wake you up and can't get back here..."

Kenzie nodded. "Fine. I'll keep mine on right here, in case you call or text." She picked it up and tapped the screen a few times. "I've turned off 'do not disturb.' So you can disturb me."

"Have a good sleep." He leaned down to her, pausing with their faces just an inch apart. He could feel her warm breath on his lips. "Sweet dreams."

He kissed her gently. Kenzie wrapped her arms around him and hugged him close, lengthening out the kiss.

"I was hoping for some action tonight," she said, indicating the empty space on the bed and giving a conspiratorial smile.

"I have to watch," Zachary said, looking toward the dark window. "I'm sorry."

She reached over and turned the reading lamp off. With the room in darkness, Zachary could see what was outside the window much more clearly. He walked over to it and stood looking out for a few minutes, watching for any movement or sign of anything that was out of place.

"Sweet dreams," he told Kenzie again, and left her in the bedroom alone.

When everyone was up in the morning, Kenzie and Zachary called Campbell to see if he had any ideas about what to do about Devon.

"Unfortunately, I agree with Buck. Devon has a permit to carry, so that in itself is not an offense. There is nothing overtly threatening in the email to you about your friend… I wish I could say there was, but you'd be asking a jury to agree that an *X* through a picture was the equivalent of a serious death threat. All you need is one juror who cut her ex out of all of their pictures without ever intending to do him any physical harm."

"He bullied and harassed Harding to death. He was the one who told him to kill himself. He was the one who said that Harding didn't deserve to live."

"But that's not the same as killing someone. Nobody is going to convict on that. Bullycide is an internet meme, not a legal charge."

"Do we have enough to get him for cyberstalking? There must be enough evidence to charge him with that."

"Yeah, I think we've got a lock on that one."

"What's the penalty for cyberstalking?" Kenzie asked eagerly, giving Zachary two thumbs up to encourage him.

Campbell sighed and didn't answer. Zachary closed his eyes. The one thing they could get Devon on, and Campbell was afraid to even tell them the bad news.

"First, we'd have to convince the FBI that it was worth their while to investigate him, since he was living in New Hampshire and harassing you in Vermont. If we could convince them to investigate him, charge him, and send him to Vermont... the sentence is two hundred and fifty dollars or up to three months jail time."

Zachary thumped his head down on the dining room table in disbelief. Kenzie touched his back sympathetically.

"Are you still there?" Campbell asked.

"I am," Kenzie said. "But I think we've lost Zachary."

He shook his head, still resting it on the dining room table. Two hundred and fifty dollars. That was what his life was worth. That was what Richard Harding's life was worth. A miserable two hundred and fifty dollars or up to three months.

"Zachary?" Campbell asked.

He didn't answer.

"Can we go ahead with it?" Kenzie asked. "Can you get the FBI to pursue it so that we can at least get him off the streets for a few months? Maybe?"

"I'll ask them, but I wouldn't expect anything to happen immediately. They'll only have a skeleton staff over Christmas, and nonviolent crime is not high on their priorities list."

Zachary decided that if he were ever going to be able to feel good about leaving Mr. Peterson alone, he was going to have to take matters into his own hands. He made a few phone calls, calling in what favors he could, in order to get a security system installed immediately. It meant extra money to get people in during the holiday season but, as far as Zachary was concerned, money was no object. He would do whatever it took to make sure Mr. Peterson and Pat were safe.

He worked on their phones and computers, cleaning off any suspicious programs, and added extra firewalls and security measures to keep them from being hacked again in the future.

"Don't open any email you aren't expecting," Zachary insisted. "Talk to the sender and find out what it is if you're not sure. Especially if it's from me or something to do with me. Don't click any links or attachments unless you are one hundred percent sure what they are and that it was really the person you think it was who sent it to you. I think you should get burner phones. Change your numbers so that he can't track you or get into your phone logs somehow. This guy is good. Really good."

"Maybe we should go back to wall phones with rotary dials," Mr. Peterson joked. "I never got a virus on one of those, and there was no need to track them, they were always in the same place."

"You'll be careful?" Zachary persisted.

"We'll be careful," Pat assured him. "You know Lorne is just joking. You don't need to worry about us."

But Zachary *was* worried. He took their car to a local shop and had them put it on a lift so that he could make sure no one had put a tracking device underneath. He checked for bugs at the house and in the car and found nothing, which just made him more sure he had missed something. He kept going at a frenetic pace all day long, getting everything done that he could. He ignored all pleas to eat or rest or sit down and visit.

When it was all done and he had nothing left to do, it was Christmas Eve.

***

Zachary sat on the bed in the spare bedroom, facing away from the door. Staring toward the window, but not actually looking out, his eyes unfocused.

"Everything is all set?" Kenzie asked Zachary brightly.

"Yeah."

"Do you think Mr. Peterson will be able to figure out the security system?"

"Pat's got it."

"Good. Well, you've had a busy day. Now you can relax."

"Uh-huh."

"You deserve a holiday."

Zachary drew in a shuddering breath. Everything was an effort, even breathing.

"And you told Ashley about it being suicide?"

"No."

Kenzie cocked her head, surprised. "I thought I heard you call her. Didn't you?"

"I called her. But I didn't tell her it was suicide."

"Oh. What did you tell her?"

"That it was an accident, just like the police said."

"Did she believe it?"

He nodded. "She paid for my expertise. I uncovered everything else. She believed me."

"That's good," Kenzie decided. "No point in laying that on her. Now she can start the grieving process."

"As long as Devon leaves her alone."

"I think he will, don't you?"

"If he doesn't, we know who he is. We'll put him away for another three months."

Kenzie chuckled. "Actually, if he's been convicted before, they can put him away for six."

Zachary didn't respond. What was the point?

Kenzie sat down on the bed beside him and took his hand. "Maybe Devon will decide to get help. Maybe his conversation with Lorne will convince him to look at therapy instead of transferring his guilt to everyone else."

"Yeah."

She looked into his face, trying to connect with him. "Where are you, Zachary?"

He blinked. Even blinking was exhausting. He wanted to go to sleep and never have to wake up again. He wanted something to take away the unrelenting pain in his chest.

Kenzie squeezed his hand. "I'm here, Zachary. You're not alone."

The Christmas lights on the neighbor's house came on.

Zachary heard the screaming. His chest burned with the smoke. He felt again the terror that he was going to smother and burn, all alone, trapped in the room that burned with the fires of hell. The sense of horror that he had done this to his family. That they were all going to die too. His throat was raw from screaming to them and from the superheated air of the room.

"Zachary." Kenzie squeezed his hand. "It's okay."

"I could never carry a gun."

"No," Kenzie agreed. She had criticized him for it before, saying that if he were going to investigate potential homicides, he should at least protect himself.

But he couldn't. Not because he was a pacifist or because he couldn't shoot, but because it would have been too big of a temptation.

"You're safe." Zachary's voice was a croak.

"We're all safe. Lorne and Pat have this fancy new security system. State of the art."

Zachary raised his head, not to look at the window sensor and motion detector, but at the smoke detector on the ceiling over the bed.

"Yes, we're safe from fire too," Kenzie confirmed. "There are no fire hazards, you know that."

"I need to see the tree."

"Come on, then." She stood up and waited for him to follow. Zachary rose slowly, every muscle in his body protesting. Kenzie put her hand on his back to encourage him. He felt like an old man walking out to the living room. A hundred years old, tottering and unsure of his feet. Mr. Peterson joined them in the living room when he saw that was where they were going. Zachary sagged into the couch and sat there staring at the decorated Christmas tree. It was still unplugged. The candles were all packed back away.

Mr. Peterson said something, all smiles, but Zachary couldn't process it. Lorne's smile faded away and he sat down across from them, saying something quietly to Kenzie. She rubbed Zachary's back. For a long time, Zachary just stared at the tree, the events of that night replaying over and over in his head. It wasn't going to happen again. He wasn't going to let it happen again. But he could never go back in time to correct his mistake or to make things right with his family.

He put his hands over his face and sat there with Kenzie and Mr. Peterson. After a while, he became aware of Kenzie shaking him, trying to get his attention. He pulled his hands away from his face, still dry-eyed.

"Zachary, why don't you call Tyrrell?"

He shook his head.

"He wants to hear from you. It might help you to get through this."

"Kenzie, no. I can't."

"Are you afraid of feeling *worse* than this?"

She did have a point. He was scraping rock bottom, it wasn't like anyone could make him feel worse than he already did.

"Not today. Not now."

"Tyrrell might need you tonight just as much as you need him," Mr. Peterson pointed out. "Do you think it's a coincidence that he wrote to you as Christmas was approaching?"

He hadn't thought of that. He thought of Tyrrell as angry, another cyberstalker like Devon, intent only on hurting Zachary, but Tyrrell had been through the Christmas Eve fire too. Maybe he was traumatized rather than angry. He had the same blood running through his veins. He had grown up, at least until age six, in the same family atmosphere. It was possible he suffered the same PTSD and depression as Zachary, especially at the time of year when he'd lost his home and half his family.

"One of us can call if you can't manage it," Kenzie said. "You don't have to do it yourself."

Zachary rubbed the tight band across his forehead. He nodded.

"Yes?" Kenzie asked eagerly. "You want me to call? Or Lorne?"

Zachary felt his pockets for his phone, retrieved it, and handed it to her.

It was probably a good thing that Zachary hadn't been eating. Waiting for Tyrrell to arrive, he felt dangerously nauseated.

"He sounded really nice," Kenzie assured him after the call. "He sounds a lot like you do on the phone."

So maybe Tyrrell wasn't angry. Maybe he was just looking to connect. But Zachary still wasn't sure that meeting on Christmas Eve was a good idea. He wasn't very good company. If Tyrrell was having a rough time, Zachary wasn't sure there was anything he could do to help.

The doorbell rang. Zachary got to his feet and moved to the door, no longer exhausted and in pain, but numb and disconnected from himself, feeling as if he were watching himself from a distance. He knew he should check through the peephole first to make sure it wasn't Devon, but he was afraid that any hesitation would keep him from opening the door at all. He drew in a deep breath and turned the door handle.

He expected to see a stranger, but Tyrrell seemed completely familiar to him. He looked just as he was supposed to. Taller than Zachary, but with many of the same features as Zachary saw when he looked in the mirror. His hair was longer and shaggier. He was clean shaven, whereas Zachary knew he was scruffy after a few days without shaving. And his eyes were Tyrrell's. Just exactly the same eyes as Zachary remembered in six-year-old Tyrrell.

Zachary just stood there, looking at Tyrrell, stunned after decades of not seeing any blood relations.

"Hey, Zachary," Tyrrell greeted, holding out a hand uncertainly.

Zachary automatically shook in response, then Tyrrell pulled him in and wrapped his other arm around him, hugging him tightly. He swore and laughed.

"Man, Zachary, it's been too long! It's been so, so long!"

Then they were both crying. Kenzie came over and closed the door and herded them into the living room. She was grinning fit to burst.

"Merry Christmas, Zach," she murmured, touching him lightly on the arm.

He didn't even look at her, completely wrapped up in Tyrrell. Tyrrell kept thumping him on the back, exclaiming things like. "Can you believe it? My big brother!"

Eventually, they both managed to land on the couch. Tyrrell stretched his arm around Zachary's shoulders, still holding him close. "I can't believe it!"

"You look good," Zachary managed to say. Tyrrell seemed healthy and happy. He was well-dressed and didn't look like someone who had spent his life barely making ends meet.

"And you look…" Tyrrell ran his hand over Zachary's head, the hair cropped close in a style that was easy to take care of with minimal fuss. "You look like crap, Zachary. Are you sick?"

Kenzie snorted, then laughed aloud. "He doesn't always look this bad," she advised.

"I just… haven't slept in a few days." Zachary rubbed his eyes self-consciously. He had seen in the mirror that morning how hollow they looked, and didn't imagine they were much better after a hard day's work. He'd avoided looking at the mirror again. And his long whiskers. He should have cleaned himself up before Tyrrell arrived, but he hadn't had the energy or will.

"You gotta sleep," Tyrrell said. He patted Zachary again on the back. "You gotta take care of yourself, you know."

Zachary sniffled and nodded agreement.

Tyrrell leaned back, letting out a long stream of air. "Oh, you don't know how long I've been waiting for this day. After the first year or two, I never thought I'd ever see you again. The social workers would never tell me anything about you. Or they'd say they didn't know. I imagine they could have found out, if they really didn't know. They just didn't want to tell me. They wanted me to just forget."

Zachary nodded.

Tyrrell looked around the room. "This is a nice place. I thought you lived farther north—"

"It's not mine." Zachary took in his surroundings. He pointed to Mr. Peterson, still sitting in an easy chair. "Lorne, this is Tyrrell. Mr. Peterson—Lorne—was one of my foster parents. It's his place."

"Oh, okay." Tyrrell nodded. "You kept in contact after all these years? That's amazing. You must have lived with him a long time."

Zachary shook his head. There was so much to tell, so much to explain. "I was only with him a couple of weeks. Not here, with him and his ex-wife."

"Zachary and I are both into photography," Mr. Peterson explained. "Zachary used to come over to develop his pictures, even after he was moved. So we kept in touch over the years, even after my wife and I separated. Pat and I bought this place just a few years ago."

"Ah. Well, you can tell her that it's very nice. Very homey."

"You can tell him that yourself." He raised his voice and directed it toward the kitchen. "You should come in and join the fun, Pat."

Pat poked his head through the kitchen doorway, grinning. "How about some Christmas cheer? Would everybody like drinks? Cookies?"

There were agreeable noises all around. Mr. Peterson got slowly to his feet. "I should help in the kitchen. What does everyone want? Egg nog? Cider? Mulled wine?"

"Wine sounds good to me," Kenzie said.

Zachary wasn't sure he'd be able to get anything down. It had been so long since he'd eaten or slept, any alcohol would go straight to his head.

"Something nonalcoholic," Tyrrell suggested. "The cider?"

"Cider it is," Mr. Peterson said. "Zachary, the same?"

Zachary nodded. He glanced over at Tyrrell.

"You don't drink?" Tyrrell asked.

"Not usually."

"I'm a recovering alcoholic," Tyrrell said frankly. "So I don't drink at all."

"Oh. I'm sorry."

"Should we not drink in front of you?" Kenzie asked. "Would that be a problem?"

"No, no," Tyrrell waved his hands at both of them. "You go ahead. And there's nothing to be sorry about," he told Zachary. "We all have our own challenges. I don't remember much about it, but I guess Mom and Dad drank, and there's a genetic predisposition for these things. I found my way through it, but I never want to fall down that hole again, so I avoid it."

Zachary nodded. He remembered them drinking. Remembered the voices getting louder and angrier as the nights wore on and they'd had more to drink. Alcohol was not something that ever brought back happy memories for him.

Tyrrell looked around. "We should turn the tree on! Old Saint Nick will be making his journey around the world soon."

Kenzie looked at Zachary. He looked at the tree, trying to decide whether he'd be able to tolerate it, since Tyrrell was there with him. But it was Christmas Eve. The tree could go up like a torch.

Even though he knew logically that history wouldn't repeat itself, he couldn't help the panic and vertigo that swept through him when he even considered the possibility. He shook his head at Kenzie and Tyrrell.

"I… I can't. I…"

"Zachary sort of has a thing about Christmas trees," Kenzie informed Tyrrell.

Tyrrell looked at Zachary, understanding dawning. "Oh. Hey, I get it. I still can't listen to *Santa Baby*. That's okay, no sweat."

Madonna's rendition of *Santa Baby* had been playing on Zachary's radio that night, just before Tyrrell fell asleep. Remembering it brought back a flood of memories. His parents screaming and fighting. Tyrrell cuddled in his arms, scared. Holding him and humming along with *Santa Baby* to put him back to sleep.

Tyrrell tightened his arm around Zachary's shoulders. "It's okay, big bro. It's all okay now."

Zachary nodded, but he didn't feel okay. Everything was closing in. He wanted to be alone, but was surrounded by people. He felt good about seeing Tyrrell, but that didn't change the fact that it was Christmas Eve and terrible things happened on Christmas Eve. He didn't want to bring tragedy down on his family and friends.

Mr. Peterson and Pat brought in the drinks, Pat also carrying a plate of Christmas cookies and treats. Zachary darted a glance at Tyrrell, worried about how he would react to Lorne and Pat's relationship. Society as a whole had grown more tolerant of gay relationships, but individuals could still be prejudiced and unkind, and he'd run into a lot of intolerant behaviors in the system.

Zachary and Tyrrell took their warm glasses of cider, and Tyrrell touched the glass to his lips and took a sip. "Oh, this is perfect! And I need one of those gingerbread cookies…" Tyrrell took one from Pat's serving platter. "Did you do all of this yourself?" he asked. "The food and the decor?"

"Mostly," Pat admitted. "Lorne's passion is for photography, like Zachary."

Pat was not the stereotypical gay decorator, with an effeminate voice and manner. Neither of the men fit the stereotypes on TV or in the media. They were just individuals, Zachary's foster father and his partner.

"You like photography?" Tyrrell turned back to Zachary.

Zachary nodded. He put his cup on a coaster on the coffee table. "Yes… but it's not my profession. Though I use it at work."

"Are you really a private investigator? I wasn't sure, when I was looking for you, if that was you…"

"Yeah. That's me. Not a lot of Zachary Goldmans around here."

"That's so cool. My brother, the private eye!"

Zachary forced a smile. "It's not glamorous like people make out. Mostly, it's sitting around watching people and writing reports."

"Don't let him play it down!" Kenzie jumped in, pointing her wine glass in Zachary's direction. "He's solved several murders in the last year or so. That's no accident. He knows what he's doing."

She and Mr. Peterson proceeded to tell Tyrrell all about Zachary's biggest cases. Zachary just rolled his eyes and sat back, knowing there was no stopping them.

Kenzie, Mr. Peterson, and Pat had all excused themselves as it got late, heading off to bed. Only Zachary and Tyrrell were left, sitting on the couch and talking quietly as the night drew on.

"You should probably go," Zachary told him. "You must have places to be tomorrow. You need to get your sleep."

"No." Tyrrell shook his head. "I'll make some calls to my friends with little kids who will be up early, then I'll have a nap. I don't have to be anywhere until dinner tomorrow afternoon."

Zachary looked at Tyrrell's hands. "You're not married?"

"Divorced. Two kids. Their mom has them this year. I'll get them for spring break."

Tyrrell had also been looking at Zachary's hands. He reached out and touched the biggest scar on Zachary's arm, tracing it gently. "Is that from the fire?"

Zachary nodded. He swallowed hard, trying to get rid of the lump in his throat.

"She said you got burned. The social worker. She said it wasn't bad, that you'd be okay."

"Yeah. I was in hospital a few weeks… probably longer than they needed to keep me, because they didn't know where to put me."

"You don't have any on your face." Tyrrell moved back and forth, staring at Zachary. "I can't see any, if you do."

"I covered my face. Trying to protect it. Trying to make a pocket of breathable air." His body remembered being trapped in the inferno, squashing himself under the couch to try to escape the flames. His muscles quivered and his heart raced.

Tyrrell squeezed his arm. "It's okay. I'm sorry. I shouldn't have brought it up."

Zachary pressed his palms over his eyes briefly. "I screamed at you to get out. All of you. Did you hear me? Did anyone get hurt?"

"I heard you. I woke up and you weren't there. You were screaming to get out and the room was full of smoke. I tried to go out to the hallway, but it was too hot and smoky. I went back and hid under the bed. Me and Vinny. They said it was good we got down low, where there wasn't as much smoke. When the fire engines came, the firefighters broke the window. They got us out. They kept asking who else was in the room, and I told them you weren't there and I couldn't find you." He stared at Zachary for a few minutes, and Zachary wondered if he too was trying to make his way through the flashbacks. Then he focused again. "No one else was burned. Just a little smoke inhalation. They got us out through the bedroom windows, then went in looking for you. None of us had to stay at the hospital. Just you."

"Did you see them all? You saw they were okay?"

Tyrrell nodded. "I don't remember a lot of the details after the fire. It was all pretty chaotic and I was only six. I remember them splitting us up; there wasn't any respite home that could take five kids. I was so scared we'd never see each other again. And we didn't. I've talked and video chatted with Joss and Heather, but we haven't gotten together to meet face-to-face. But me and the little kids stayed together until we were teenagers."

"Do you still talk to them? Vinny and Mindy?"

Tyrrell nodded. "Not as much as I should, but yeah, we have each other's numbers."

Zachary didn't ask whether any of the others wanted to meet him. He assumed that if they did, Tyrrell would have said so.

"So you're not going to go home tonight?"

"Do you want me to leave?"

Zachary shook his head.

"Then I'll stay." Tyrrell patted Zachary's leg and gave him another hug, smiling.

Eventually, the sky started to get lighter. Zachary let his breath out.

"It's morning," Tyrrell said. "It's Christmas Day."

Zachary closed his eyes, feeling the peaceful stillness of the house. No fire. No disaster. Just his family and friends around him, seeing him through the tunnel.

"Merry Christmas, T."

"Merry Christmas, Zachary."

They sat in silence for some time, talked out and comfortable with just letting the quiet surround them.

Zachary got up from the couch. His clothes were sweaty and sticking to him. He wasn't sure when he had last changed. Mr. Peterson and Pat had offered him a change of clothes, but he hadn't wanted to wear something that wasn't his. Too many years of hand-me-down clothes shared through dozens of foster children. He only wanted what was his.

He bent over and plugged in the tree.

"You're sure you're okay with that?" Tyrrell asked.

"Yeah. If something was going to happen, it would have happened last night."

Tyrrell grinned. "You know that's crazy, don't you?"

"I know."

"You know what we never did?"

"No. What?"

"We never built that snowman."

Zachary remembered holding Tyrrell and trying to calm him while their parents raged at each other, yelling and hitting and throwing things around.

"Do you think Santa will come?" Tyrrell had asked.

"No!" Zachary laughed and rubbed Tyrrell's head. "Santa doesn't come here, silly."

"But tomorrow's Christmas."

"Yeah. Tomorrow's Christmas. No school. Maybe we'll build a snowman."

Tyrrell snuggled against him. "A snowman? Will you help me?"

"Sure. We'll all do it."

"We'll make it so big. Taller than me."

Zachary shook his head at the memory. "I can't believe you remember that."

"You said we could build a snowman."

"I don't think I can make one taller than you anymore."

"It doesn't have to be."

They got on their coats and shoes and gear and went outside. When Kenzie got up, that's where she found them, building a snowman.

At breakfast, Pat managed to cajole Zachary into eating a Christmas orange and a few bites of freshly-baked cinnamon rolls. The bun was so sweet it hurt his teeth, and after barely having eaten anything in the days before Christmas, his stomach wasn't ready for anything so rich.

"It's really good," Zachary told Pat. "I just… can't eat much in the morning."

"You need to get some weight back on," Mr. Peterson observed. "You're skin and bones."

"It's not that bad. I'll bulk back up. Just not all in one day. Next time… I'll have dinner."

"You can't stay today? Pat already has the bird in the oven, and his family is going to be coming over this afternoon. The more the merrier."

"I need to get home and get showered and changed. I'm not going to make a very good impression on Pat's family if they think I'm some homeless person you just plucked off the street."

"They'd like to meet you."

"Next time."

"My mother said you're probably the closest thing to a grand-child she's going to get," Pat said, grinning. "I think that means she's finally accepted that I'm not going to switch teams."

"What about your sister?"

"She doesn't want to marry or have kids."

Zachary couldn't understand how anyone could not want a family of their own. It was funny to think of Pat's mother calling Zachary her grandchild. In a tortuous way, she was sort of right. Zachary was the former foster son of her son's partner. Pat had been more of a parent to Zachary than the former Mrs. Peterson, strange as that seemed.

"Tell your mom I'm looking forward to meeting her, but we have another engagement today." He looked at Kenzie, who nodded. "We set up a visit with… a friend of mine who is spending his first Christmas without his mother. I don't want to let him down."

Finally showered, shaved, and dressed in clean clothes, Zachary answered his door and let Kenzie in. She had done a better job than he of looking after herself when staying over at Mr. Peterson's, so she really didn't look that different from what she had when he had dropped her at her house. Different clothes and some makeup were the only changes he could spot.

"You look much better cleaned up," Kenzie approved. "Some concealer to hide the bags under your eyes wouldn't be a bad idea…"

"No, thanks."

She laughed. "I'm driving. I know how little sleep you've had lately, you're a menace on the road."

"Besides, you want to drive your car."

"A convertible isn't the most practical thing during Vermont winters, but she's closed up tight. We're not going far. We'll stay warm."

They did, and before long, they were at the Salters' home, where Zachary could smell roasted turkey and the fixings before they even opened the door. Vera greeted both of them with a hug and a kiss on the cheek. She called Rhys, who must have heard them ring the doorbell anyway and didn't really need to be told they had arrived.

Kenzie and Zachary sat down, and it was a few minutes before Rhys came into the room.

He was dressed in neatly pressed trousers, a white, collared shirt, and a Christmas sweater that looked both ugly and uncomfortable. He raised a hand in greeting. He was smiling, but his eyes were sad and bloodshot.

"Rhys! Merry Christmas!" Kenzie jumped up to give him a hug and a kiss on the cheek.

Rhys looked flustered and Zachary figured if it weren't for his dark skin, he would have been blushing furiously. What teenage boy wouldn't have a crush on Kenzie and get all embarrassed over a kiss?

Rhys reached for Zachary's hand, and instead of just giving him a polite handshake, he clasped Zachary's forearm and pulled him to his feet. He kept a strong grip on Zachary's forearm, a gesture Zachary took to mean *brother* and *stay strong*. He hugged

Zachary with the other arm, held him for a moment, and then released him.

Rhys nodded and licked his lips. "Merry Christmas."

Zachary gave him a warm smile. Rhys was going through his own hard time, but he was holding up well. It was good that they had made an effort to be there for him. He would be strong for Zachary, and Zachary would be strong for him.

"Merry Christmas, Rhys."

Rhys nodded and looked Zachary in the eyes for a few seconds, clearly imparting that he was glad that Zachary was there. Zachary wasn't just another guest at the table, but someone Rhys needed. He remembered the conversation with Rhys, discussing how they were both broken, and the light that had come into Rhys's eyes when he understood that he and Zachary were both part of the same special club. Both broken inside, even if they looked normal on the outside. Rhys needed someone from that club there with him for Christmas. Someone who knew what it was like to miss his mother being there on Christmas Day and to mourn the life he might have had, if things had been different.

Zachary rubbed his stinging, gritty eyes.

"Let's sit down," he told Rhys. "You can show me what you got."

Sign up for my mailing list at pdworkman.com and get Gluten-Free Murder for free!

PREVIEW OF THEY THOUGHT
HE WAS SAFE

1

The little family gathered around the dining room table was about as far from a traditional nuclear family as one could get. Lorne Peterson had been Zachary's foster father for a few weeks when he was young, following the house fire that had been the last straw in the break-up of his biological family. But Zachary and Mr. Peterson had kept in touch, connected in part by a love of photography and his former foster father's darkroom facilities.

Mr. Peterson—Zachary tried, but could rarely bring himself to call him Lorne—had gone through his own family dissolution a few years later, when his wife had become aware of his alternative relationships. They had lost their certification to foster, and separation and divorce followed soon after.

Zachary remembered the initial shock when he had stopped in to visit Mr. Peterson and get some film developed and he realized that Pat, the other man in the apartment, was not a neighbor who had stopped in for coffee, but Mr. Peterson's partner. He had known that Mr. Peterson was seeing someone named Pat, but had mistakenly assumed that Pat was a woman. More than twenty years later, Lorne and Pat were still together, and society had changed enough that they were able to live together openly in the mainstream rather than keeping their relationship quiet.

Pat was between Zachary and Mr. Peterson in age, still muscular and vital, though he was definitely looking more distinguished than he had in his twenties, gray creeping in at his temples and fine lines mapping his face. Mr. Peterson's deeper wrinkles all pointed up, ready to burst into a sunrise when he smiled. He was losing his hair, and the fringe that was left was almost pure white. But even as his body got older, he remained energetic and young at heart.

They had been a constant in Zachary's life for two decades and, despite the fact that Mr. Peterson had only been his foster parent for a few weeks and Pat never had been, they were the closest thing to family that Zachary had. He hadn't kept in touch with any of his other foster siblings or parents, and much of his adolescence had been spent in youth centers and group homes. With his severe ADHD and PTSD, he hadn't been an easy kid to parent.

Tyrrell's face at the table was a new one. In spite of the fact that he was Zachary's biological brother, they had not seen each other from the time that Tyrrell was six until he and Zachary had been reunited on Christmas Eve.

As Christmas Eve was the anniversary of the fire that had destroyed their family more than thirty years previously, it was always a dark time for Zachary. Some years he had almost not made it through the holiday. Being reunited with his brother had been the fulfillment of what he had thought was an impossible dream. He had been sure that he would never see any of his biological siblings again. Even being a private investigator, he had never looked for them, never daring to interfere with what might be happy lives to remind them of the horrible thing he had done in causing that fire.

Tyrrell's facial features were similar enough to Zachary's to recognize a family resemblance, though Zachary's face was still gaunt, not yet filled out following his pre-Christmas depression. Tyrrell's hair was dark like Zachary's, but longer and shaggier. He was clean-shaven. It was his eyes that Zachary found startling. In spite of the hard life that Tyrrell had been through, they were still the shining blue eyes of the six-year-old brother he remembered.

They gathered around the table to exchange stories of Zachary's and Tyrrell's separate lives, comparing notes and getting to know each other again. Zachary needed an environment where he felt safe to share in spite of any flashbacks or surges of emotion brought up by the retellings. A restaurant or bar would just not have worked. Some of their experiences were similar, and others were not. Tyrrell had been younger at the time of the family's dissolution, and therefore less damaged than Zachary, and he had been able to stay with the two younger kids for most of his childhood, so he'd had that constant in his life. Zachary had been alone, bounced from one family to another so quickly that he'd been known to return to the wrong family after school, forgetting where he was supposed to be.

But in spite of the smiles around the table, Zachary knew there was something wrong.

At first, Zachary hadn't been able to put his finger on it. He thought that maybe Mr. Peterson and Pat were just awkward having a new 'son' at the dining room table. They were used to Zachary and his quirks, but Tyrrell was a recent addition and they didn't know enough about his past to know what might trigger him, or about his interests to know what questions to ask to encourage his participation in the conversation.

But it was more than that.

There were a number of looks exchanged between Lorne and Pat that didn't seem to follow the rhythm of Tyrrell's participation in the conversation. Mr. Peterson put his hand over Pat's as they ate, something Zachary had rarely seen him do at the table. Their natural cheer was diminished, as if there were something pulling them away from the conversation to think sad thoughts. Like someone who had recently lost a loved one but was trying to act unaffected.

He watched the two of them more closely, but didn't call them out in front of Tyrrell. Obviously, whatever was going on was something they didn't want to share with Tyrrell. Maybe not with Zachary either.

Tyrrell didn't know Pat and Lorne like Zachary did, and didn't seem to notice anything amiss. He tried to catch Zachary's eye.

"Do you remember that?"

Zachary hadn't realized how distracted he had become from Tyrrell's story. He licked his lips. "Uh… sorry… I missed that."

Tyrrell looked at him for a minute, nonplussed. He shook his head. "About time to top up your Ritalin?"

"Uh… not taking any ADHD meds right now," Zachary admitted. "Sorry."

"I didn't mean…" Tyrrell flushed pink. "I wasn't serious. It was just supposed to be a joke. Because you were distracted."

Zachary flashed a look toward Mr. Peterson and Pat, noting that their hands were again touching, and Mr. Peterson was giving Pat a questioning look as he thought Zachary was occupied by a separate conversation. Zachary swallowed.

"I try to only take them if I really need to focus on something. I don't like to have to take them all the time, and they can interfere with other meds. So I just take them when I really need to."

"I didn't mean you to take it seriously…"

"What were you talking about? That I missed?"

Tyrrell looked like he didn't want to cover the same ground again. Mr. Peterson put down his fork and jumped in.

"It was about your sister Jocelyn. I gather she was sort of a second mother to you guys?"

Zachary nodded, glad to segue to something in the past rather than focusing on the issues he still battled. "Yeah, she was really bossy. I resented it, because… well, who do you think got most of that bossiness? It wasn't the little guys; she was pretty patient with them. But me… she figured I was old enough that I should have figured out how to behave myself. We were supposed to pay attention to her and fly straight, but… I was always going off-script."

Tyrrell chuckled. "Is that what you call it?"

Zachary felt his own face get warm. "I tried, but… I wasn't any better at following her rules than I was anyone else's." He included Mr. Peterson and Pat in his broad shrug. They had either experienced or heard the stories of some of his more disastrous choices.

"Joss was a little bossy," Tyrrell admitted. "But she really helped me to figure out what I was supposed to do. I really wished that we'd been able to stay together when we went into foster care. She would have been able to help me to figure out the rules when I was in a new home. I often heard her little voice in my head, telling me how to behave properly, when I was trying to sort it out."

Zachary often had too many little voices in his head, and they all told him different things. But it wasn't usually until *after* he'd impulsively done something that he actually heard them. The voices of Joss, his parents, his social worker, or some other authority in his life, telling him that once again, he'd done something exceptionally stupid and that there were going to be consequences.

Zachary shrugged and looked down at his plate. He ate a couple of bites, forcing himself to eat despite the bubble of anxiety in his stomach from trying to figure out what Mr. Peterson and Pat were so worried about. As he'd told Tyrrell, he was off of his ADHD meds, so he actually had an appetite, and Pat was a good cook, but the unspoken tension in the room was getting to him.

"Have you had any contact with her?" Mr. Peterson asked with interest.

"A little," Tyrrell said. "Mostly just email or social media, you know. We haven't gotten together face-to-face. I think… she's got her own life and isn't that interested in reconnecting. It can be hard… stirring up old memories. She's got her own family now."

"You guys should have a reunion, get everyone together. It sounds like you know where everyone is now."

Tyrrell nodded slowly. He glanced sideways at Zachary. "I have ways to contact everyone now. But I'm not sure if everyone wants to get together. They're all living their own lives."

"But you grew up with the younger ones. You guys must have a pretty good relationship."

"We were together until I was fourteen or something, so yeah, we have a lot of shared memories, but then we didn't have anything to do with each other because we were in different homes until we were adults. It's a real hodgepodge of relationships."

"I can't imagine what it must be like not to know where your siblings are," Pat contributed. "I just have one sister, and we've always been in contact, even if she didn't particularly approve of my 'lifestyle choices.' It would be hard, not even knowing where they were."

There was a suspicious crack in Pat's voice that set alarm bells ringing for Zachary. Pat didn't usually get emotional about his family. He laughed about their attitudes, mentioned them now and then, but even when his father had died, he hadn't cried about it. Not in front of Zachary, anyway. With the number of times that Zachary had broken down around Pat, Pat certainly shouldn't have felt awkward about shedding a few tears in front of Zachary.

Zachary studied Pat closely, and then Mr. Peterson. Lorne apparently caught the significance of the look. He made an infinitesimal shake of his head, which might have even been unconscious, and Zachary knew it wasn't the time to ask what was going on.

"I guess it's a different experience," Tyrrell agreed, "but I've never known anything else, so for me, that's just the way families are. You spend a few years together, and then you don't have any contact for a decade or more. Now with the internet, you have these opportunities to touch base again and find out what people have been occupying themselves with. We're all adults now, so it isn't like we're looking to live together as a family again."

"I'm glad you reached out to Zachary," Mr. Peterson said. "It's been really good for him to have contact with someone from his family again."

Zachary nodded reflexively.

"I think everyone needs to know that they have somewhere they belong," Mr. Peterson went on. "Not just somewhere like this," he spread his hands to indicate his home, where Zachary was a welcome part of the family any time, "but biologically, too. I've heard that a lot of people who are foster or adopted kids really miss that biological connection, even if they never met their biological family before. There's just a hole where they feel like they don't belong or aren't a part of the family who raised them."

Zachary let his eyes linger on Mr. Peterson for a few moments. It was only natural that, as a foster parent, he would be aware of the needs of foster kids to find some kind of genetic connection. But he didn't want Mr. Peterson to feel like he hadn't been a good enough parent or friend to Zachary.

Tyrrell gave a shrug. "I guess so. I always knew I had biological siblings out there. Even parents, if I wanted to look for them. But I was more interested in building a family of my own. Getting married, having kids. I guess that was my way of having a genetic connection with someone. My own kids."

Zachary felt a pang. He hadn't told Tyrrell his own history with his ex, Bridget, and the issues that she'd had with having children. Zachary had always thought that he would have a family, a house full of kids to remind Zachary of the family that he'd lost. To make up for the pain that he'd caused.

Even though Bridget had said from the start that she didn't want kids, he'd thought that she would change her mind. That biological clock would start ticking, she would see what a great father Zachary would make, and she would decide it was time.

He'd been sadly mistaken and things had not ended well.

Mr. Peterson flashed a look at Zachary, knowing the history. Maybe that too was part of what he had read. How kids with no biological heritage longed for children of their own. Maybe it was an established pathological desire.

2

They got through the evening. Zachary found the time went much more slowly than usual as he watched Mr. Peterson and Pat, waiting for a flash of insight into what was going on with them. He was intuitive, skilled at reading body language and facial expression, and he knew Lorne and Pat well, but he couldn't quite put his finger on what was going on.

After saying his goodbyes, he walked out to his car, and waited until Tyrrell got into his and drove away. Then he returned to the house.

Pat opened the door, looking at Zachary with surprise. "Forget something?" he asked, looking behind himself to see if Zachary had left a book or bag.

Zachary shook his head. He hesitated. "I just wanted to see if there was something I could do…"

Pat looked at him for a minute, then stepped back. "Come in."

Mr. Peterson came around the corner. "Oh, Zachary. What's up? I thought you were on your way."

Pat looked at him, communicating something by his manner. Mr. Peterson nodded slowly. "I guess I should know better than to try to get anything past you." He led the way to the living room and they sat down. Mr. Peterson normally liked his easy chair, and Pat was usually back and forth, preparing coffee or checking something in the kitchen, playing the part of the diligent host. But they both sat down together on the couch, holding hands again.

Mr. Peterson looked at Pat. "You want to start?"

Pat blinked, looked down, then nodded. "Sure." He cleared his throat. He looked at Zachary, gaze steady. "A friend of mine is missing."

"Oh." Zachary thought about that. "I'm sorry. How long has he been missing? Have you talked to the police?"

"I talked to the police... they weren't really that interested. They said that they would look into it, but as far as I can see, they haven't done much. They said they would get back to us if they found anything, but..."

"You haven't heard anything back from them," Zachary finished. "They can keep their investigations pretty close to the chest, sometimes. If you're not the next of kin, they don't have any requirement to report back to you. They haven't said anything?"

"They don't think there's any foul play. They think that he just... left town."

Zachary nodded. "Could he have?"

"He didn't," Pat said with certainty. "I know Jose, and he didn't leave town. He would have said something to me if he'd been planning on leaving. Even if it was something unplanned, he would still have called."

"Where do you know him from?"

Pat looked at Mr. Peterson, and then back at Zachary. "We know him from the community. He's gay. Someone we get together with now and then to do something with."

They didn't often talk about their social life, so Zachary didn't know how large their group of gay friends was, or how long they had known this Jose. Zachary had never heard either of them mention him before.

"How long has he been missing?"

Pat swallowed and rubbed his forehead. Mr. Peterson patted

his back and filled in the details. "As far as we can tell, it's been a week since anyone has seen him."

"A week." Zachary didn't like that. He could understand the police not being too concerned if it had only been a day or two, but a week should have been raising some red flags. "Have you talked to his work? His family?"

"He doesn't have any family here. He has a wife and kids back in El Salvador, he sends money home to them. Here, he doesn't have anyone… steady. Just friends, casual encounters."

"He's gay but he has a wife and kids in El Salvador?"

Pat shrugged and nodded. "Sometimes it happens that way."

Mr. Peterson had previously been married to a woman and had foster kids, so Zachary supposed he shouldn't have been surprised. People chose to do the socially acceptable thing, and then later decided that they couldn't maintain appearances.

"And work? Does he have a job?"

Pat nodded and took over again. "He did day labor, cash pay, but it was with the same company every day, not going from one job to another. I talked with the foreman and he said that Jose just stopped showing up."

"Was he surprised about that?"

"No… but that doesn't mean that he was right. If you had a worker coming in every day and then they just stopped coming without a word, wouldn't you be concerned?"

"I would," Zachary admitted. "But I don't deal with day laborers. I guess they probably have a pretty heavy turnover. Is he… legal?"

"No. Undocumented."

"So if there was trouble, he might have just disappeared."

"He could… but like I said, he would have at least given us a heads-up that something had happened."

"If he could. But sometimes there isn't any warning, they just get arrested and put into a facility awaiting deportation. You don't know that he would be able to call you. Or that he would. He might have been limited in the number of calls that he could make, or he might have figured there was no point. You couldn't do anything for him, so why bother?"

"I still think he would have told us if he could."

"Did the police check in with ICE? See whether he had been picked up in a sweep?"

"They haven't gotten back to us. I think if they had found his name on a list like that, they would have at least said that he was okay, even if they didn't give us any details."

Zachary nodded. In theory. But sometimes the police dropped the ball and didn't call back, especially if it were just a random friend and not the next of kin. Sometimes they got distracted by other cases or bogged down, and just clearing the case was all they could do, without making a bunch of reports to the friends or family.

"You don't think he went back to El Salvador? What if his wife said she needed him to come back? She or one of the kids was sick. Something that sounded like an emergency."

"He would have let someone know." Pat shook his head. "He didn't live by himself. Most of these illegals don't make enough money to get a place of their own. Especially when they're sending as much home as they can. So he had roommates. He didn't tell them where he was going. He just didn't come home one day."

Zachary found himself pulling out his notepad to start making notes. His brain was grinding through the possibilities. If Jose hadn't gone home, then ICE was still the most likely possibility. Someone had tipped them off and he had been nabbed on his way home from work, at a bar, or even at the grocery store.

But there were other possibilities. He was mugged or had an accident, and was in the hospital somewhere. Maybe under his own name and maybe as a John Doe. Similarly, he could be in the morgue. Going home to El Salvador was less likely. He would probably at least have told his roommates what was happening if he were going back home. There would be no reason not to tell them. He would have had to make arrangements; he wouldn't have just been able to hop on a plane and fly back in a couple of hours. Zachary scratched down a few thoughts. He looked up to see Mr. Peterson and Pat watching him intently.

"Do you have the name of the officer who investigated it? A case number?"

"Yeah. Just a minute." Pat got up and retreated to the bedroom to get the details.

Mr. Peterson gave Zachary a smile. "Thanks for this, Zachary. We've been very worried."

"You should have told me. I could have gotten started on it earlier."

"You have a lot on your plate. One undocumented worker disappears… it's not exactly at the top of the priority list."

"Not for the police. It would have been for me."

Mr. Peterson smiled. "Thank you."

They waited for Pat to return with the information about the policeman. "He and Pat were pretty close?"

"They clicked. Sometimes you just meet someone that everything falls into place with. You start a conversation with them, and it's like you've known them your whole life. You know?"

Mr. Peterson didn't sound jealous, but Zachary couldn't help wondering just how far the friendship went. He had never seen any cracks in the relationship between Mr. Peterson and Pat, but people hid that kind of thing. Zachary hadn't known that Mr. Peterson and his wife were getting divorced until he had shown up at the house one day to be told by Mrs. Peterson that her husband didn't live there anymore. He had seen, before that, that the two of them were not terribly compatible. They had very different personalities and viewpoints. If Mr. Peterson had had his way, Zachary probably would have lived with them longer than he had. Maybe not for years, but a few more weeks. They would have tried for longer to work things out. Mr. Peterson understood Zachary and his issues better. His wife had only been concerned about Zachary's behaviors and how they might affect the other foster children. As a mother, of course that was something that she had to consider.

Pat returned with a piece of paper. He handed it to Zachary. Detective Dougan, a phone number, and a case number.

"Thanks. Tell me the information you can about your friend. His full name, where he worked, where he lived, anyone else in your group I can talk to."

Pat sat back down. He pulled out his phone. "His name is Jose Flores. He worked for A.L. Landscaping." He read off a phone number and address for Zachary. "The roommate that I talked to…" He tapped around on his phone for a minute. "His name was Nando Gonzalez."

"Do you know him?"

"No. I hadn't ever met him before. I hadn't ever been in Jose's apartment. But I knew where it was. We had picked him up before and I knew what the apartment number was. So I just went and knocked on the door…"

Zachary processed this. He tried to envision what had happened, and how Nando might have felt about the broad-chested white man showing up without warning at his door. He would have been nervous. Anxious about being turned over to Immigration. Suspicious of whether Pat were actually a friend of Jose's, or someone playing a part. Nando probably wouldn't have told Pat everything he knew. Even if he knew from Jose that he and Pat were friends, he probably would still have hung back. Illegals had to be wary even of friends. There was no telling what Pat's true motivation might have been.

"Do you mind me looking into it? Going back and talking to him?"

"No, of course. Go ahead. I'd really like to know what happened to him. I'm worried. He wasn't that kind of guy, you know, the kind who would just disappear. I know some people do that. But Jose… he was dedicated to his job. He wanted to make things work in America. He wanted to help his wife and kids come here."

"This roommate that you talked to, he wasn't someone from your community, then?"

"No. We didn't know him."

"The two of them were not a couple?"

"No." Pat gave a smile and shook his head. "I doubt that he knew Jose was gay."

"Why not? Had he not… come out?"

It seemed like an antiquated term in a society where sexual orientation was no longer supposed to be taboo and gay marriage was legal. Was there still a reason for men and women to be in the closet and hide their orientation from their families and friends?

"It's different for men of color," Pat said slowly. "There is a belief that the word 'gay' only applies to white men. That it's not just sexual orientation, but race and class as well. The type of gay men that you see on prime-time TV. White, limp-wristed, lisping, middle-to-upper-class, sweater-wearing men. And people like Jose… aren't that. So they tend not to even identify as gay."

"Really?" It had never occurred to Zachary that the term meant anything other than a same-sex attraction. "I… I had no idea."

"How would you?" Mr. Peterson gave a smile. "Unless you spend a lot of time in those circles, you don't really hear what people think or what their prejudices are."

"So how would he identify himself?" Zachary asked curiously. "If he wouldn't say that he is gay, because only white guys are gay, then he would say that he is…?"

"MSM is a term they have borrowed from medical literature. During the initial years of the AIDS epidemic, medical practitioners found that a lot of non-whites said that they were not gay, even though they were having same-sex relations. So they had to change their language in order to properly identify the risk factors. Not 'are you gay,' but 'have you had sex with men?' MSM was the medical shorthand. Or WSW for the women."

Zachary wrote MSM down so he wouldn't forget it when he started to talk to people that Jose knew who might be part of the gay—MSM—community. Language was a powerful thing, and he didn't want to risk offending someone who might have information to share. Say the wrong thing, and he might never hear anything more from a witness.

Pat handed Zachary a photo. A group of men around a table. Pat and Lorne and others Zachary didn't recognize. Pat pointed to the Hispanic man beside him.

"That's Jose."

He was well-dressed, not what Zachary would have expected for an illegal worker. He had on evening wear, like the other men, a suit or dinner jacket and blue tie. He had a wide, pleasant smile, and looked comfortable, part of the group. Zachary raised an eyebrow at Pat, and when he nodded, kept the photo.

"Have you talked to his wife?"

"I don't know how to reach her. We never talked about it. I don't know her name or where in El Salvador she lives."

"Did *she* know that he was… MSM?"

"I doubt it. A lot of men like him keep it pretty quiet. Other than the people that they hook up with, they don't tell anyone. They live two lives, and keep them very separate."

"How did you meet?"

Pat and Mr. Peterson looked at each other. Not in a way that suggested they had something to hide, but just that they had to think about it and might need a memory jogger.

It was Mr. Peterson who answered first. "I think… the first time we met up was at a club downtown. There was a very popular lounge singer who was doing a night there… it was very busy, a lot of people wanted to see him. We went well ahead of time to get a table. The place was so packed, they were asking patrons to share tables. Jose ended up at our table, and we struck up a conversation."

"That's right," Pat's face cleared. "I'd forgotten all about that. We've done so many other things together. It was just one of those cases where everything fits together, and it was such a comfortable conversation… by the end of the night, it was like we had always been friends."

"And you've spent a lot of time together since then? How long has that been?"

"About... four months... five?"

"And the three of you together, or just Jose and you?"

Pat raised his eyebrows. "I'm devoted to Lorne, Zachary. This was not a hook-up."

"So the three of you?"

"Yes, the three of us. Usually other people as well. A group of guys getting together at a bar or club, or even a museum or gallery. Christmas shopping together. Just... things that friends do together."

Zachary nodded, getting a more clear picture of the relationship. "Can I talk to one or two of your friends? Or would that be intrusive?"

There were several seconds of hesitation, the silence drawing out.

"I'll have to talk to them first," Pat said eventually. "I'll get you names and numbers once I've had a chance to."

"Okay. Did the police talk to anyone else?"

"I don't know who they talked to. They didn't ask for the names of any other friends. Just for his boss at A.L. I think that's where the investigation stopped."

They Thought He Was Safe, Book #5 of the *Zachary Goldman Mysteries* series by P.D. Workman can be purchased at pdworkman.com

ABOUT THE AUTHOR

Award-winning and USA Today bestselling author P.D. (Pamela) Workman writes riveting mystery/suspense and young adult books dealing with mental illness, addiction, abuse, and other real-life issues. For as long as she can remember, the blank page has held an incredible allure and from a very young age she was trying to write her own books.

Workman wrote her first complete novel at the age of twelve and continued to write as a hobby for many years. She started publishing in 2013. She has won several literary awards from Library Services for Youth in Custody for her young adult fiction. She currently has over 50 published titles and can be found at pdworkman.com.

Born and raised in Alberta, Workman has been married for over 25 years and has one son.

Please visit P.D. Workman at pdworkman.com to see what else she is working on, to join her mailing list, and to link to her social networks.

If you enjoyed this book, please take the time to recommend it to other purchasers with a review or star rating and share it with your friends!

facebook.com/pdworkmanauthor

twitter.com/pdworkmanauthor

instagram.com/pdworkmanauthor

amazon.com/author/pdworkman

bookbub.com/authors/p-d-workman

goodreads.com/pdworkman

linkedin.com/in/pdworkman

pinterest.com/pdworkmanauthor

youtube.com/pdworkman